GOOD TO BE
Home

Books By Leah Dobrinska

Love at On Deck Café
Good To Be Home

It's...
GOOD TO BE
Home! ☺

With love,
Leah

LEAH DOBRINSKA

This book is entirely a work of fiction. Names, characters and incidents portrayed in it are either the work of the author's imagination or are used fictitiously. Any resemblance to actual persons, living or dead, businesses, companies, events or localities is entirely coincidental.

Editing: Jenn Lockwood

Cover Design: Ana Grigoriu-Voicu with Books-design

Author Photo: Beth Dunphy

Library of Congress Control Number: 2022902675

ISBN: 978-1-7374483-2-7 (paperback) | 978-1-7374483-3-4 (ebook)

For my mom and dad, with all my love.

Prologue

ENTERTAINMENT MAGAZINE

Review: *Inspired Interiors* – Pilot Episode

Inspired Interiors debuted on HoSt Network on Wednesday evening. While it was filled with the time-tested home and design show elements (a family needs home renovation and décor advice, they call in the expert, they're pleased with the results), the entire episode fell flat.

Newcomer Isabel Marshall took center stage for much of the show, designing the kitchen, dining, and living room spaces for clients Josh and Peg Ellis. While it's obvious Isabel has been highly trained in design—her resume boasts that she passed the prestigious National Council for Interior Design Qualification (NCIDQ) exam after having only the minimum two years of on-the-job experience—her delivery leaves much to be desired. She was stiff and mechanical, regurgitating facts and design best practices but not sharing anything new or "inspired" with her audience or the homeowners.

Ms. Marshall's so-called experience is not enough to

carry a TV show. Perhaps she should spend some more time creating a home of her own before she tries to impart her "expertise" onto others. After all, as viewers, we don't need book knowledge spewed out at us. We need real-life tips for making our houses into homes. We're sorry to say, but we didn't see that in this pilot episode. Inspired Interiors *did not live up to its title.*

Review Summary: Inspired? More like insipid.

Chapter 1

"TELL ME ABOUT MAPLETON."

Isabel Marshall choked on her coffee. The latte she was drinking sailed down her wind pipe, sending her into a coughing jag. She stood to avoid soiling the white linen of the couch that was perfectly staged at the house she was designing and put the back of her hand to her mouth to keep the beverage from dribbling out onto her upmarket blouse.

"I'm sorry, what?" Isabel had never mentioned her hometown to Horatio McMillan, the producer of her TV show—not in the two years they'd been working together. She was sure of it.

Horatio arched his eyebrows, making circular gestures with his hands, as if to stir up her memory. "You know. Mapleton, Wisconsin. Where you grew up. I hear there's an opportunity for some work there, and I want to jump on it."

Isabel shot an accusing look at Grace Bartal, her executive assistant.

Isabel had been on the phone with Grace yesterday when a call came through from Julia Derks, who lived in Mapleton. Isabel hadn't talked to Julia since she'd left her hometown and moved to Los Angeles four years ago.

That wasn't a dig at Julia in particular. Isabel hadn't kept in touch with much of anyone. Instead, she'd been working her tail off, spending countless hours networking with the who's who of LA's fashion and design world, painstakingly making a name for herself.

When her design blog caught the eye of the Home and Style Network, she was offered a starring role in her own TV show, and Isabel jumped at the opportunity. After one negative review nearly sidelined her before she had even started, Isabel had gone on to film the most watched debut season of a home design show in HoSt history.

Sometimes, she couldn't believe she was in her second year of filming. Other times, it was as if she'd been at the grueling uphill climb of production forever. It was a constant grind to find clients, to film the show, to make everyone—the network, her producer, and her clients—happy.

Not that Isabel was complaining.

This was the life she wanted. So what if it was becoming like a never-ending game of Monopoly where instead of trying to convince her brother to give up Boardwalk, she was out here in real life, trying to land the biggest names with the biggest budgets. This was the dream. She'd never admit to anyone that, though this was everything she wanted, something felt a little...off.

It didn't matter. She was here, and she was doing it.

So, when Julia called yesterday and proposed that Isabel come to Mapleton to design the houses her fiancé was renovating before they put them on the market to sell, Isabel had no intention of agreeing to the proposition. Her reasoning was two-fold.

First, Mapleton was the antithesis of a design hub. Second, it would be far too awkward to face those whom she left behind.

She'd told Grace she didn't want to go, and Grace said she'd get the PR team to handle it.

Now, Grace was staring at the ceiling, out the window, at her shoes—anywhere to avoid eye contact with Isabel. The coward.

Isabel turned to Horatio and tried to play it cool.

"I don't think that would be a good idea, H. Mapleton is in the middle of nowhere in northeast Wisconsin. I can't imagine it would film well. It's the backwoods and on the back end of all artistic and creative trends. I wouldn't be surprised if the village's website hasn't been updated since the invention of the internet."

Horatio gave her a dismissive wrist flick. "I don't care how refined the Village of Mapleton is. It's home to you, isn't it?"

"Well, it's where I grew up, yes. But—"

"Then it's home. Listen, Isabel. You know I believe in you. I love the work you're doing, but we got the ratings of the first few episodes of this season, and they aren't as strong as last season's."

Isabel's stomach dropped to the floor, and the acidic taste of panic rose into her throat.

"We need to switch things up," Horatio pressed on.

Isabel narrowed her eyes. "But HoSt said it wanted me to focus on upscale home redesign this season. It's how they marketed my entire show. And that's what we're giving them."

After the success of the show last season, the Home and Style Network had been adamant about the direction of her series going forward—as many high-end properties as she could land, and the bigger the budget, the better.

"I know that, but whether HoSt admits to it is another story. The reason people tune in to the show is because of *you*. But you can only hold the viewers' interest so long if what you're talking about and working on isn't what they're looking for. What better way to keep them engaged than by giving them more of you? Something totally out of the box. A special in your hometown is what you need. A chance to give fans a taste of your roots and what makes you, you. It's also genius PR to give back to a small-town community."

It made sense, but Isabel's head felt woozy. She'd left Mapleton and made a name for herself. In the process, she'd basically sidelined her family and friends, putting them on the backburner while she worked herself silly over the past couple of years. She'd told herself her family should understand—cut her some slack, even. After all, she was the one doing the big-city, exciting work.

Now, she didn't like the thought of returning home only when she needed something—like the prodigal daughter. It made her feel a little slimy about how she'd treated those she left behind.

Eventually, she'd have to reconcile with them. She *wanted* to. But she thought she could kick that can down the road a little bit farther. Besides, she should be able to figure this out on her own.

"Horatio, there has to be another way. What about designing a different style home? Or a bigger celebrity's home? I think I saw Oprah at the gym the other week. I could go and try to find her…"

Isabel trailed off. She didn't particularly like sounding absurd, and that was exactly how she was sounding.

"Why are you so opposed to going home?" Grace asked.

Isabel shook her head. "I don't consider Mapleton my home anymore."

And they probably don't want to claim me, either.

The last time she'd seen her parents in person was three years ago when they made a weekend trip to LA. She'd had to work while they were here, and she'd been a bit of a diva. She wasn't proud of her behavior, but in her defense, she'd been on the cusp of a big career break.

Horatio waved his hand in the air between them. "Your home is always your home. Besides, this could be great for you. I'm picturing you working on five houses in Mapleton. We can air the episodes back to back for a whole week around Christmas. I've already pitched it to the network as your own "home for the holidays" special. If we leave on Monday, we can film throughout August and get back with enough time to keep up with our regular production schedule. We'll take a skeleton crew with us. Grace will obviously come along and serve as your design assistant, and we'll have the camera and production team members. But you two will have to do most of the leg work."

"Leave on Monday?" Isabel hadn't heard anything he said after that. Her voice came out an octave higher than usual. "You've got to be kidding me! I have so much to do here. And the book—it's not going to write itself."

Isabel rubbed her temples, the familiar ache setting in as it did every time she thought about the book project.

Thanks to the attention her show received and some well-placed connections within the network, Isabel had landed a publishing deal for a home and design book. Her first draft was due in mid-September. Very few people knew that she'd made plans to donate fifty percent of her earnings to a local nonprofit that worked to get families into homes. She didn't want the publicity or the praise that came along with a gesture like that. She just wanted to do a good thing. She didn't need the money, and this was a way she could pay it forward.

Unfortunately, Isabel couldn't organize her thoughts, and every time she sat down to put words on paper, she ended up deleting them and walking away. She was trying not to get worked up, but the looming deadline nagged at her, and she was afraid if she didn't come up with something to write about, the organization she was so excited to support wouldn't make much from her pitiful efforts.

Isabel started pacing. A trip to Mapleton would eliminate any time off she so desperately needed to try to write.

Horatio clicked his tongue. "Get on board with this, Isabel. I'm going to make it happen. Grace will call your contact and let her know we're coming. We'll work everything else out from there. Books have been written in cities other than LA, you know."

Isabel glanced up at the ceiling and blew out a breath. "I guess I don't have a choice."

"That's the spirit." Horatio chucked her shoulder with his knuckles as he bustled into the other room, shouting an order to his assistant.

Isabel spun to face Grace, her discomfort at the thought of going home manifesting itself in frustration. "How could you? When you said you'd handle Julia's call, I thought that meant you'd shut it down, not that you'd bring Horatio in on it and start planning a homecoming trip to Mapleton."

"Come on. Can you blame me for digging into the prospect here? It's my job. And you haven't been home since I've known you. I researched Mapleton, and it's cute. It does have a decent-looking website, by the way." Grace raised a shoulder as if this whole situation wasn't that big of a deal.

Isabel snorted. There was no way Grace was looking at the right website. Her home town was nothing if not old school, and certainly no one there was on the cutting edge of graphic design.

"All I'm saying"—Grace held up her hands in defense—"is that I think Julia's call was providential. Mark my words, a trip back to small-town Wisconsin might be what you and our show needs. I predict you'll love being home. It might even help unstick that writer's block you've been suffering from."

Isabel sunk down onto the couch as the realization of what Horatio said about the show's ratings hit her. "I can't believe I'm getting negative reviews. It makes me not want to write a book at all."

Anytime bad press cropped up, Isabel couldn't help but think of the initial review in *Entertainment Magazine*. While she'd developed thicker skin over the past two years, that first bad review always ate away at her. Fortunately, the general public hadn't agreed with the magazine's take, and Isabel's popularity had soared during season one, but still.

Grace stared her down, pointing a finger at her chest. "Don't do it, Isabel. I won't have you spiraling on me. You are not allowed to self-destruct. The most recent reviews weren't bad, per se. More like constructive criticism. And what do we always say?"

"All press is good press." Though she gave Grace a wobbly smile, Isabel didn't think she'd ever actually believe those words.

"Exactly. Besides, Horatio's just being proactive," Grace assured her. "And his plans are gold. I, for one, am excited to see your hometown. I know viewers will be, too."

Isabel shifted her jaw to the side, helpless to prevent her mouth from contorting into a grimace. Sure, it would be nice to see the sights in Mapleton again. It was the people she was worried about. Because the question was, would *they* really want to see *her*?

"Chin up, buttercup. It's going to be fantastic. I'm going to go get to work planning our trip. I need to call Julia again and coordinate with her and her fiancé. I'll have travel itineraries ready for you by the end of the day."

"Great." Isabel tried to muster up some enthusiasm, but all she felt was trepidation.

"Isabel, we need you in hair and makeup." Hilde, her no-nonsense, never-smiling stylist, stood with her hands on her hips. Her snappy tone jolted Isabel out of the fog of dread she was slipping into.

She hurried over to the makeup chair. But as she sat back and let Hilde go to work—playing up her dark eyes with warm eye-shadow tones and blowing out her chestnut hair in beachy, oversized waves—a ball of nervous energy ping-ponged around Isabel's insides, and deep from where she'd buried it underneath the lowest valve of her heart, the image of a man with the kindest green eyes resurfaced.

Isabel blinked it—and him—away.

"Hold still," Hilde scolded.

"Sorry." Isabel pressed her lips together. For once, she was grateful for Hilde's brisk chastisement.

Because dwelling on Daniel Smith would only torture her.

Chapter 2

DANIEL

DANIEL SMITH RELAXED INTO the leather couch at On Deck Café. As a freelance writer, Daniel got to set his own hours and create his own office. The quaint café on Mapleton Avenue was his location of choice. The friendly hum of villagers gossiping with each other and the playful banter between baristas provided the perfect background noise for his work.

Today, he'd snagged his favorite seat—one with a view of both the front door and the counter—and he was determined to be productive. He pulled up his planner to see what was on the docket as the bell over the front door to the café jingled.

Daniel jumped up to help Kristy Klink, who was struggling to keep the door open while also pushing a stroller with her daughter Caroline in tow. Daniel held the door so Kristy could maneuver her stroller all the way inside.

"Thanks, Daniel," Kristy beamed. "Getting around used to be so much less complicated."

"No problem at all." Daniel reseated himself as Julia, the owner of the café, came around the counter and began doting on Caroline. Daniel listened with half an ear to Kristy and Julia's conversation while he started researching content for a piece he was writing for *Wisconsin Magazine*. He'd been given a broad topic: Fall Fun. He set to work perusing area websites and city social media pages to glean what sort of events were happening around the state in the next few months. Before long, he was drowning in a list of apple orchards and pumpkin patches, hay tractor rides and corn mazes.

"So, I called her up. I never in a million years imagined she would answer. She's such a big star now that she has her own TV show."

Daniel snapped his head around when he overheard Julia. She couldn't have been talking about who he thought she was talking about, could she? Then again, who else could it have been? It wasn't like Julia Derks from Mapleton, Wisconsin knew a hefty number of TV stars.

"What did you say to her? Was she nice?" Judging from her pizza pie-sized eyes, Kristy couldn't get an answer fast enough.

"Yeah, she was. A little rushed." Julia cocked her head. "I'm sure she's extremely busy. I mean, she's crazy famous. But she promised she'd consider what I said, and she told me she'd get back to me."

"Oh my gosh. That's so exciting," Kristy squealed. "Can you imagine if *the* Isabel Marshall actually came home to Mapleton? This little town wouldn't know what hit it."

Daniel stared straight ahead at his computer even though the words swam across the screen in front of him, meaningless.

Four years had passed since Isabel Marshall left town, carrying with her his broken heart. Since that time, he'd refused to let himself dwell on her, or on the what-ifs of their relationship. They weren't meant to be. That's what he told himself.

But the pain lingered, less than an inch under the surface. The mere mention of her name was like a scratch that started Daniel bleeding, and there was no way he could focus on fall fun now. Daniel closed his eyes, and when he opened them again, the Times New Roman font on his screen came into focus. He pretended to busy himself with work, but his total attention was on Julia and Kristy's conversation.

"How soon do you think you'll hear back?" Kristy asked, taking a sip of her iced coffee.

Julia shrugged. "Who knows? Samson doesn't have a ton of time to spare. He wants to finish up the houses and stage them before listing with Ford this fall, before the rush of the holidays."

At the mention of Ford, Daniel stiffened. Ford Marshall was Isabel's older brother and a local real estate agent. Ford and Isabel were thick as thieves before she left town. After she left, Daniel and Ford bonded over their common hurt where Isabel was concerned. Over time, that shared pain had hardened and was easier to throw around, make fun of, and deal with.

"That makes sense." Kristy nodded.

Caroline dropped her sippy cup, and Kristy bent to retrieve it. When she did so, Julia's gaze met Daniel's before he could look away.

"Daniel, did you hear my news? Well, I guess it's not news yet. She probably won't come. But you knew Isabel, didn't you?"

Now that was a loaded question.

Here was the thing about Isabel Marshall... Even in his memory, her face was still as crisp as the fresh page of a notebook on the first day of school. Four years without seeing Isabel may as well have been four seconds. He could picture her as if he'd seen her just today. As if she'd just kissed him goodbye and walked out the café door ten minutes before.

If only...

When he let his head drift to thoughts of her, he couldn't help but to get sucked in. It was like she was a tornado, and he was a helpless house of straw. If he remembered the pools of her eyes, he'd be lifted off the ground like it was nothing, and then, before he could blink, an image of her wide, glistening smile would sneak up on him and tear him apart. The recollection of her candy-apple cheeks, flushed red from a compliment he bestowed on her, and the taste of her full, soft lips sent every last fiber of his being scattering like debris in a storm.

And *poof*. Daniel was a goner.

That was why he didn't let himself picture her. He didn't let himself think of her. He couldn't. It was a disaster waiting to happen. Anytime he flirted with her memory, his head sounded a piercing warning, blaring at him to get to an interior room with no windows and lock it down.

So yeah, he knew her.

He cleared his throat, afraid the two keen women in front of him would point out the blush he felt crawling up his cheeks.

"I used to know her well, yes." *Understatement of my life*, he thought to himself. "But I haven't spoken with her in years."

Julia nodded. "I don't think many people have. When she left Mapleton, she didn't look back."

Kristy furrowed her brow and tipped her head at Daniel. "Forgive me if this is overstepping, but didn't you two date?"

Daniel cringed, running an absent hand through his trim-cut hair. He did not want to do a deep dive into his dating history here and now. Half the town was currently sipping coffee and listening in on their conversation, but he could hardly ignore Kristy's inquiry without making it more awkward.

"That was a lifetime ago."

"That's right!" Julia smacked her forehead. "How could I have forgotten? You two were together in college. When did you break up?"

"When she left town," Daniel ground out.

Saying it out loud was both painful and embarrassing. Knowing the woman he thought he was going to spend the rest of his life with chose an out-of-state adventure over him wasn't the type of memory he wanted to relive.

But all the deafening warning sounds in his head were helpless to halt the vision that formed before his eyes—as clear as the blue sky on that fateful day...

"So, you're just going to leave?" He stood looking at the most beautiful girl he'd ever known, the only woman he'd ever loved, as she ripped his heart out.

"I have to get out of this town, Daniel. If I stay here now, I'll end up here forever, and I can't do that. I've got to go and see what's out there. Come with me." Isabel spoke earnestly. She honestly thought he could leave and follow her out west.

Maybe in another life.

"Izzy, I belong in Mapleton. My grandpa is here. I can't abandon him. Not after everything he's done for me. You can't ask me to do that."

"So, you're willing to let me go? Your grandpa wouldn't want you to put your life on hold for him. He'd be fine here. They'll take great care of him at the assisted living facility. And you'll call and visit, of course." Her hazel eyes flashed with emotion—sadness and resolve all rolled into one. Daniel feared he wouldn't be able to convince her to stay.

"How can you say that? I can't leave him here with no family to look after him. This is an impossible choice for me. You have to see that." Daniel could barely breathe. The thought of losing her was suffocating, but the fact that she couldn't grasp what his relationship with his grandfather meant to him made him upset for a whole different reason.

"So you've made up your mind?" she asked.

"I can't leave my grandpa. I have an obligation to him here. Why can't you stay? You'll make it big no matter where you are. I know it."

"There's no way you can know that, Daniel." Isabel looked at him desperately. "I'm going to go stir-crazy here. What does Mapleton have to offer me?"

"It has me, Izzy. Us. Isn't that enough?" Daniel reached for her hand, trying desperately to hold onto her.

Her eyes clouded with tears before she jerked away. "Yes and no. You know I love you, but I've got to go. If you aren't coming, then it's best if we end things now."

Her words hit him like a right cross. "Izzy, please."

"No, Daniel. I'm going. I'll, I'll...see you, I guess."

Without so much as a goodbye hug or kiss, she climbed into her little red Honda and drove away. Her taillights faded along with any hope for a happily ever after.

Chapter 3

DANIEL

"YOU REALLY HAVEN'T TALKED to her in all these years?" Kristy's question lured Daniel from the painful reminiscence.

"There hasn't been a need to." Daniel kept his voice light in an attempt to seem indifferent.

If they knew the number of times he longed to call her and tell her about something he thought she would love, they'd think he was pathetic.

He never made those calls. What did he know about what Isabel loved anymore?

"But wouldn't it be an exciting homecoming?" Julia said to no one in particular.

Several of the café's patrons concurred.

Daniel listened as they talked about their favorite episodes of Isabel's show or the latest tips they'd gotten from her blog, grateful to be out from under the town's microscope.

"She has a book in the works," Marge Wilson informed them.

Marge would know. The woman ran Mapleton through her many volunteer positions. Daniel hadn't heard that bit of news, but it didn't surprise him. Everything Isabel touched turned to gold. She was always destined for big things. The fact that she'd built a small empire in the four years she'd been away was evidence she accomplished what she had set out to do. He guessed she didn't regret leaving him, not with everything she'd done in the time they'd been apart.

The residents of Mapleton claimed her as one of their own, their fondness overshadowing the fact that she hadn't been back to town in so long. But they hadn't experienced the pain of her leaving as he had.

That was why, contrary to what Julia and the rest of the town thought, *exciting* was not the word he would use to describe a potential reunion with Isabel. More like *uncomfortable, dreadful, embarrassing...*the list didn't stop there.

He'd only watched a few of her shows. Any more would have been torture. Daniel squirmed in his seat, but the ringing of Julia's cell phone stopped his thoughts in their tracks.

"Oh wow, this is an out-of-state area code. It's the same as Isabel's!"

"Answer it!" Kristy shrieked before tossing her daughter's sippy cup on the counter, scooping Caroline up and bouncing her on her hip to keep her entertained.

The chatter in the café dropped to a hush. All the patrons turned as one to listen in as Julia took the call.

"Hello," Julia answered.

A garbled voice he didn't recognize came through from the other end of the line. At least it wasn't Isabel. Daniel relaxed.

"Okay. Are you serious? Wow! Yes, I understand." Julia's mouth hung slightly open. She shot Kristy a look Daniel couldn't read, but then she gave a thumbs up to the patrons in the café, and he gulped.

"Of course. Let me write it down, and I'll email you right away with Samson's contact information so you can coordinate schedules." Julia snatched a pad of paper and a pen from near the register and scribbled furiously.

"I can't wait. We are thrilled. Yes, I have half the town here. Tell Isabel we say, 'Hello!'" Julia laughed her trademark laugh. "Thank you so much for the call. You, too. Buh-bye."

Pulling the phone away from her cheek, Julia looked out into the café, eyes wide as saucers. "Isabel Marshall is coming home!"

Kristy whooped and swung Caroline around in celebration.

Caroline's giggles would have usually made Daniel grin, but in this moment, it felt like someone had plunged a hand into his stomach and grabbed a fistful of his digestive tract, squeezing it tight.

He had to get out of the café. Shutting his laptop, he clutched his coffee and rose to leave.

"Daniel, are you done for the day?" Julia asked, stepping away from where she'd embraced Marge in a celebratory hug.

He made up a lie on the fly as he moved to the door. "I've, uh...got lunch plans with my grandpa."

"Oh! How nice! Say hello to Gus for us," the friendly barista yelled after him.

Daniel grunted as he let the door slam behind him and walked into the stagnant, summer air. The late-July humidity pressed against him, and the branches of the maple trees that rose high over Sunrise Park stood immobile. Daniel could relate—he couldn't get the air to move in his lungs, either.

Isabel Marshall—*his* Izzy—was coming home.

He shoved that idea aside as he hopped in his car. She wasn't *his* anything. Whatever they once were was over, and he put the nail in the coffin after she left as much as she had by leaving.

Daniel turned east out of the parking lot and onto Mapleton Avenue. He told himself to relax his shoulders as he passed familiar landmarks on his way to his grandfather's apartment at Colony Elms, the assisted living facility in town. The mature trees lining the road shaded his drive. The village still held onto a hint of patriotic flair from the Fourth of July Festival it had hosted earlier that month. Red and white flowers cascaded from hanging baskets affixed to the streetlamp posts.

Daniel waved to Kenneth Wynert, the town's mailman, as he hurried along on his route. He passed the stately home of George and Mary Ellen Vander Kempen. Its crisp, black shutters pinned against the clean white siding always reminded Daniel of Holstein cattle on the local farms.

He drove by the red brick village administrative office building and the library. Across the street was the town's water tower, painted in a fresh coat of sky blue.

As Daniel approached the outskirts of the east end of the village, he skirted the new housing development before veering onto a side road. He drove another mile and pulled into a parking stall outside his grandfather's unit at the assisted living facility. The large, single-story, cream-colored building sprawled before him. Several residents sat in wheelchairs and on benches in the courtyard under the shade of a wooden pergola. He half expected to see his grandfather among them.

"He's inside. The game's almost on," LeRoy told him when he asked after Gus.

"Which we all know, since you can practically hear his radio out here," Cheryl snorted.

Daniel gave her a forced smile and walked ahead, catching a glimpse of his reflection in the glass, automatic doors. His broad shoulders were more hunched than usual, and the bubbles of panic in his dark, forest-green eyes betrayed his unease. Daniel looked away and scraped his hand through his short hair.

Upon entering the building, the blast of air conditioning soothed his warm, agitated skin. He strode down the hall to his grandfather's room. Cheryl wasn't wrong. Gus's radio was turned up so loud Daniel could hear the pre-game broadcast of the Milwaukee Brewers' baseball game from halfway down the hall.

Gus Keller was a die-hard baseball fan, and Mapleton was a baseball town. Daniel's grandfather rooted for the local teams as well as Wisconsin's major league franchise. Daniel looked at his watch. It must have been a noon start. Despite the unsettling morning he had, Daniel smiled as a familiar sense of peace and contentment washed over him. Being in his grandpa's presence had that effect on him. Daniel's parents died in a car accident when he was only three years old. His grandfather, Gus, and his grandmother, Cathy, took him in and gave him a full life.

Daniel knocked on the door to room 144 before entering. Gus sat in his recliner, facing the television screen. The on-screen announcers were muted, and the radio sitting precariously on an end table alongside the chair was turned up to full volume.

His grandpa always preferred the radio broadcast. The static mingled with the announcers' voices was the soundtrack to Daniel's childhood.

His grandfather caught sight of Daniel, and a smile spread across his wrinkled face. "Daniel, my boy. Good to see you."

"Hi, Grandpa." Daniel walked over and gave his grandpa a hug. He casually turned the dial on the radio down a few notches. The neighbors were fairly indulgent around here, but annoying them unnecessarily wasn't advisable. He made a mental note to have his grandpa's primary care doctor check his hearing aids at next month's checkup.

"What brings you around? Going to watch the game with me?"

Daniel pulled out one of the dining table chairs and sat down in the small space with Gus. "Would you mind? I could use the company."

His grandfather turned his full attention to Daniel, studying him with his wise, brown eyes. "What's going on, Son?"

Daniel looked away, hesitant to let Gus see the emotion he knew was written all over his face.

"Izzy's coming back," he said, willing his voice to stay steady. He darted a glance at his grandpa to see his reaction.

Gus's forehead creased, and he rocked in his chair. "Well, I'll be. What brings her back to town?"

"Work, I guess. She's going to design the homes Samson has been renovating."

Gus tipped his head to the side. "Makes sense, I suppose."

"Yeah, but Samson and Julia are my friends. Mapleton is *my* town. She all but abandoned this place. Now what? Does she think she can waltz back in as if the last four years haven't happened? I don't like it."

Daniel slumped back in his chair, crossed his arms, and stewed like an entitled teenager.

"Are you finished?" Gus asked after a moment.

Daniel gave a reluctant nod. He repositioned himself in his seat, ready for his grandpa to chastise him for his attitude. He deserved it, but he couldn't help himself. If only unloading his gripes with Isabel made him feel any better.

Instead, Gus lifted a knobby finger and pointed it at Daniel's heart. "How are you feeling about seeing her again? I mean, how are you really feeling, Danny?"

Daniel scrubbed his hands over his face, fighting to get his emotions into check. "It doesn't sound like my idea of a good time."

"And why is that? Because you don't like her anymore, or because you do?"

Daniel opened his mouth to respond and deny any lingering feelings for Izzy, but his grandfather went on before he could get a word out. Which was for the best. Gus would see right through his façade.

"You know, I always wondered why you didn't follow Isabel to LA."

Daniel frowned. How were they even having this conversation? "I told you, Grandpa. I wasn't going to leave you behind."

Gus rested his elbows on the arms of his chair and steepled his fingers. "I remember what you told me, Danny, but I always suspected there was something else holding you back. Perhaps a little bit of fear?"

Daniel scoffed. "I wasn't afraid. I'm not afraid of Isabel, Grandpa." After four years, the denial came so naturally he almost believed it himself.

"If you say so." His grandfather leveled him with a look, the cavernous creases around his eyes deepening as he tightened his gaze. "But you can't sit here and tell me you've moved on from her."

Daniel winced and turned away.

"All I'm suggesting is that you don't let any fears you may or may not have keep you from exploring any remaining potential there."

Daniel turned Gus's words over in his mind as his grandpa changed the subject, talking Daniel's ear off about the Brewers' left fielder and his back-to-back walk-off home runs over the weekend. He was grateful Gus didn't push him.

Truth be told, it didn't matter if Gus was right about Daniel's feelings for Isabel, even if Daniel was reluctant to admit it. What Gus didn't understand was that there wasn't any hope for the two of them, no matter what Daniel's heart wanted. Because his grandfather didn't know the full story, and Gus wouldn't be proud if he found out what Daniel had done.

At that thought, a shot of guilt ripped through Daniel, and the walls of the small assisted-living room his grandpa called home seemed to close in on him.

Someday, he'd tell his grandfather the truth. But not today.

Chapter 4

Isabel

"So, who'll we see when we get to your house?"

Grace sat in the passenger seat of the rental car, staring out the window with the excitement of a golden retriever puppy as Isabel navigated the back roads on the way into Mapleton.

Isabel arched her brow. "We? You'll be seeing no one. I'll be seeing my parents."

She wasn't even sure her parents would be home. She'd texted them that she was headed back to town, but she hadn't given them a specific ETA.

Grace pouted. "Come on. What are you going to do, make me wait in the car?"

"Yes, actually. That's exactly what I'm going to do."

"No way. I didn't come all this way not to meet your folks. I'm sure they're lovely people."

Isabel bit her lip. She didn't want to come out and tell Grace she was embarrassed by her humble home, but that was a part of it. She'd all but shed her small-town roots in an effort to fit in with her swankier clientele. Grace had never known her other than in the capacity of a well-established designer. She wasn't sure how she would react to seeing where Isabel came from—how it would color Grace's opinion of her.

"I don't know why it matters so much to you," Isabel hedged.

"Don't be silly. It matters to me because we've been working together for two years. I consider you a friend, and I'd like to see who made you, you."

"I made me, me." Isabel kept her eyes on the road, ignoring how prideful she sounded. She'd never meant to get to this point—being a woman on an island. But that's what had happened. And she'd told herself it was better this way. Isabel didn't even let herself think about home because if she did, the twisting in her gut felt an awful lot like regret.

But regret? No way. She loved her life in LA. She had everything she could ever dream of—well, almost everything. She didn't have her family, and she didn't have—

Grace harrumphed. "Don't give me that malarkey. I know all about Isabel Marshall, self-made design icon. And I'm proud of you, you know that. But I want to meet the people who formed you into the woman who was able to drive out to LA by herself and take it by storm."

Isabel was silent as she drove up and over a hill. The base of her sternum ached with a desire to see those people, too—*her* people. But she was afraid they'd hold the past four years against her, and then what would she do?

"Please." Grace stretched out the word, folding her hands together in prayer.

Isabel let loose an exaggerated sigh. "Fine. But we're not staying long."

She may as well satisfy Grace's curiosity before the rest of the production crew arrived. Hopefully, she'd be placated, and Isabel could deflect attention away from her childhood home for the rest of her time here—while somehow also making peace with her parents.

She fought the urge to moan. This was going to be impossible.

Grace was oblivious to Isabel's inner crisis. She pumped her fist in the air. "Yes!"

Isabel shook her head as she eased the car over one final hill, and the trees of Sunrise Park came into view.

"Welcome to Mapleton, Grace. Population two thousand, one hundred, and thirty-three," she said, parroting the sign along the side of the road.

Her friend's eyes were glued out the window. "So, this is it?"

Isabel tapped the brakes and coasted for a beat, remembering the local police force was only so happy to pull over drivers who failed to respect the in-town speed limits. She pressed the automatic window buttons and rolled them down, inhaling the scent of the village—all riverwater musk and freshly mown grass—for the first time in what felt like a lifetime.

"This is it," she echoed. A thrill fluttered in her chest as she found herself explaining landmarks to Grace with a hint of fondness in her voice.

"Over there is the town's swim lake. It's a man-made pond surrounded on all sides by sand. Best place to cool off in the summer. And this is Sunrise Park." She pointed to a dense clump of trees, their branches swaying as a gust of wind swept through Mapleton. A walking path wove in and out of the woods. A pair of women dressed in neon wind suits were out for a morning stroll. Beyond them, she could barely make out the Squirrel River. Its blue-brown current ran leisurely along the north side of town.

"This is gorgeous, Iz." Grace craned her neck toward the windshield. "Hey, are those baseball fields?"

Isabel nodded. Beyond the trees and flanked by the river were the village's baseball diamonds.

"Mapleton is big into baseball," she explained. "The town hosts a ton of tournaments. And this must be Julia's café. She was starting to renovate the building as I left town. Wow, it looks amazing."

Isabel stared in awe at the crisp, honey-colored wood shingles accented with black trim and shutters. The white picket fence along the lot line gave the building a story-book vibe. Cedar flower boxes brimming with pink and red blooms enhanced the effect. The parking lot in front of the café was almost completely filled. Business must have been good.

"It's seriously darling. I cannot wait to meet Julia in person!" Grace exclaimed.

Isabel's gaze hovered on the refurbished café as she drove by. From the looks of it, things in Mapleton had changed. A shiver of insecurity ran through her. Where did she fit here anymore? *Did she fit here?*

She did a double-take when a man with a familiar frame walked out of the café, and then she shivered for a whole other reason.

Daniel Smith held his hand up to shade the sun from his eyes—Isabel's favorite of his facial features—and squinted at her car as it passed by.

Isabel's cheeks burned. She found herself holding her breath as she ratcheted her gaze back to the road in front of her, gripping the steering wheel for dear life and sinking down in the leather seat, trying to hide herself.

"You okay?" Grace was staring at her with a crinkled brow.

Isabel chanced a look in the rearview mirror.

Daniel had turned and was walking toward a vehicle, his back to her car. A woman had followed him out of the café, and Isabel caught a fleeting glimpse of his profile as he smiled at whomever she was.

A strong shot of jealousy slithered across her stomach. She sat up straighter in her seat, actively ignoring the unsettled feeling in her gut.

She could hardly believe it. What were the chances she'd see Daniel before she'd even been in town for five minutes? Then again, this was Mapleton—not a very vast expanse. She was bound to run into him at some point. A tiny part of her had been hoping that he'd lost some of his good looks over the last four years. Apparently, that wasn't going to be the case. She'd seen the way his biceps bulged from beneath his short-sleeve shirt. Yes, they *were* defined enough that she was able to ogle them, even just driving by, which proved her point.

And was he dating someone?

Isabel caught sight of Grace, who was waiting on her response, out of the corner of her eye, so she masked her dismay. "I'm fine. Totally fine."

Grace crossed her arms and sat back in the seat next to Isabel. "If you say so, but I'm not sure I believe you."

They passed the town water tower, tinted a pale blue with *Mapleton* stenciled on it in navy paint, and Isabel focused on her breathing. She needed to pull herself together. Her reaction to Daniel was probably the result of her shock at such an unexpected sighting. That was all. Good for him if he had a girlfriend. He should. He was a good man.

And she *was* fine. She had to be. Because she had other things to worry about.

"I'm just really anxious about seeing everyone again. Especially my family," Isabel admitted as she turned right off of Mapleton Avenue and drove two blocks down Crabapple Street. "Here we are."

She pulled to the curb in front of her parents' modest two-story, saltbox-style home. The siding was light yellow, and the navy shutters looked a bit more faded than they did four years ago. Her mom's begonias hung in baskets from the shepherd's hook positioned near the front door, just as Isabel remembered. The "We Are Marshall" sign her father brought home after the movie's premiere was staked in the woodchip-filled berm to the right of the house.

"This is cute," Grace said.

Isabel eyed Grace, trying to gauge her sincerity, because Isabel couldn't help but look at the house and see all it was lacking.

"I'm serious!" Grace assured her. "I can't wait to see inside."

"Well, you're about to. Here goes nothing," Isabel mumbled as she opened the door and climbed out, stretching her stiff limbs. Her heart pounded as she walked up the short path to the front door and knocked before she could second-guess herself.

Grace stayed a few paces behind her.

Though she'd given her a hard time about coming in, Isabel was thankful she was here. Isabel didn't know if she would have had the nerve to come at all if Grace hadn't forced her, and Grace could be an excuse to leave if things got too tense.

As Isabel put an escape plan in place, the front door swung open, and only the screen separated her from her mother, Val Marshall.

Her mom looked about the same: pear-shaped, brown hair that was turning gray along her scalp line, wearing a worn Mapleton Shredders T-shirt and last season's blue jeans. Fashion icon she was not.

Val blinked once, squinting her eyes as if bringing the scene in front of her into focus. Isabel couldn't tell whether or not Val liked what she saw until her mom shoved open the screen door and bull-rushed her.

"Galloping grasshoppers! Isabel Marshall, as I live and breathe!"

Isabel couldn't help but let a small laugh escape as she was engulfed in a hug. It was a nervous laugh, to be sure, but there was some degree of relief in the fact that her mother didn't take one look at her and slam the door in her face.

"You're home. You're actually home? Oh my goodness, let me look at you." Her mom pulled away and studied her face.

"Hi, Mom."

"You're beautiful. Prettier in person than you are on TV, even, I'd say! Look at your brows! Are they tattooed on? Oh, and I love your longer hair. Very chic." Val prattled on without pause. "Oh, my word. We didn't know when we'd see you. And I told the whole town, 'I'll believe it when she gets here.' But now, here you are! You could have called to give us a head's up. Then again, that's not really been your style as of late, now has it? Well, never mind that for now. Come in, come in."

Isabel absorbed the slight jabs about her lack of communication as her mother grasped her hand and tugged her inside. She was already formulating excuses and defenses as they walked together into the cramped living room.

"Dave! Come down quick," Val hollered up the stairs. "You'll never guess who's here."

Isabel wandered forward, taking stock of the space. Not much had changed here in four years. Her mom and dad hadn't updated the 1970s pea-soup green carpet. It clashed with their faded orange-and-brown floral couch and leather rocker recliner. The white brick on the fireplace that stretched across the whole side wall of the room had potential, but the mantel was chock full of her mother's knick-knacks.

"Take a seat, take a seat."

Her mom fluttered about like an overactive hummingbird, her chirps interrupting Isabel's internal critique of the room.

"What can I get for you two? And clearly, my Isabel has forgotten her manners since moving out to California. I'm Val Marshall, and you are?" She held out her hand to Grace.

"Grace Bartal. It is an absolute pleasure, Mrs. Marshall."

Isabel rolled her eyes so far back into her head she worried they might get stuck.

Grace shined her teacher's-pet smile at Val. "A glass of water would be wonderful."

"That's good for me, too, Mom."

"Be back in a jiffy, then."

Her mother dashed to the kitchen, and Isabel plopped down on the couch, wishing she could climb into the chimney and escape.

The cuckoo clock on the wall blared, and Isabel suppressed a groan. It was all so kitschy.

And that, *that* was the reason Isabel had left Mapleton four years ago. There was a total lack of design acumen going on here, and had she stayed in her hometown, she would have been spinning her wheels. She needed the bigger stage to stretch her design wings and fly.

Out of the corner of her eye, she glanced at Grace as her friend sat down next to her, her head on a swivel as she took in the room. What must she be thinking? And what would the rest of the crew think of Isabel after seeing where she grew up? They'd think she was a fraud. Then again, Isabel didn't sense any condemnation in Grace's gaze, just curiosity.

"Izzy."

Isabel jumped at the sound of her childhood nickname.

Her father, Dave Marshall, stood at the base of the steps, smiling at her.

"Hi, Dad."

She rose and went to him. He hugged her, and she smiled, too. He smelled like leather and the laundry soap her family always used.

He smelled like home.

A lump formed in Isabel's throat. She cleared it away, stepping back.

Her dad studied her. "It's good to see you, pumpkin. It's been a long time. Too long."

Her mother bustled into the room, holding two glasses filled with ice and water. "Oh good, Dave. You heard me. Here you two go." She handed one glass to Isabel and gave the other one to Grace. "Let's sit. We have so much to catch up on."

Isabel obeyed, sipping some water to cool her burning throat.

"We can't stay long, but we wanted to pop in." She didn't know what to say—what her parents wanted to hear.

Grace put her hand on Isabel's arm, patting it twice. "Actually, we have plenty of time."

Isabel flashed her friend a cease-and-desist look, but Grace avoided her attempted eye contact.

"We don't have much to do for the rest of the afternoon. Isabel's team doesn't arrive until later tonight or tomorrow, and she doesn't really start work until they all get situated."

"'Isabel's team.' Golly. Aren't you fancy now, Iz? Much too fancy for us, that's for sure." Val sounded breezy, but Isabel detected a layer of hurt underneath her words. She opened her mouth to try to head her mom off, but Val had turned her attention to Grace. "How do you two know each other? And Grace, dear, are you single?"

Isabel sucked in a mortified gasp. "Mom!"

Grace's eyes danced with amusement. "It's fine. I'm actually Isabel's assistant. And yes, Mrs. Marshall, I am single. But always ready to mingle."

She winked and was rewarded with a knowing smile from Val.

"Grace was one of the first people I met when I landed the TV show gig. She's got an impeccable eye for design, too." Maybe if Isabel buttered Grace up enough, she would stop getting all chummy with her parents, and they could leave. Isabel already felt like she needed to regroup.

"How nice." Her mother clasped her hands with delight. "Thanks for taking care of our Izzy. Someone's had to."

Isabel bit the inside of her cheek. "Mom, I—"

"It's been wonderful to get to know her over these years. She's remarkable." Grace swooped in to save her, giving her a warm nudge.

In spite of herself, Isabel's lips ticked upward.

Isabel's dad nodded from across the room. "We could have told you that. She's always been destined for big things, our Isabel. It's too bad we no longer have a front-row seat to what she's doing. It's been hard to lose touch."

Isabel's stomach clenched. If she thought they could avoid the elephant in the room, she'd thought wrong. Her dad wasn't one to mince words.

"I've been super busy, Dad, and—"

"We tune in to your show every week. We're always happy to see you doing your thing." Though Val had all but started it, she evidently didn't want to have this conversation in front of Grace, so she changed the subject. "But now, Izzy, what about you? Are you single?"

Isabel closed her eyes for a second before glancing at her mom. "Yep. I am."

"There's always Tad Darling to consider." Grace took a sip of her water, unruffled as could be.

Isabel resisted the urge to smack her.

Her mom was all over the name drop. "Tad Darling? *The* Tad Darling? Star of that new sit-com? What's it called?"

"*Brighter Days,*" Grace supplied.

Her mom snapped her fingers. "That's it." She cocked her head at Isabel. "What's going on between you and Tad?"

"Absolutely nothing, Mom. Believe me." Isabel liked Tad well enough. He was respectful, interesting, and Hollywood handsome with jet-black hair that fell in a swoop across his forehead. They served as each other's dates to business events, but beyond that and the occasional weekend dinner date over the past six months, Isabel rarely saw or thought about Tad. For that reason, things had remained strictly platonic between them. That, and Isabel had never felt the spark with him.

Her mom screwed up her mouth, but then shrugged. "Well, that's a shame. Then again, maybe that'll work in your favor. Before you leave Mapleton, you could both be fixed up right nice. There are a lot of wonderful gentlemen in town, you know." Val directed this last line at Grace, who nodded, looking wide-eyed and convinced.

Isabel protested, even as the memory of a specific man from Mapleton crowded into her thoughts. One drive-by sighting of Daniel had left Isabel feeling more of *something* than all her time spent with Tad combined.

"Mom, I don't need a man to—"

"Believe me. I know. You don't need anyone, Iz. I got it." Val swiped her hand through the air. "But all of Mapleton is absolutely thrilled at the thought of you coming here to do some filming."

"We're very excited, too," Grace answered for her, arching an eyebrow in a pointed way. "Right, Isabel?"

Isabel nodded, putting on a serene face. "Just thrilled."

"Maybe we could film some shots here. You know, show people where you came from?" Grace surveyed the cramped living room, as if assessing its lighting for production.

"What? No!" All the serenity she was faking fled as Isabel shot a look around. How could Grace suggest such a thing? Was she not sitting in the same room? Didn't she see how awful it all looked? Nothing matched. Nothing coordinated.

At Isabel's outburst, her mom frowned and looked down at her hands, twiddling her thumbs as she pinched the rest of her fingers together.

A cold rush of shame doused Isabel, and she tried to recover. "I mean, I'm sure we'll have plenty of footage at the actual houses we're designing. I doubt there'll be time for extra filming here."

"Well, how long are you staying?" Val asked, returning a staunch gaze to Isabel.

"My producer thinks we can accomplish everything we need to accomplish in a month."

"Here for a whole month!" Her mother's jaw dropped open. "Wowzers. I'll make up your old bed with fresh linens, and we'll even turn on the air conditioning for you."

"I actually have a room at the hotel in Turner."

The look her mom and dad exchanged—a mixture of exasperation and disappointment in their gazes—told her she may as well have stuck her foot directly into her mouth. But the truth was, she hadn't known if her parents would want anything to do with her, so she'd made other plans.

Her mother faced her and scowled. "Nonsense, Isabel Marshall. I don't care how long it has been since you were back in Mapleton or whether or not you believe it's only necessary to call home a couple times a year. When you are in town, you will stay in this house. It is your home."

Grace was watching their exchange, undoubtedly cataloging each line, each show of body language, so she could pummel Isabel with questions later. Her dad was similarly studying her from his recliner across the room.

"Okay. I-I mean, if you're sure. But just so you know, I'm going to have a lot of work to do for the show. I don't know how much I'll be around." Isabel raised her shoulders to her ears and let them drop in a shrug, trying to temper her mom's expectations.

"I don't care if I don't see your cute little hiney at all while you're here, busy as you may be, but your head will go to sleep on that pillow in your room upstairs. That's my final answer."

When her mother set her mind to something, little could be done to sway her. Come to think of it, Val was where Isabel had inherited some of her own tenacity.

Isabel let loose a shaky breath. "Okay, then."

This was her chance to try to make amends with her parents. Ready or not.

Chapter 5

ISABEL

AFTER A COUPLE MORE minutes of small talk and working out logistics, Isabel went to fetch her bags.

Grace trailed her to the car. "Your parents are great."

"Yeah. They are." And that knowledge only made Isabel miserable at the moment.

"It's really nice that you can stay here." Grace pressed on. "It'll be such a good chance for you to reconnect."

"I know, Grace." Isabel's voice held a bit of annoyance. She pressed her lips together. Grace didn't deserve that. "Sorry. It's a lot, you know? You saw the house I grew up in. Don't you understand why I left? This is like the antithesis of a creative well. And now both of my parents are giving me a severe "you abandoned us" vibe. And don't even get me started on Ford."

"Who's Ford?"

"My brother."

"Is he hot?"

Her friend was trying to lighten the mood, but Isabel couldn't summon any good humor.

"Stop," she whimpered.

"What? It's a fair question." Grace nudged her shoulder. "What's the deal, then?"

Isabel swung the key ring around on her finger. "Ford and I were close, but we've drifted. I imagine he'll be about as happy to see me as I am to see a spider in the shower. I'm sure he thinks I ditched him."

"Did you?"

"No. Yes. I don't know. None of it was on purpose. This is such a mess. And this is why I didn't want to come back here." She hooked her thumb over her shoulder, gesturing to her parents' house.

"Just relax, Isabel." She smirked. "Or should I say, Izzy."

Isabel wrinkled her nose. She'd dropped the childlike nickname the second she crossed the state line, rebuilding herself as Isabel Marshall, a professional design expert. Izzy Marshall was a young, naïve creative with no direction for her craft.

Then again, a small part of her missed being just Izzy, but Isabel didn't know what to do with that realization. It was throwing her completely off balance, because she wasn't that girl anymore.

"Listen," Grace said, undeterred. "All I'm saying is, you shouldn't sell your parents or your town short. If you give it a chance, I'm sure you'll be inspired in Mapleton as much, if not more, than you are in LA. Maybe that inspiration will hit you in different ways. And it's easy to see your parents are proud of you. Maybe let them in a little bit, yeah?"

Isabel popped the trunk and didn't respond. She hoisted her bags out of the car before reluctantly giving Grace the keys. She hugged her goodbye and stood on the porch, waving as Grace drove off.

"Well now," her mom said from behind her. "Let's get you settled."

"I'll take your bags." Her dad grabbed the suitcases from her hands, and Isabel turned and trailed them both into the house.

Dave led the way up the stairs. Isabel remembered which boards creaked and which boards didn't, thanks to all the times she'd snuck in and up to her room after curfew. Back then, one wrong step and she would have been busted. Now, she couldn't help but think she was only one slight misstep away from having the past four years blow up in her face.

"Here ya go, pumpkin." Her dad set down the bags at the foot of her bed.

Isabel walked into the room she'd grown up in and turned in a circle. Her small writing desk sat in the corner with a lava lamp plugged into the wall. The faded pink comforter on her bed was folded neatly and accented with white throw pillows. The lace curtains she'd sewn herself hung on either side of the window over her bed. The corners of her Backstreet Boys poster had curled further, but otherwise, nothing had changed. This room was like a time capsule of her high school years.

"I'll let you get situated. Dinner will be at six o'clock." Her dad shut the door with a soft click. The hallway floor squeaked as he walked downstairs.

Isabel's heart stuttered as she sunk down on her bed and stared into space. Her dad sounded like the concierge at a hotel, so formal and starched. Is that the way she held herself? As if she wanted to be treated as nothing more than an unfamiliar guest?

Isabel felt like there was a ratchet strap around her stomach that kept getting clicked another notch tighter. The guilt was catching up with her.

She thrust it away, sitting up straighter. She wasn't going to be ashamed of the life she built. As she looked around at her humble beginnings, she squared her shoulders. She was proud of what she had made herself into. She wouldn't apologize for her success.

She flopped back on the bed then, pressing the heels of her hands into her eyes. What she *did* need to figure out was how to balance that success with the other areas of her life she'd all but neglected. She just wasn't sure how.

After a moment, Isabel sat up again and slid her laptop out of her computer bag, turning it on to get to work. As the screen lit up, Isabel bit back a curse. She'd forgotten to ask her parents for their Wi-Fi password, and she was too drained to face them again right now.

Wait a minute.

Isabel frowned, leaning closer to her screen and peering at the illuminated bars of the Wi-Fi icon. She was online. But how was that possible?

Isabel checked her settings, and a surge of affection for her parents hit her square in the chest, choking her up. *Of course* her parents' internet network was unrestricted. That was so typical of them—of all of Mapleton, really. Everybody trusted everybody. Her parents wouldn't password protect their network because why would they care if a neighbor hopped on and used it once in a while? They knew everyone on their street, so there wasn't a second thought given to the potential for stolen information.

Isabel would have to charge her phone and work from her wireless hotspot. Her parents may not have had information to guard, but she did. If anyone found out she was staying here, they could easily hack the network and see all her future blog post ideas and her book draft.

Not that that was anything to write home about.

The familiar flare of panic hit her, unsettling her stomach like bad cheese. Isabel was getting desperate to figure out what direction she was going to take her book. Her draft deadline was less than two weeks after she was scheduled to return to California, which meant she'd have to work out the kinks here.

Isabel sighed. She'd worry about all she had riding on the book later. Right now, she needed to write and schedule a blog post.

Her blog, *Inspired*, was her baby. It was the first thing she'd poured her heart into out in LA, and it was what had landed her the show on the Home and Style Network. While everything else about her career had taken off and required multiple employees, Isabel still wrote every one of her blog posts herself.

Isabel closed her eyes, shut down her wandering thoughts, and forced herself to focus. Five minutes later, she started typing, processing life through her words as she so often did.

...So I guess what I'm saying is, sometimes plans change, and you have to roll with it. If you get stuck in a design rut, or if

you are working around a fixture that you can't move and don't particularly love, don't be afraid to pivot. Let your creativity take over, and you'll be surprised at the solutions you come up with. Maybe it's placing an enlarged family photo on a fireplace mantel to add warmth and personality, or choosing a paint color you hadn't previously considered that'll help to tone down a bold bathroom tile. Whatever challenge you're facing, know I'm rooting for you. Have fun with it, and be sure to share your results or the solutions you've come up with in the comments below. Until next time, dear readers, happy designing.

Love, Inspired

Isabel always smiled when she saw the signature on the bottom of her blog posts. It started as a pithy attempt to keep her anonymity. When she was new to LA, despite wanting to make a name for herself, she was terrified of anyone finding out her identity. So, she signed her posts "Inspired." It stuck, and now, even though everyone knew it was Isabel Marshall who ran the wildly successful blog, she kept her old signature as a small tribute to how far she'd come.

And, if she was being honest, because she was still a little uncomfortable in her own skin.

Isabel proofed her post and scheduled it to publish before she shut down her computer and leaned back on her bed. But she was too fidgety to get comfortable.

No sooner had she stood and started pacing the room than the little voice inside her head that Isabel usually referred to as her instinct rang out loud and clear.

Take your own advice.

Isabel paused in front of her window and looked out over her parents' front yard. This trip home was a significant pivot, one she felt completely ill-prepared to make. But like she'd written, deep down, she knew she should make the most of it. And that started with making up for lost time with her parents. She was rusty, but she needed to figure out how to make this pivot with grace.

Chapter 6

Daniel

Daniel leaned back in his chair and blew out a frustrated breath. He should have known better than to think he was going to be able to be productive today. Not with all the ruckus surrounding him.

On Deck Café was pulsating with energy. Everyone and their brother was dropping by the café, or what they'd taken to calling *Ground Zero*, ever since Julia made work of shepherding Isabel to Mapleton. Rumors were swirling about when the villagers thought they might catch their first glimpse of the hometown-girl-turned-big-star.

"Well, I heard from Nancy, who spoke to Val herself, that Isabel arrived yesterday afternoon. She's staying with them on Crabapple Street." Marge's voice carried across the dining room.

"Of course she's staying with them." Mable Glasheen crossed her arms. "That's her home. Where else would she go?"

The answer to Mable's question was lost in the grinding of ice behind the counter. Julia was working overtime alongside her business partner and best friend, Amanda, to fill all the orders.

Daniel turned to his computer screen. He needed to do something, anything, to keep his mind occupied. Unlike the elated anticipation felt by everyone else in the café at the thought that they could see Isabel, in the flesh, at any moment, Daniel was unnerved. He was equal parts excited to see her and filled with dread. No matter how they had parted, and no matter what had happened in the interim, half of his heart would always belong to Isabel Marshall.

His grandpa was right: he hadn't moved on from her.

Daniel repositioned his chair so his back was to the rest of the café. He hated to be antisocial, but he had enough thoughts of Isabel on his own without the town's speculations added in. He retrieved his headphones from his backpack and got to work.

Opening up his to-do list, he groaned. He really needed to tackle his article for *Brides of Wisconsin*, the state's premier wedding magazine. But in his present frame of mind, he could hardly think about weddings or brides without conjuring up an image of Isabel—dressed in a white gown, with baby's breath tucked in her copper-colored hair, walking toward him at the altar.

Get a grip, man.

Daniel pressed his index finger and thumb into his closed eyes. He could do this. He was a business professional. He'd written about weddings dozens of times, and this would be no different. Besides, it would only be more of a challenge after he saw Isabel for himself.

His topic for this article was *shopping for a bridal gown*. His editor wanted him to touch on how many bridal gowns the average bride-to-be tries on before finding "the one," and how a bride knows "the one" when she sees it.

Obviously, he didn't have any first-hand experience in this department, so Daniel would need to crowd source. He could ask on the *Brides of Wisconsin* social media platforms and come up with an accurate survey of the brides in the area. Another option popped into his head, and he ripped out his headphones.

"Hey, Amanda!"

Daniel flagged down the barista. Seth, another barista at On Deck Café and a friend of Daniel's, proposed to the feisty redhead a couple months before. Seth was a cool guy. Come to think of it, Daniel would love to hear his thoughts on the wedding-planning process, and that gave him an idea, inspiration percolating for an entire series of articles. But he tabled the thought for now, turning his attention to Amanda, who finished wiping down an adjacent table and joined him.

"What's up?" She balled up the rag in her hands.

"Could I interview you for some first-hand commentary on your recent bridal gown hunt?"

"Gosh, I guess." Amanda tucked an errant curl underneath her bandana. "If it would help."

"It would be a huge help," Daniel assured her.

"Okay. I'm in."

"Thank you so much."

Smiling to himself, Daniel put his headphones back in and started typing away. His upbeat playlist was successfully drowning out the chatter of the rest of the café, and his faith was restored in his ability to be productive.

After getting an introduction and outline organized, he paused, extending his arms in front of him and cracking his knuckles before getting back to work. He clicked the keys in time to the music until he felt a hand come to rest on his back. Simultaneously, he smelled the scent of honeysuckle that he only ever associated with one person.

Daniel's stomach turned inside out, and the hair on his neck stood up. He took out his headphones and turned to see Julia. Standing behind her was none other than...

"Isabel."

Her name came out as an exhale. Daniel wasn't sure if he'd spoken aloud. His heartbeat thudded so loud in his ears he could barely hear anything else.

"Hi." Daniel stood up, banging his knee on the table and sloshing coffee out of his mug.

"Hi." Isabel stared back at him, glowing like the first glimmer of the sun at the end of a long, gray winter.

Daniel looked away, directing his gaze to Julia, who had started talking.

"Sorry to interrupt your work," the bubbly barista chattered, "but we're slammed. Can I steal these chairs? Or is there any chance Isabel and her friend here could share your table for a bit? They're waiting on Samson to arrive."

His eyes flicked to Isabel. After all this time, she still took his breath away. She wore her reddish-brown hair longer than she used to, but it fell in familiar, flawless waves near the tips. Her dark, deep-set eyes were framed by soft, full eyelashes. Her skin still looked milky smooth, dusted with a few freckles around her nose.

Daniel dragged his attention back to Julia. "Sure."

"You're the best, Daniel. Thanks!" Julia hugged him and hustled behind the counter. "We could not be happier you're here, Isabel!" she called over her shoulder.

Isabel waved to the hurried barista and turned to him. "I'm so sorry to intrude, Daniel."

He hadn't heard the sweet sound of her voice saying his name for four years, and Daniel was sure his heart was on the verge of combusting. He wouldn't be surprised if smoke started seeping out from between the buttons on his shirt. He attempted to play it cool as she looked him up and down, but it was terribly difficult not to stare at her.

"It's no problem at all. Please sit. Daniel Smith, by the way." He held out his hand to the woman with Isabel, proud of himself for keeping his voice relatively even.

The woman returned his handshake and stared at him with a look of blatant curiosity. Her sharp blue eyes were emphasized by the baby-blue blouse and white capris she was wearing. Daniel had the sinking suspicion that, whoever she was, this woman was about to read the situation between Isabel and him like an open book.

"Where are my manners? Daniel, this is my assistant, Grace Bartal. Grace, Daniel Smith, my—" Isabel hesitated, as if unsure how to categorize him. Her flushed cheeks betrayed...something. Was it nerves? Embarrassment? An ounce of remaining attraction? He didn't know. Whatever it was, it only made his blood knock harder through his veins.

He released Grace's hand and, out of a habit he didn't think would ever die, filled in Isabel's blanks.

"Isabel and I go way back."

Grace smiled easily at him and nodded. "Nice to meet you."

She scooted into her chair first. Isabel followed her lead, and there she sat, across from him. Daniel sunk into his seat and shut his laptop, fumbling for a napkin to sop up his spilled coffee. He hadn't the first idea of what to say to Isabel. The silence stretched between them—enough to fill four years.

"So…" Grace's gaze flitted from Isabel and Daniel. "This is quite the establishment. Is it always this packed?"

Daniel glanced behind him for the first time. Julia's dining room was at capacity. He recognized many people from town, but mixed in were a lot of new faces.

"It seems like you and Isabel brought some friends who are making it more crowded than usual, but yes, to answer your question, Julia runs one of the best businesses around."

"I couldn't believe it when we drove by for the first time," Isabel interjected, respect filling her tone. "This building didn't look anything like this when I left."

"Julia's a testament to what someone can do if they stick their heart and soul into a business in this town. The villagers respond in kind and support her through and through."

Isabel sat up straighter. Her mouth flattened into a long, thin line, and her eyes narrowed almost imperceptibly. But Daniel noticed. Just like he noticed that she was picking at the hangnail on the side of her thumb, which meant she wasn't as cool, calm, and collected as she was trying to appear.

He refused to back down from her, so he held her cutting gaze. He hadn't meant to ruffle her feathers, but what he said was true. Julia had made something of herself in Mapleton. Isabel could have done the same thing if she would have chosen to stay.

If only she would have chosen to stay.

Grace babbled on, either oblivious to or intentionally ignoring the silent tension that ran taut between Isabel and Daniel. "The coffee is delicious. I'm sure that helps."

"It's the best around," Daniel agreed.

"So we've gathered." Isabel motioned to his computer. "Were you working?"

"Yep. This is my office. Business is good." He tipped his head to the packed café.

When he looked back at Isabel, he was rewarded with the slight upturning of her lips, the strain of the previous moment diffused with his joke. They never were the sort of couple who fought and stayed mad at each other. Other than when she left town, they'd always been on the same page.

"What do you do?" Grace sipped her drink and studied him.

Thank goodness she was here. Daniel's thoughts were hanging dangerously close to the rim of the cliff called *memories*. If not for Grace, he was sure he'd make a wrong move and find himself careening over the edge.

He already knew how the crash landing felt.

"I'm a freelance writer. Mostly content marketing stuff and articles for the local paper and magazines around the state. I've worked with a couple of national publications over the years, too. But for the most part, it's a modest gig."

Grace gave an appreciative nod. "Sounds like a great job to me. Working here, flexible hours. What's not to like?"

Daniel chuckled. "That's exactly how I feel."

"Hey, you could give Isabel some pointers. She's got a book in the works."

Isabel's gaze dropped to the table between them, and the thumb-rubbing ramped up. She was uncomfortable with this topic.

Picking up on that, Daniel kept his response subdued. "I heard through the grapevine about your book deal. Congratulations. That's really impressive. I'm sure you don't need any help from little old me."

Isabel shot him a look, a smidgen of worry flashing across her eyes before she smiled and hid it. "Thank you. I've got some work to do, but it's a great opportunity. I'm hopeful that it'll all come together."

Daniel frowned. Something was up with the book project that was affecting Isabel's confidence, which was unexpected. When it came to design, décor, and her work, Isabel had never *not* been confident. Before he could press her on it, Isabel changed the subject.

"What are you writing about now?"

"Actually, I was working on an article for *Brides of Wisconsin* magazine." Daniel's hands were suddenly clammy.

Isabel's sculpted brows rose, and her perfectly shaped lips quirked. "Wow, what makes you a wedding expert these days?"

She was teasing him, and gosh, had he missed the way she teased him.

One time in college, he'd gotten a parking ticket for leaving his old Chevy in a street parking spot overnight, and Isabel hadn't let him live it down for weeks. She badgered him relentlessly, calling him her little law-breaker and pretending to debate whether or not she was comfortable dating a criminal. He'd let her take her digs until, one time, he played along and told her with a record like his, she might be better off without him.

He could still picture the shocked look on her face. She'd jumped into his arms, wrapping her legs around his waist in a move that he'd seen repeated too many times on the reality TV show *The Bachelor*—which he'd only ever watched for work, by the way.

"Daniel Smith," Isabel had said. "Don't you *dare* say I'm better off without you *ever* again, you hear me?"

Daniel had kissed her square on the mouth then, and they'd laughed.

But that was a long time ago. And as it turned out, Isabel *was* better off without him—or at least that was how it seemed when she'd made the choice to leave him and not come back.

Until now.

Daniel realized Isabel was waiting for him to answer her question.

"I have a standing commitment to write an article a month for the magazine, so I guess you could say I'm an expert of sorts. My editor tells me the readers enjoy hearing a male perspective, and I never mind digging into the wedding industry—photographers, flowers, venues, ceremony locations, cakes. The opportunities for interesting articles are endless. This month, it's all about bridal gowns."

"God bless you, man," Grace said wryly. "I don't know that I would have the gumption to wade into the taffeta, organza-filled world of weddings and write about that sort of thing."

"Well, thanks." Daniel gulped down some of his coffee before meeting Isabel's eyes.

She held his gaze for a beat before peering around the rest of the café, and Daniel had to work to swallow the pesky sensation in his mouth that tasted a lot like fresh-brewed desire.

Curse his runaway brain for dragging up thoughts of the past. And curse his traitorous heart for still yearning for the woman sitting across from him after all these years.

You don't even know her anymore, his head tried to reason with his heart. *But you want to*, his heart thudded back.

Daniel ran his hand along his neck, squeezing the skin that covered the top of his spinal cord, hoping to force some composure into his nervous system.

"So," he said, "what are you two up to today?"

"Samson's going to show me around the houses they want me to work on. I'll try to get a feel for them before we plan out our filming schedule. Then, I got roped into dinner at my parents' house tonight." Isabel heaved a sigh.

Daniel itched his top lip to hide his frown. Isabel had never been much of a family girl. Well, that wasn't entirely fair. She loved her family, but she hadn't thought twice about leaving them. It was a significant difference between the two of them. Isabel's family had always been there, in her corner, whether she wanted them there or not. She didn't know any different. He doubted she could comprehend the depth of loneliness she would experience if they were no longer around, supporting her.

He, on the other hand, understood life was fragile. Although he didn't remember losing his parents because he was so young, he was always extra thankful for his grandparents' willingness to take care of him and give him a stable home life growing up. And when his grandmother passed away, it hit him hard. He wished he could make Isabel see what a gift her family was, but she'd have to come to that conclusion on her own.

"Isabel Marshall?" Samson's deep voice sounded behind Daniel, and the general contractor stopped at the end of their table.

Isabel and Grace rose to greet him.

Daniel stood and took a step back, allowing the trio to chat and make introductions. As they turned to go, Samson shook Daniel's hand.

"Good to see you, brother. Let's get together soon."

"You got it. Name a time."

"I'll be in touch." Samson turned to lead Isabel and Grace out of the café, stopping to drop a light kiss on Julia's smiling lips.

"Wonderful to meet you." Grace turned to Daniel. "I love this town already. Good people, all around."

"Can't argue with you there. See you."

Isabel lingered as Grace walked away.

"It was nice to see you." She didn't meet his eye. "Thanks again for making room for us."

Daniel nodded, and they stood there, alternatively staring at each other and the floor. The awkwardness was so thick between them Daniel could have wrapped it around himself and used it as a shield. Maybe he should do just that—try to protect his heart.

Finally, Isabel spoke. "Look, are we okay?"

Just like that, she sliced right through his defenses. He'd always struggled to say no to her, and he hated the thought of causing her pain or making her uncomfortable, so he smiled. He might have been okay, but it was a lot more complicated than that—too complicated to get into in the middle of the café.

"We're good."

She offered him a full smile, and his pulse skipped in response. She held out her hand. "Friends?"

"Friends." He clasped her fingers and ignored the shudder that her touch sent coursing through his body. "I'm sure I'll see you around, Isabel. Tell your family I say hello, and good luck on site."

"Will do. Bye, Daniel."

With that, she walked out of the café, stopping to greet a couple villagers with her Hollywood smile in the process.

Daniel eased himself into his chair, slightly stunned at what had just transpired.

At least their initial meeting was over, he reasoned. It was sort of like ripping the Band-Aid off. Now that he and Isabel had seen each other, he could lay low. He'd be cordial when they came into contact, but there was no reason to seek her out. He wasn't sure his heart could handle much exposure to her. She shone like the sun, and he was wary of getting burned.

Daniel ran a hand through his buzz cut and opened his computer, clicking the touchpad to wake up his screen. Images of wedding gowns popped up before him, and one of them may as well have reached out and taken a cheap shot to his solar plexus.

Isabel could say she wanted to be friends, but she would always be more to him than that.

Despite what he'd said and what he'd done.

Chapter 7

ISABEL

ISABEL TRAILED GRACE AND Samson into the parking lot of the cute café, hurrying over to her rental car.

"You can follow me," Samson said as he climbed into the cab of a large black truck.

Isabel shot him a thumbs up and sat down behind the wheel. The second she put the key in the ignition, Grace was all over her, giving her no chance to smooth out her frayed nerves.

"What's going on with you and Daniel?"

Isabel tried to hide her flinch by glancing out the window. "Nothing," she lied. "I haven't seen him in four years."

The truth was, when Isabel saw Daniel sitting there with his back to the café, headphones in, typing away at his computer, she was instantly transported to their college days and the countless times she had snuck up on him in the library, looking just like that—a little rumpled, with concentration etched all over his face. She used to plop herself down in his lap and wait for a kiss.

What threw her off was how drawn to him she still was after all these years. Sure, he'd changed a bit. His eyes, for example, held a hint of wariness at the sight of her. She'd noticed it immediately, and in the depths of her heart, where she'd tucked away all of her feelings for him, a sad wail rang out. She hated that he looked uncertain in her presence.

Whose fault is that?

She didn't know if she wanted to answer that question. She'd told herself it was his, but wasn't she partially to blame?

Grace steamrolled ahead. "But four years ago. Something was going on, wasn't it?"

It was pointless denying it. Grace would weasel it out of her—or worse, she'd weasel it out of someone else in Mapleton—eventually. Isabel may as well get out in front of the story.

"Fine. We dated."

"I knew it." Grace clapped her hands, decidedly smitten by the idea. "You guys were adorable with your awkwardness."

Isabel moaned. "It was awkward, wasn't it? Gosh, I knew this trip was a terrible idea. Daniel is just another reason why."

Daniel. The man she hadn't been able to replace with work or any number of swanky LA dinner dates these past four years.

"Oh, come on. Was it so terrible to see him?"

"Yes! Yes, it was terrible."

"He wasn't sad about seeing you, that's for sure."

Isabel shook her head. "There is no way Daniel was happy to see me."

"Why not?"

Isabel waved a hand, as if that could wipe away the memory. "I wanted him to come to LA with me, and he wouldn't. He made his choice then, and nothing's changed."

Isabel would do well to remember that. Even if Daniel—with his wide shoulders and kind heart—did look as downright delectable as ever, stirring up those old feelings was pointless. The ending would be the same.

Grace sat forward in the passenger seat and turned to face Isabel, mouth agape.

"I had no idea. I can't believe you didn't tell me any of this. You have a jilted lover who, by the way, is very attractive. He's got that hipster-writer look down to a science. And coupled with the muscles that were framed by his t-shirt?" Grace licked her lips.

"Grace! Stop!"

Isabel's face burned, but Grace wasn't wrong. Daniel had the understated confidence she always found attractive. He was an impeccable mix of a deep-thinking mind and roguish good looks. Like a cross between Matthew Macfayden as Mr. Darcy and Sean Connery in his young, James Bond days. By his olive skin and light-brown hair, you'd never guess he spent most of his time behind a computer screen. He kept his hair cut in a high-and-tight style, more typical of military men and athletes than creatives. Isabel always liked that he didn't fit the conventional, bookish mold.

But she wasn't about to admit that to Grace. She'd have a field day.

As if sensing she'd taken this line of questioning far enough, Grace sat back in her seat. "Alright. Fine. I'll drop it. But there's no way Daniel has. Mark my words."

Isabel didn't respond, and Grace turned her stream of commentary to how picturesque the town was and the charming welcome they'd received from Julia and the rest of the café patrons.

When they arrived at the first property, Isabel hopped out of the car, anxious to get to work and out from under Grace's scrutiny.

"Well, what do you think?" Samson pointed to the home in front of them.

"It's lovely," Isabel answered honestly as she took in the Dutch Colonial with its trademark gambrel roof. She didn't see a lot of this style in California. "Can we take a peek inside?" she asked, her brain whizzing with ideas.

"Of course."

Samson led them on a quick tour, and Isabel made mental notes of the layout, finishes, and color schemes she'd like to see implemented. Grace shadowed her with her tablet in hand.

When they were finished, they walked down the street to the second property. This house was darling, as well—a story-and-a-half bungalow with a cute front porch stoop. Samson had installed brand-new siding in a classic navy blue. The crisp white shutters made the perfect contrasting statement, and the charcoal dormers were a nice touch. Isabel was impressed with his taste.

"Did you pick the color scheme here?" she asked as they entered through the restored front door.

"Yeah. But Julia helped." Samson blushed. "She loves these old homes. The café building used to be rundown, too, and she poured blood, sweat, and tears into restoring it, so she knows what it takes. I've got the manpower to do a job more quickly, but I like her input."

Isabel nodded. "She's got a good eye. The café is stunning."

"You have no idea what that'll mean to her when I tell her." Samson shook his head. "Especially coming from you."

Isabel brushed off the compliment, and after touring the house, they drove down a block and a half to the third home, a square two-story. She liked the lines of this one, though the house itself was basic.

"You can do a lot with a blank slate like this."

At Grace's remark, Isabel nodded. She was right. Isabel could picture four different ways to make this house come to life.

"A statement color on the front door will really pop."

Grace clicked out notes. "Chartreuse would be unexpected, but pretty."

Samson stared between the two of them. "You two have quite a system."

Isabel glanced at Grace who beamed at Samson.

"We've been doing this together for a while. We complement each other well. Isabel is the driving force behind the operation, but sometimes I see things she misses—opportunities, past regrets—and can bring them to her attention."

Grace winked at Isabel who stifled her groan. While Grace was right, the double meaning of her words wasn't lost on Isabel.

Leave it to Grace to draw Isabel's thoughts straight back to Daniel.

"Can we see inside, Samson?" Isabel asked, ignoring the look Grace was giving her.

"Definitely."

As she followed the contractor, she narrowed her gaze at Grace.

"Behave yourself," Isabel grumbled.

"What?" Grace widened her eyes in faux innocence. "Did I say something untrue?"

Isabel pressed her lips together, but Grace just laughed. "Come on."

The fourth house they visited was another bungalow. This one had a creamy brick exterior, and Isabel knew she wanted to dress it up with cedar window boxes like the ones she'd seen at Julia's café.

The fifth home was the largest of the five and turned out to be Isabel's favorite of the bunch. It was a ranch-style home with a sprawling front porch and a ton of windows.

"I'll have my work cut out for me if I'm going to get this all done in a month," Isabel said as they gathered outside of the fifth home.

"We all appreciate you lending your expertise to these projects. It's been a labor of love, so it seems only fitting to have one of the town's own putting the finishing touches on it."

Sparring surges of guilt and gratitude crept up Isabel's spine. Everyone was thrilled she was here, and they were being so kind. It was more of a homecoming reception than she could have ever hoped for. And yet, she didn't deserve it.

Pivot.

The word echoed in her head.

She had a chance to make things right—to earn this goodwill. All she could do was try.

And even if it stung that her family wasn't going to let her past behavior slide, she could appreciate that the town was willing to give her a pass.

Isabel smiled at Samson. "I'm looking forward to getting to work. I'll start at the Dutch Colonial."

"Perfect. I've emailed Grace all the information you should need, but please don't hesitate to call or text if there's anything else I can do to help move things along. I'll be bouncing between job sites during the day, and we'll be meeting with some of your TV people soon."

Samson made a face, and Isabel told herself not to laugh. She didn't want to make him feel bad over his obvious discomfort at the idea of "TV people," namely her producer and camera team. She remembered her first day on set. She'd been a nervous wreck, convinced she looked like a fool and no one would want to watch her show in a million years.

"Don't worry." She softened her expression, willing her eyes to exude a friendly sort of comfort. "The producer of our show, Horatio McMillan, is a great guy. This was all his idea—well, his and Julia's."

Affection flooded Samson's features at the mention of his fiancée. It was sweet and pure and made her want to cry.

An image of Daniel's face resurfaced, popping into Isabel's head like a swimmer coming up for air. Isabel worked to dunk the memory of him back into the watery depths of her mind. Out of the corner of her eye, she caught a glimpse of Grace, who was staring at her with a smirk on her face. Isabel shot her an exasperated look. She so did not have time to deal with Grace's meddling right now. And she certainly was too busy to entertain the thought of what this reunion with Daniel might mean for her nonexistent love life.

Chapter 8

ISABEL

THAT NIGHT, ISABEL FLEW down the back roads from Turner to Mapleton. She and Grace had been at Grace's hotel all afternoon, working on their game plan for the first week of filming, and now Isabel was running behind. The last thing she needed was to be late for the mandatory family dinner her mother was preparing. That would tank her plans to get back into her parents' good graces, and her brother Ford would be there, so she really didn't want to give him one more reason to be annoyed with her.

She had given him a couple years' worth of reasons.

Isabel careened around a curve and over a shallow hill. She gasped and slammed on her brakes as a deer jumped out into the road, not fifteen feet in front of her.

"Are you crunching my cucumbers right now?" Isabel muttered to the dash, bringing her breathing back under control only to suck in an exasperated snort. She'd been in town for a couple days, and she already sounded like her mother.

Great.

She stared the deer down for thirty precious seconds, silently praying it would move out of her way. Finally, it trotted off into the field on the other side of the road. Isabel floored it and made it to her parents' house only a minute after six.

A fancy BMW she didn't recognize was parked in the driveway. She thought this was going to be a family dinner. Who had her mom invited? Isabel gripped her purse and hurried in through the front door.

"Hi, honey." Her mom, dressed in her trademark denim shorts and a fully tucked in t-shirt, rose from the hideous sofa to greet her.

"Hey, Mom."

Isabel was smashed in a hug before she could say any more.

"Your dad and brother are out on the deck. Come on." Val dragged Isabel outside. "Look who finally made it."

"Hi, pumpkin." Her dad waved at her with his spatula from behind the grill.

"Hi, Dad. Hi, Ford." She smiled, but her stomach gurgled with anxiety at the sight of her brother.

"Sis. Welcome home."

Ford may have said it, but his chilly tone told her he wasn't actually welcoming her anywhere except to the near side of his cold shoulder.

Isabel's smile slipped.

Val clapped her hands. "This is everything I've dreamed of for the past few years. The whole family under one roof!"

"Is someone else here?" Isabel asked, recovering from Ford's icy blast. "I didn't recognize the car in the driveway."

"That's mine," Ford said, a sharp edge to his tenor.

"You drive a BMW?" Isabel couldn't keep the shock out of her voice.

"I do."

"Since when?"

Ford scowled at her. "Contrary to what you may think, not all of us had to leave town and disown everyone from our pasts to be successful."

Isabel recoiled from the verbal slap. She'd expected it, but that didn't make it hurt less. She held up her hands, shaking them back and forth in surrender. "I didn't mean anything by what I said. It's a sweet car. I just had no idea."

"You wouldn't have any idea, would you? You haven't bothered to reach out much more than to say 'Merry Christmas' through a text last December."

Val stepped forward. "Ford, that's enough. We don't need to get into this."

"Mom, come on. What did you expect? That I'd sit here and act like we're all one happy family? No way. Isabel left. She *left*, Mom. And then she couldn't be bothered to stay in touch." Ford stopped to take in a breath. "That doesn't magically all go away because she came back."

Nobody said another word. Val glanced alternatively between Isabel and Ford, a silent look of desperation on her face, as if she was pleading for someone to say something to diffuse the situation. Dave focused on the steaks he was grilling. Isabel couldn't form a sentence because stupid tears were trying to strangle her, and the stoic look on Ford's face didn't invite any sort of apology, even if she would have been ready with one.

"Steaks are done." Her dad broke the uncomfortable hush that had settled over them.

"Oh, thank goodness. Let's eat." Her mother shuttled them inside.

Once they were all seated with food on their plates, Isabel figured it was safe to engage her brother. Maybe steak would put him in a better mood. A girl could hope.

"So, how's the real estate market in Mapleton these days, Ford?"

"Fine. The usual."

"I bet you're really good at what you do."

Ford was excellent one-on-one with people, and he was a great listener—easy to trust.

"Thanks." His response was so short she didn't try to carry the conversation beyond it.

Val chimed in to fill the void. "Ford's working with Samson on his project, too."

That got Isabel's attention. It was partly her project now. "Really?"

Ford gave a curt nod. "As soon as you're done with the houses, I'll list them for sale."

"Wow, so we'll be working together, then." The thought of joining forces with her brother filled Isabel with excitement. Perhaps that was what they needed to right their rocky relationship. "I love working with realtors in LA."

"I'm sure you do." Ford's tone was cool. "But I won't need anything from you except to know when you're finished."

The family lapsed into prickly silence again, only interrupted by Val's attempts at forced conversation about the weather, the town's Fourth of July festival, and the prospects of the high school baseball team winning the summer league state championship.

Isabel refused to let Ford see how much his resentment affected her, but the air of indifference she put on in the face of his constant looks of betrayal was only a thin veil. She didn't trust herself to keep up the act for long.

Isabel moved a piece of steak from one side of her plate to the other. "You know what? I'm not feeling the greatest."

"Was the food undercooked?" her dad asked.

"No, no. It was great, Dad. It's just been a busy day. I have a headache. I'm going to go rest." Isabel shoved back from the table. "Good night."

Her throat throbbed as her feet pounded up the stairs. She closed the door to her room behind her, collapsing in a heap on her bed and letting the tears fall. Her face burned hot and sticky with embarrassment and anger.

She deserved Ford's treatment toward her—at least in part. But they were siblings. Shouldn't her brother give her a break? See that she was trying and cut her some slack? He used to be her biggest fan.

Ford had called every week when she first moved to LA. For a couple months, she'd answered, and the two talked for an hour or so about what she was up to and the differences between life in Los Angeles and in Mapleton. But as she started spending her time with the "in" crowd and her commitments piled up, she'd let his calls go to voicemail more often than not. Soon, he'd resorted to texting to see if she was available. Eventually, their communication fell off altogether.

She'd struck up conversations here and there—when she thought of it—but she was usually met with one-word answers to texts or phone calls that fizzled out after a minute or two.

It had all been too little, too late, and Ford had given up on her.

Isabel grabbed for a pillow and hugged it to her chest, but no amount of squeezing would wedge out the truth. She'd taken Ford for granted, and now she had to face the consequences.

Isabel stood and started pacing around her small room. This was everything she was afraid of and exactly why she'd been reluctant to come back to Mapleton. She was content to do her job and live the dream in LA, but she couldn't ignore those she had left behind when they were standing right in front of her. Coming home was forcing her to face everything she didn't want to face.

Isabel padded to the small desk in the corner of her room and logged in to her blogging platform. She sat thinking for a long time before she started writing anything. Eventually, her fingers took over, and she began working through her feelings by putting words on the page.

...I guess what I'm trying to say is, sometimes you'll make a mistake. Maybe it's a little mistake like picking the wrong paint color, or perhaps it's a big one like buying the wrong house. Whatever it is, remember you are in control. You can make a change. You can dig in and right the wrong. Repaint the room. Make the house your own. You have the power to create your own design, your own dream, your own destiny. Lean in to that power, and you can't go wrong. I can't wait to see what you do with it. Until next time, dear readers, happy designing.

Love, Inspired

Chapter 9

ISABEL

THE NEXT MORNING, ISABEL awoke with a fuzzy head, still unsure of the best way to approach her brother and the rest of her family. She rejoiced at the thought of losing herself in her work. The Dutch Colonial called to her from down the block, and she practically skipped through the doors.

"Wow, someone's in a good mood this morning. Did you have a nice dinner with your family?" Grace hugged her hello.

"Hardly." She ignored the displeasure splashed across Grace's face. She didn't want to get into a discussion about it. "Come on. I'm itching to get started."

Isabel and Grace prepped all morning for filming. Isabel chose a color scheme, and they brainstormed ways to accentuate the architectural details that made this house what it was. Isabel was neck-deep in a vision of creamy drapes and pastel wall art when Grace got her attention.

"I'm starving." She plopped down on the window seat in front of the bay window.

Isabel checked her watch and puffed out a surprised gasp. "How is it one o'clock already?" If Ford could see her now, Isabel wagered he'd understand that this was why she never called home. Her days got away from her, and her time was not her own. "Let's grab lunch. We can run to Hal's."

"Who's Hal?"

"Hal is the owner of the diner with the most mouth-watering food in town." Isabel strung her purse over her shoulder. "Let's go."

Less than five minutes later, they walked into Hal's Diner, and Isabel was hit by the smell of fried cheese curds, beer-battered fish, and a whiff of the lemon cleaner Hal used to buff his bar—each scent making her more nostalgic than the last.

Not much had changed at Hal's in the past four years. The Formica tables sat spread out over the scuffed cherry wood floors. The dark panel walls were covered with faded newspaper clippings detailing local sports teams and community news.

"Isabel, is that you?"

Isabel turned to see the owner of the diner, Hal Davenson, approaching her from the swinging door leading to the kitchen.

"Sure is." Isabel smiled at the older man. He was a little more weathered than when she had left, but his eyes still twinkled. When she was a girl, he used to add extra fries to her plate every time her family came to eat here. "I told my friend this is the best place in town to eat."

"Well, aren't you as sweet as ever." Hal kissed her cheek. "But you know we're about the only place to eat in town, so that's not saying much."

Isabel laughed and introduced Grace as Hal seated them at a table.

Without a look at the menu, Isabel rattled off her order to the college-aged waitress who introduced herself as Sylvie.

"I'll have that right out for you, Ms. Marshall. I am just thrilled to see you."

Isabel flashed her a friendly smile. The few other patrons eating a late lunch were staring. She spotted Daniel seated at a table in the corner. He was very obviously *not* looking in her direction, but of course he was here. Everyone was everywhere in Mapleton.

Isabel fiddled with the packets of butter stacked in towers alongside the salt and pepper shakers. "This is weird."

"What is?"

Isabel jerked her chin. "All of them. I don't know what to do with their attention."

"They're proud of you."

Isabel shifted in her seat, a mixture of emotions swirling around her insides.

"Isabel." Grace stretched across the table and put her hand on Isabel's arm. "You know that's a good thing, right?"

"Of course." She was thrilled to have Mapleton's support, but the competing remorse she had over how she'd abandoned those closest to her made it difficult to fully enjoy the rest of the town's pride. She shot a quick look in Daniel's direction.

He was sipping an iced drink, and his food was pushed off to the side to make room for his computer. He was so absorbed with his screen he didn't see her staring.

Isabel blinked. She shouldn't *have been* staring. She had enough on her plate with a job to do and a messy family situation to work out. Right now, she needed to put all her focus on that.

Not on how Daniel's brow still furrowed in the most endearing way when he was concentrating. She'd bet she could still identify every single shade of green that speckled his eyes.

She was sort of pathetic like that.

She shook her head and faced Grace. "Anyway, let's talk shop. Now that we have a tentative plan for the Dutch Colonial, I'm thinking we're going to need to hit up a flea market or a vintage sale and find some distinct pieces."

If she could stay focused on work, she wouldn't have to face the people of Mapleton—in other words, Daniel—and the feelings that being around them—ahem, *him*—dredged up.

Grace flicked her gaze to where Daniel was sitting and rolled her eyes but mercifully let Isabel's deflection go. Instead of pushing it, she retrieved her ever-present tablet to take notes. "What sorts of things were you thinking?"

Isabel talked through what she hoped to find but paused when the door to Hal's opened, and her show's producer walked in.

"Horatio!" She waved him over.

His eyes lit up, and he marched in their direction. "Isabel. Grace. Great to see you both. How're things here?"

Horatio scraped a chair over the floor to their table and dropped into a seat between them.

Isabel gave him a rundown of what they'd accomplished this morning and of her plans.

"I like it." Horatio nodded, tapping his chin. "I'll want to film your trip to the antique store. It'll be textbook 'down-home' footage. I think it'll land well with your audience. I must say, this is the handsomest little town I've ever seen."

"It is more charming than I remember." Isabel smiled up at Sylvie as the waitress dropped a sizzling Reuben sandwich in front of her. She tucked her napkin into her lap and returned her focus to Horatio. "When did you get in?"

"Just this morning. I had to take a later flight. The network wanted to have a final discussion about what exactly we were doing here."

"Is everything okay on that front?" Grace asked, and a wave of nausea hit Isabel at the reminder of the tenuous position her show was in. With all the hoopla from Julia and the café patrons surrounding her homecoming and the stickiness of her situation at home with Ford and her parents, she'd almost forgotten the whole reason she was in town was to drum up interest in her show because the reviews for this season hadn't been up to par.

"Oh, yes, yes." Horatio shrugged off their concern. "Don't you worry your pretty little heads about it. Now, can you shop this weekend for those vintage pieces?" Horatio asked, slurping on the lemonade Sylvie dropped off for him.

"I thought we'd go first thing Saturday morning. There used to be a huge warehouse called Vintage Market out east of town where vendors have different booths."

Grace typed a search into her tablet. "I see it here. 'Vintage Market – Antiques, Renewed, Refurbished.' Looks awesome."

Isabel nodded. "I used to spend hours walking the aisles of that place. If we go early, we'll have a better chance of finding what we need. You'll film with me, right, Grace?"

Horatio scrunched his nose. "Grace? No, no, no. That's all wrong."

"What do you mean?" Isabel did a lot of her shopping with Grace. All of it, as a matter of fact.

"We need to play up the *home* angle of this visit. That's what I've pitched to the network, and that's what they'll want to see delivered. You'll have to find someone from around here who can go shopping with you. Your mother, a friend, or really anyone from town who is willing."

Oh no.

Isabel sat stiffly in her chair. That was not a good idea.

"What about Daniel?" Grace tossed out the suggestion from across the table as if she was merely commenting on the weather when, in reality, his name sent a bolt of electricity piercing through Isabel's heart.

"Who's Daniel?" Horatio's ears perked up while Isabel shot daggers in Grace's direction, trying to silently tell her to shut her over-eager mouth.

"Isabel's friend."

"No one," Isabel said at the same time.

She needed to work on communicating with her eyes.

"He's right over there. We could ask him now."

"What? No! I can't ask Daniel Smith for a favor after seeing him yesterday and speaking to him for the first time in four years."

The thought of how presumptuous she would come across made her stomach churn.

"Let's get him over here and let the man decide for himself. Everyone around here seems more than accommodating," Horatio said.

"Daniel!" Grace held up her hand and motioned for him.

"Grace!" Isabel shushed, feeling like someone had stuck an ice cube down her shirt. She wanted to crawl out of her skin.

Horatio dropped his voice. "Relax, Isabel. I can ask him to join you on behalf of the show. We could even pay him."

"Pay him?" Isabel squeaked. "I don't think so." That was a surefire way to offend Daniel.

"Uh, hi." Daniel stopped next to where Isabel was sitting.

She jolted upright, knocking into the table and rattling the ice in all their drinks. She grimaced. "Daniel, hi. Nice to see you again."

Heaven help her. She sounded like a morning talk show host.

Horatio coughed.

"Right." Isabel gestured to her producer. "Daniel, this is Horatio McMillan, my show's producer. Horatio, this is Daniel Smith."

"Excellent to meet any friend of Isabel's." Horatio held out his hand, and Daniel shook it. Something flashed across his face, but Isabel wasn't fast enough to log it.

She couldn't help but wonder if Daniel had ever seen her show. She didn't know what she wished for more: that he had or hadn't. If he had, he would have been able to see right through her to all her insecurities. He always could. He knew her better than anyone else. But if he hadn't...well, that hurt, too. Because if that were the case, she must not have meant as much to him as he did to her.

"I have a favor to ask you." Horatio charged ahead, oblivious to Isabel's inner turmoil. "Nothing major. We need some help with the show."

"What sort of help?"

"We're hoping you wouldn't mind going on a little local adventure with Isabel this weekend. She has some shopping to do at Vintage Market, and we'd like to film her there. Are you interested in joining her?"

Isabel dragged her gaze up to Daniel's face. His lips had parted in surprise, and he cast a quick look in her direction. She watched his Adam's apple bob as he returned his focus to Horatio.

"Umm, yeah. Alright. I could probably make that work." Daniel's voice was quiet. "If that's what you need."

He directed that last line toward Isabel, not Horatio, and Isabel credited the multiple years of experience she had of always being "on" for her ability to keep a calm expression on her face. She ignored the mischievous look Grace was giving her, instead smiling at Daniel until Horatio spoke, drawing their attention.

"That's wonderful! We can't thank you enough." He rattled off details, setting the schedule for Daniel and herself for this upcoming Saturday.

Isabel busied herself by taking a giant bite of her sandwich. She closed her eyes to savor it, and at the same time, the reality of the situation slammed into her. She'd be spending a day with Daniel.

In front of the camera.

She hardly recognized the flutter of nervous anticipation in her chest—it had been so long. And she no longer got panicky when cameras were rolling, which meant those butterflies that were alternatively soaring and dive-bombing inside her?

Those were for Daniel.

Chapter 10

DANIEL

DANIEL ARRIVED AT VINTAGE Market at seven o'clock sharp on Saturday morning. The warehouse sat less than a mile outside of Mapleton. Horatio had told him to look for the yellow tent where he'd find Grace. She'd have the paperwork for him to sign and get him equipped with a mic pack.

For the past three days, Daniel had tried not to dwell on how weird it would be to be on camera. That was Isabel's forte. Not his. He also decided not to think too much about why he was the one who was asked to do this. He was sure there were more than a few people in Mapleton who would have bent over backward to have this opportunity. If Isabel hand-selected him, what did that mean? Was she doing it out of pity, to try to clear the air? Was she trying to prove to herself and to him that they were friends? Or was he the only available one? He could have been her third or fourth option, if others she asked had prior commitments. But merely being the understudy was a depressing thought, so Daniel shoved it aside.

He'd almost said no when Horatio had asked him to film with Isabel. They had agreed to be friends, but he knew what he was getting himself into. If he spent time with Isabel, he was going to fall for her all over again. The work he'd done to move on from her these past few years would be erased, and when she left town in a month, he'd have to start the grieving process anew. It would be torture.

But he was a glutton for punishment apparently, because here he was.

Grace stood, waving both arms above her head like a ground control officer to draw his attention from across the parking lot.

"Hi, Daniel. Good to see you again," she said as he approached.

"You, too. What am I in for?" Daniel figured if anyone would shoot him straight, it was Grace.

"Don't worry. I'll walk you through everything you need to know now. Then, you can join Isabel inside with our hair and makeup team."

At Daniel's grunt of alarm, Grace held up her hands to placate him. "Nothing to be intimidated by. We'll probably add some powder so the lights don't make you shiny. You don't have much hair to gel, so that makes our stylist's job easy. Anyway"—Grace clapped once—"let's get you taken care of."

Twenty minutes later, Daniel may as well have signed his life away. Grace must have presented him with fifteen different nondisclosure agreements and various other contractual documents before hustling him inside.

Daniel had visited Vintage Market in the past, and things inside the warehouse looked about how he remembered them, aside from a few extra standalone lights. Near the register, he caught a glimpse of Isabel perched on a stool. A woman materialized in front of her, wielding a makeup brush. The makeup artist was dressed in head-to-toe black with jet-black hair to boot, and Daniel's anxiety spiked.

"Over here we go," Grace directed. "This is where I leave you. Horatio should be by any second to walk you through what to expect with filming, but like I said, don't worry. Be yourself. You'll be great. This is Hilde, our makeup artist extraordinaire."

Hilde turned and looked him up and down. The woman's stare made him wish he was a turtle so he could tuck his head into his shell and hide.

"Hey." Isabel waved from behind where the black-haired scary lady stood taking stock of him.

"Hey, yourself."

"You can sit here." Hilde grabbed a stool and scooted it next to Isabel. "I'll be right back." Without another word, she turned on her black high heel and strode away.

"Is she always so—"

"Intense? Yes. Yes, she is. I was terrified of her on my first day, but she keeps me looking good on camera, so I can't complain."

Daniel held his tongue. Isabel didn't need any extra help looking good on camera. Not in his opinion. The couple of times he'd seen her show, he thought she looked a little too made up. He was used to seeing her more relaxed. It wasn't that he was opposed to makeup, but it wasn't Isabel's style—or it hadn't been.

It is now.

He reminded himself that he didn't know much of anything about Isabel's style these days. The two sat in silence, waiting for Hilde the Intimidator to return.

"Thanks for agreeing to this," Isabel said after a minute. "I was going to shop with Grace, like I usually do, but Horatio wanted the hometown segment to feature someone from Mapleton, so he and Grace put their heads together, and that's where you came into the picture. I appreciate you being a good sport about it."

Well, that answered his question at least. And Isabel must not yet realize he couldn't say no to her. The only time he did was the worst day of his adult life.

"Happy to help."

Isabel threw him a dazzling smile, which disintegrated from her face the second Hilde reappeared.

"No smiling yet. Your foundation will crack and crease!" the woman scolded. "And you." She turned to face Daniel. "Let me see you."

Hilde pinched his chin between her thumb and pointer finger and turned his head this way and that, inspecting him as if he were a melon in the produce section and she was checking for bruises. He sat ramrod straight but flicked his eyes to Isabel, who was trying not to laugh.

"Good bone structure. You'll do. Just a little powder." Hilde took a brush and dipped it into a bowl of gunk before attacking his face with it.

Daniel choked as whatever it was she was dousing him with went up his nose.

"What is this stuff?" he coughed.

"Matte finishing powder. To help with your oily t-zone."

"What's a t-zone?" Daniel asked aloud. He shut his mouth when Hilde gave him a look that could freeze the devil himself. "Never mind," he mumbled.

A giggle escaped from Isabel, and it startled Daniel. Her laugh was like the strain of a long-forgotten favorite song, conjuring up all sorts of feelings as it floated by. It was a sound he still heard in his dreams, but that version paled in comparison to the real thing.

The first time he'd gone out of his way to make Isabel laugh was their freshman year of college. Before then, they'd only been high school acquaintances, knowing of each other but not really knowing each other.

Early in their first semester of undergrad, they'd met up to study—just two Mapleton kids, away from home, seeking the familiarity that they'd left behind. Daniel was enrolled in Shakespearean Drama 101. He'd asked Isabel what Shakespeare's favorite song from the movie *Frozen* would have been, and when he'd delivered the pun, "Ham-Let it Go," she'd burst into giggles. They went back and forth with bad, literary dad-jokes until a librarian came by and scolded them for being too loud. Not long after that, he'd asked her out to dinner, and they'd been inseparable for the next four years.

Now, Hilde turned and shot Isabel a look of condemnation. She clamped her mouth shut, but the second Hilde turned her back, she narrowed her gaze at Daniel and stuck out her tongue.

Daniel's lips twitched. He was thankful he could still make Isabel laugh. He decided that would be his goal. Isabel may have been famous now, with makeup teams and producers directing her every move, but underneath that fame, he bet she was still the girl he once knew. He'd have a little fun finding out if he was right.

"Good morning. Good morning. Good morning." Horatio joined them. He was a short, balding man with dark, round spectacles.

"Good morning, H," Isabel said as Hilde stepped aside.

He nodded at Isabel before turning to Daniel. "I can't thank you enough for being here. Let's get to it. We're going to let Isabel take the lead. She said she used to come to Vintage Market all the time, so she knows her way around. The plan is to have cameras trailing you two as you walk around. We'll have others filming at the ends of each aisle. What I need from you is to act like they aren't there. Be natural, and we'll have the greatest chance of getting the authentic footage we're going for. Once we roll for a while, we may cut in and tell you what we need from you. More energy, to pace yourselves, yadda yadda yadda. But don't worry about that until you have to. Just follow Isabel's lead."

Daniel shot Isabel a look out of the corner of his eye, and she lifted a light shoulder. This must be par for the course for Horatio.

"Think you can do that?" Horatio asked him.

"I'll give it my best go." Daniel didn't want to overpromise.

"Excellent." Horatio slapped him on the back. "We'll start rolling in ten. Take your marks outside when Hilde's done with you so we can shoot you entering the building. We'll record a voiceover later, introducing the market and having Isabel talk about you, so talk between yourselves like you normally would. It won't matter what you say at this point."

Daniel barely heard his last sentence since Horatio was already making his way back across the room.

"Should I salute him or something?"

His question elicited another soft giggle from Isabel.

"He does act like a drill sergeant on occasion, that's for sure." She hopped down from her stool and leaned over to kiss Hilde on each cheek.

Daniel wasn't certain if he was expected to do the same.

"You may go, too," Hilde said to him before turning her back and stalking away.

Okay, then. No kisses required.

"Horatio is the best in the business," Isabel said as they walked to the front doors. "He's taken me under his wing these past two years, walking me through the ins and outs of the television world. I'm not sure where I'd be without his expertise. He's taught me everything I know and is the fundamental reason the show was renewed for a second season."

"I'm sure you had something to do with that," Daniel said. He was rewarded by Isabel's smile.

"Thank you for saying that."

They walked out the doors, and someone from the tech team came over to check their mic packs.

"Wires are hot," Horatio said through a blow-horn. "Recording started."

"Careful. Anything you say from now on can and will be used against you," Isabel kidded.

"Way to make me feel right at home," Daniel said dryly.

Isabel laughed, and Daniel relaxed.

"And...rolling!" Horatio boomed. For a small man, he'd mastered the art of projecting.

"Alright, here we go." Isabel walked back to the front doors. The yellow tent was moved farther off to the side of the building. Daniel figured it was out of the shot. He quickened his pace so he could open the door for Isabel.

In a fit of muscle memory, he settled his hand on the small of Isabel's back. "After you."

She tensed before relaxing again, offering him a soft smile, her gaze both tentative and appreciative.

Daniel smiled back, trying to mask the fact that his stomach had somersaulted at the simplest touch of his hand on Isabel's gauzy shirt.

He'd heard it said that the cameras didn't lie, and if that was true, he was completely toast. Because when this episode aired on national television, everyone was going to be able to tell that he was off his face for the woman next to him.

Chapter 11

DANIEL

THEY STOPPED AND STOOD in the entryway, and Isabel took a deep breath and gazed around the market.

"Gosh, I love this place. It smells the same as always."

Even in the dim light of the warehouse, Isabel's eyes held a joy-filled glint, and when they landed on him, Daniel thought he might be able to fly.

He took a minute to look around, trying to ground himself. "Like a mix of sawdust and cinnamon."

"Exactly." She inhaled one more time before clapping her hands. "Okay. I am dying to get started."

"What are you on the hunt for?" Daniel asked, shadowing Isabel down the first aisle.

Her eyes roved around, taking in every little detail of the first few vendor booths that greeted them. "We're working on this precious Dutch Colonial. You know the one? It's right on Mapleton Avenue in the center of town. The home has so much character, and Samson and his team have done a ton of work to make sure that shines through, so I want to play it up with some antique pieces."

Isabel was good at this. On the first take, she'd managed to talk up the home, the contractor, and explain why she wanted what she did. Daniel listened as she went on.

"First things first, I need a buffet for the dining room. I'm thinking something with curved legs that'll sit up off the ground a bit. The room isn't oversized, so we need to give the allusion of space by keeping the floor open."

Daniel nodded as if he understood what she meant.

"As far as finishes, I'm open to whatever we find. That's the fun of a treasure hunt, isn't it?" Isabel beamed up at him.

He cocked his head to the side. "Whatever you say."

She nudged him, her face awash with good humor. "Come on, you can't tell me you aren't having a good time."

She was right. He couldn't. Her energy and excitement were contagious. But he didn't want to let her off so easily, so he raised his eyebrows. "Jury's out."

"Well then, I'll have to show you what fun antiquing is. Wait until we find exactly what we need. It's quite the adrenaline rush."

She marched farther down the aisle and started pointing out pieces to him.

"Something like this, but it can't be so deep." She motioned to a massive black piece of furniture that looked like a dresser to him. "And I don't want it to sit directly on the floor."

"Gotcha." Daniel turned from her to survey the vendor booths closest to them. "So, do you go antiquing much in LA?" He stopped to inspect a lampshade with fringe tassels on the bottom. Isabel's back was to him, and he casually put the lampshade on his head.

"Not as much as I'd like." She was preoccupied and shuffling through some smaller items on top of a bookshelf. "A lot of our clients have a vision for what they want, so it's easier to custom order the pieces they need. This is different because these houses haven't been sold yet."

"So you get to have a little bit more fun?" Daniel bent down to inspect an old school desk. If he was casual about it—like his headpiece was nothing out of the ordinary—Isabel would crack up when she saw it, and that was what he was going for. Chip Gaines had nothing on him.

"I always have fun designing for my clients," Isabel answered.

Very diplomatic, Daniel thought.

"But this is a special treat, yes." She turned to him as she said it, and out of the corner of his eye, he saw her hand go to her mouth when she took in his "hat." She snorted in a much less diplomatic way before she stifled it.

He stood to face her. "What?"

"That's an interesting look you've got going there." She swished her finger back and forth.

"Oh, this old thing?" He doffed the lampshade like one would with a top hat, giving her a small bow before winking. "Yeah, I like to have fun, too."

Isabel giggled before shaking her head and rolling her eyes. "Believe me. I remember."

Daniel nodded, holding her gaze for a second longer but not saying anything more. The memories between the two of them were personal, special. He was content to think of them in his own head, knowing she was doing the same. And he succeeded in making her laugh on camera. So far, this TV gig wasn't so bad.

Isabel took off down the aisle, and Daniel put the lampshade back on the desk before hurrying to keep up with her.

When Isabel stopped suddenly, he bumped into her back. The honeysuckle scent of her skin and the floral tones of her shampoo filled his senses. A zip of longing ran from his head to his toes, even as he rushed to ease back. "Whoa, sorry."

"Someone is all of a sudden really anxious to find a buffet," Isabel quipped.

"I take this work very seriously." Daniel crossed his hand over his heart. "Scout's honor."

"Well, then. I need your expert opinion on this piece." She pointed to the rear of the booth in front of them.

Daniel leaned forward to see what had caught her eye. It was a robin's-egg-blue buffet with curved gold accents that parroted the slim curve of the legs.

"I love the Queen Anne legs." Isabel's voice was laced with fondness.

"Queen who?"

"Queen Anne. Technically, the curved leg you see on this piece is called a cabriole leg, but it was first made popular in the late seventeen hundreds during Queen Anne's rule, so it's more commonly called a Queen Anne leg."

The only legs Daniel was noticing were Isabel's, but *that* wasn't an appropriate comment to make on television. So he settled for a more generic response.

"I'll take your word for it. It is a striking piece. Will the color work in your design?"

He'd been picturing something neutral, but he didn't have the slightest clue what look she was going for inside the house.

Isabel chewed on her lip, tipping her head from side to side as she stared down the piece. She bent to rub a hand across the smooth top surface. "I think so. We can make this blue a focal color and work with it in the rest of the design. That's why I like to shop early, so I know what I have in my décor arsenal."

Daniel could tell she inserted these little bits and pieces of advice in their conversation for the benefit of her audience. These tips were why people loved her show.

Isabel walked up to the piece and opened one of the side doors before sticking her head inside and inhaling.

Daniel snorted. "What in the world was that for?"

"What, smelling it?" Isabel asked, standing upright. "You always have to smell it before you buy it."

Daniel squinted at her. "Why?"

"Some of these old pieces smell...well, old. The last thing you want is to buy something and get home and have it stink up all your fine china—or worse, your whole dining room." Isabel plugged her nose with one hand and waved her hand in front of her face for effect.

Daniel grinned at her. "Again, I'm going to take your word for it. You seem to be equally as passionate about Queen Anne design details as you are about the smell test, so I won't argue."

Isabel shot him a cheeky grin. "Alright, we're taking this one. Gosh, would you look at the gorgeous rounded edge? This will be perfect!" Delight enhanced the already striking angles of her face as she untied the tag from the buffet and pocketed it. "On to the next piece!"

"And cut for a moment!"

Horatio's voice startled Daniel. He hadn't realized the producer was tailing them so closely. In fact, he'd forgotten all about the cameras and the fact that they were on TV. Go figure.

Isabel turned to her producer as Hilde bustled forward to touch up Isabel's makeup before turning the powder brush on Daniel. He held his breath this time.

"This will only take a second," Horatio said. "You guys are brilliant. I almost didn't want to stop you. Your rapport is so natural. It's translating great on camera. We're going to have so much footage to choose from. Isabel, Grace scoped out the other end of the warehouse, and she thought there might be some options over there. We won't have enough time to have you walk through the whole building—even though that would be wonderful—so let's take her advice and move that way now. Next up is a fireplace mantel, correct?"

Isabel nodded as Hilde spun the lid of her loose powder closed and got out of the way. "I trust Grace's vision. We'll head over there." She turned and walked in the direction Horatio pointed.

Daniel followed along, pocketing the pleasure he felt in knowing that Horatio thought he and Isabel were natural together and saving it for a rainy day.

As they approached another aisle, Horatio hollered out, "And rolling!"

"So, what's next?" Daniel asked.

"I need to find a mantel for the sitting room. There's no fireplace, but I always think even the illusion of one brings warmth to a room. And having a mantel is great for decorating since it gives the homeowner another surface to work with."

She turned down the row of booths in front of them, and out of the corner of his eye, he spied a fake fuzzy tarantula in a booth filled with knick-knacks. Isabel bypassed the vendor. Sure, they wouldn't find a fireplace mantel in there, but this he could use. He snatched the fake spider and held it behind his back.

Isabel's eyes roved through the furniture pieces on either side of the aisle. "Holler if you see anything you think would work."

"Will do." Daniel approached her from behind and bided his time. When she bent down to shift a sizeable tan crock out of the way, Daniel dropped the spider onto her shoulder.

She rose and frowned. "Rats. I thought this might work, but the dimensions are all wrong." Her focus was on the mantel in front of her.

"Um, Isabel. Don't panic." Daniel pretended to be apprehensive.

"What is it?" She turned in his direction, and her cheek brushed up against the spider.

The result was as he expected. Isabel's eyes bugged, and she let out an ear-piercing shriek, throwing her hands in the air before raking them through her hair, dislodging the spider, and in a fit of terror, she sprinted behind Daniel, gripping his arms and using his body as a shield.

Scratch that. The result was better than he expected.

Daniel chortled. "Gotcha. You should have seen your face."

Isabel swatted him before placing her hands on her hips. Her hair was mussed, and her eyes sparkled with a mixture of relief and giddiness. Daniel couldn't remember the last time he'd seen anything so beautiful.

"Daniel Smith, how dare you? You know I hate spiders!"

"I do know. That's why I couldn't resist."

"I could have had a heart attack. Then you would have been sorry."

Isabel's pout was as fake as the spider he'd placed on her shoulder, so he laughed at her. Eventually, she joined in until they were both wiping tears from their eyes.

"Remember what they say about payback."

"We'll see if you've still got it," Daniel challenged. "Hey, what about that?"

Isabel hesitated, staring him down with her hands still on her hips, as if she wasn't sure whether he was pulling another prank on her.

"No, I mean it. Check out that mantel."

Daniel pointed to a weathered mantel that caught his eye, and Isabel turned and walked up to it. He helped her move things out from in front of it before they both stepped back and studied the find. It drew his attention because it mimicked the ornate legs of the buffet (What could he say? He had legs on his mind), but it was a little more worn thanks to the chipping white paint and exposed gray wood.

Isabel pressed her finger to her cheek, her eyes scanning the piece.

"What do you think?" Daniel asked, anxious for her opinion.

"It's spot-on." Isabel faced him, a sly smile on her lips. "Are you gunning for my job?"

Daniel whipped his head back and forth. "No way. I just thought it sort of looked like the other thing we found. But it's different enough—if that makes sense."

"You're exactly right. I find when selecting pieces for the same house, you want to avoid being matchy-matchy. Complimentary shapes work well, but do you see how this mantel looks much less formal than the buffet? It'll work really well in the family room of the Dutch Colonial. Good job, Daniel." She turned and held up her hand for a high five. He slapped his against hers.

"I learned from the best," he said and earned himself another smile.

· ♥ · ♥ · ♥ · ♥ · ♥ ·

Thirty minutes later, they'd secured a third piece, some sort of corner shelving unit with drawers on the bottom. Isabel told him she'd replace the hardware to make it fit with the rest of the space. They'd also found some framed prints for the walls in the entryway of house number three and a hutch to put in the kitchen of the fourth property.

"Cut! Great job, everybody." Horatio led them all in a round of applause. "We got more than what we needed. Daniel, we may need to offer you a full-time gig. And Isabel, being home looks good on you! You were sharing all sorts of new and interesting insights into your design process. You two together? Dynamite!"

Horatio bustled off, and Grace appeared to relieve them of their mic packs. "He's right. You two together are something else."

"We made a good team back in the day," Isabel said, not making eye contact with Daniel.

"Maybe you still do," Grace coughed.

"What was that?" Isabel asked.

"Nothing." Grace raised her voice slightly and pinned Daniel with a look. "That wasn't so bad, was it?" she asked.

"No, not too bad." Behind Isabel's back, Daniel tipped his chin in question at Grace.

Grace shook her head, but the smile on her face spoke for itself.

The three walked together to the front entrance of the market. Regular customers were flitting in and out, and the clerks were busy ringing up purchases. Isabel waved goodbye to the crew and walked outside with Daniel while Grace went over to thank the employees for their help.

"Daniel, I owe you."

"Don't be silly. I was happy to help."

"I mean it. You've got to let me return the favor. Is there anything I can do?"

Daniel couldn't think of a single thing. With Isabel's eyes on him, all other conscious thoughts seemed to have made a jailbreak from the confines of his head. "Really, I don't need—"

"You could help out at the Sunday brunch after church tomorrow."

Daniel and Isabel turned at the sound of the voice behind them.

Marge Wilson stood off to the side. Where had she come from? Daniel hadn't heard her approach. Maybe that was Marge's secret to knowing everything that went on in Mapleton—her white, silent-sole, arch-support shoes.

"Pardon me. I couldn't help but overhear. Isabel, if you're looking to lend a hand, Daniel has been coordinating the brunch we put on each weekend. It's a free meal for those in need. You're always looking for volunteers to help cook and serve, aren't you, Daniel?" Marge stared up at him, a matter-of-fact look blanketing her face.

Daniel blinked, feeling slightly dazed. He *was* always looking for volunteers, but he didn't expect Isabel to help him out with that.

"I would be glad to help." Isabel swung her gaze around toward him. "What do you need me to do?"

Marge shuffled past them before Daniel could respond, and he swore he heard her say something that sounded like, "Wait 'til I tell Val." But he couldn't be sure.

He turned his attention to Isabel, shaking his head. "Sorry. That's so...so—"

"Small town?" Isabel supplied with a smile. "I know."

Daniel nodded and couldn't help but smile. "Are you sure? You really don't owe me a thing."

Isabel tipped up her shoulder. "I know, but this is something I can do. I'm not working tomorrow, so I insist. Just tell me what you need."

The promise of seeing Isabel again the next day did something funny to Daniel's stomach. He relented and filled her in on the details before they said goodbye.

As she strode to her rental car, Daniel took a moment to observe her.

She held her head high and looked every bit the style icon she was in fashionable, cropped jeans, heeled booties, and a flowy, dark-blue tank top. But in many ways, this morning proved to him that Isabel was the same woman he once knew and loved.

And if the thundering in his chest at the sight of her walking away from him was any indication, he might just love her still.

Chapter 12

ISABEL

ISABEL DIDN'T REMEMBER THE last time she had been so nervous.

Well, that wasn't entirely true.

It was yesterday.

Yesterday, she had been this nervous to film with Daniel. And evidently, she hadn't learned her lesson. Because here she was again, feeling all jumbled up inside, and it was her own fault.

She didn't know what she'd been thinking when she'd agreed to help out at the church brunch. Maybe she hadn't been thinking—at least not with her head. The fact of the matter was, she liked spending time with Daniel.

And that was the problem. She needed to get her feelings under control—shove them back into a friend-zone-shaped box—because nothing had changed about their circumstances. Her life was in California. His was here.

It didn't matter that he made her laugh in a way few other people did. Or that they still finished each other's sentences. Or that when he looked at her, she felt like someone saw the real her for the first time in years.

She opened the door to Our Lady of Good Hope Church and pushed those thoughts away. She'd have to figure out her heart later. Right now, she had promised to help out at Sunday brunch, and she couldn't do that by waffling around outside, hung up on a boy.

The church's atrium held the faint scent of chrism oil. There must have been a baptism at nine-thirty mass. The choir was singing the offertory song in the chapel, so she silently turned and made her way downstairs to Fellowship Hall.

Isabel tarried outside the doorway to the hall and steeled herself. She could do this. It was for a good cause. And Daniel was her friend. They were *friends*.

She squared her shoulders and turned the corner. The open gathering space was empty except for a lone figure. Daniel was across the room, wearing a white apron over his straight-legged khaki pants and white polo shirt. The low hum of disco music reached her ears as Daniel danced around the kitchen with his back to her, doing his version of the hustle and singing to whatever song was playing.

Isabel's pulse skipped a sizzling trail up and down each of her limbs.

"Friends," she muttered to herself. It didn't matter that he was absolutely irresistible.

Did. Not. Matter.

Daniel spun in her direction for a four-step turn and dropped the wooden spoon he was using as a microphone. It fell with a clatter to the floor, and the sound jarred the hearts out of Isabel's eyes.

Daniel's face turned bright red. "How long have you been standing there?"

Isabel grinned, stepping farther into the room. "Oh, long enough."

Daniel ran a hand through his hair. "You're early."

"And it's a good thing I am, too." Isabel couldn't help teasing him. "If this is the show you're putting on before working hours, you're doing a disservice to the community by not advertising it. You'll draw a crowd with moves like that."

Daniel pressed his eyes closed for a brief moment before he shot her a wry smirk. "I guess my humiliation can serve as payback for the fake spider trick yesterday."

"Something like that. But if it'll make you feel better, we can listen together. I'll match you, bad dance move for bad dance move." Isabel crossed to him, and she smiled when she recognized the song. "The Bee Gees. Nice. That explains the *Saturday Night Fever* impression."

Daniel slapped his palm against his face. "Can you forget you saw that, please?"

"Uh-uh. It's seared in my mind."

Daniel's cheeks turned a slightly deeper shade of red, and he glanced away from her, wiping what she guessed were sweaty hands on his apron.

For some reason, his reaction made her relax, made her feel bold. She was grateful she wasn't the only one affected by this—whatever *this* was.

"You know, the only thing that would have made your little routine better was a partner." She didn't think twice about reaching for his hand. She lifted their arms up and twirled twice underneath the arch they made. "Voila!" She shot him a goofy smile and dropped into an overdone curtsy to let him know she was only giving him a hard time, and she was more than willing to match his embarrassment.

Daniel's eyes took on a playful gleam. "Then you better let me lead."

Isabel gasped when he tightened his grip on her hand and spun her out in a move that, had she been wearing a flowy dress, would have sent it flaring out around her like an open flower. When he pulled her back in and dipped her with the smoothness of a young John Travolta, Isabel wasn't laughing at him anymore. In fact, the intensity of his stare had made her mouth go drier than an LA summer.

Daniel had a firm grip on her waist and her shoulder, and she was suddenly very aware of how much she missed being held in his sure, strong arms. This confident, take-charge Daniel was all kinds of attractive to her.

So much for getting her feelings for him under control. Now, a crazy part of her brain sort of wanted him to bend down and kiss her.

But the song ended and, with it, the moment, saving Isabel from herself.

Daniel cleared his throat as he hoisted her upward, making sure she was settled on her feet before letting her go. "You've been practicing your moves. You think you can dance and work?"

"I'm a pretty adept multi-tasker." Isabel tugged at the hem of her shirt, trying to sound and appear put together, even as her heart felt like it was coming undone.

"Good." Daniel pointed toward several long tables in a line at the near side of the dining space. "Here's where we do the food. If you want to help me get the warmers out, we can go from there."

Isabel followed Daniel's lead, and they worked alongside each other with ease, chatting about the brunch and what she could expect. If Isabel kept her focus on the tasks in front of her and not on the man next to her, she could almost pretend that her racing pulse was just a normal part of the anatomical makeup of her circulatory system.

"How long have you been coordinating this?" Isabel asked as she stacked coffee mugs on the table.

"Going on a year now." Daniel hoisted a giant coffee urn up from a lower cabinet and set it on the table next to the mugs. "The whole town pitches in, really. Julia will bring coffee to fill this up." He tapped the urn. "But it's my job to get enough volunteers to staff the actual brunch each week."

"Marge seems to be second-guessing your abilities."

Daniel shot her a chagrined look. "Yeah. You really didn't have to agree to come by today. Sorry again that she roped you into helping."

"I'm not sorry." The words were out of her mouth before she thought them through. The truth had a way of sneaking out. But she wasn't ready to face it yet—or to face the expression she couldn't quite read on Daniel's face. "I mean, I know better than to say no to Marge," Isabel hurried to add.

Daniel smiled at her, and Isabel's stomach felt like the gooey center of a slightly under-baked chocolate chip cookie. How was she supposed to act when she was so obviously still drawn to him? Her body—her heart—wanted nothing more than for her to throw herself at him, to beg him to still love her, or to love her again. But her head kept telling her not to get involved. It felt like she was splitting in two.

Daniel surveyed the room. "We should start seeing folks in about fifteen minutes. We'll get some of the post-mass crowd and our regulars from around the community who are in need of a warm meal."

Isabel nodded, tucking her hair behind her ears.

Daniel's playlist shuffled through two more songs as they worked in silence, but then Daniel powered down his Bluetooth speaker as other volunteers trickled into the hall, each carrying a dish to pass.

Most of them seemed to know where to go without being told, but they still checked in with Daniel and had a kind word of greeting for Isabel, too.

Marge arrived and recruited Isabel to help her fill the coffee cylinder. "Julia couldn't make it today, so you're in charge of refilling mugs after everyone gets through the line. Think you can handle that?"

"I'd be happy to." Isabel smiled, assuming the position by the coffee urn Daniel had set up.

Marge nodded and strode off on other business.

Fellowship Hall filled in no time. Her parents arrived, and they waved from where they began serving an egg bake to the guests lined up at the far end of the food line. Isabel hated that she had no idea this was a part of their weekly routine. She hadn't bothered to find out.

But she didn't have much chance to dwell on her failures as a daughter right now. She turned her attention to filling cups of coffee for the steady stream of visitors. Soon it was challenging to even make small talk with those who came through the line over the din of surrounding conversations.

Isabel was helpless but to keep one eye on Daniel as brunch progressed—her and everyone else.

All the guests seemed to know him and want to talk to him, and he had a kind word, an inside joke, or a complex handshake for everyone there. At one point, he stopped and scooped a baby into his arms, tickling his belly and then scooting him onto his hip, giving a young mom a chance to eat her meal with two hands.

Isabel's heart shot to her throat at the sight, and she had to beat back the strange urge to cry.

Fortunately, Marge returned to her side and shooed her out into the hall to refill coffee. She was forced to turn her back to Daniel as she made the rounds, which was a relief. She wouldn't have been strong enough to look away on her own, but she needed the chance to regroup.

She circled the room, topping off mugs and greeting those she recognized. She made it to the last line of tables and was about to turn back to the buffet when she noticed a teenaged girl who was sitting alone. She had a coffee mug next to her seat.

Isabel switched directions and walked toward the girl, who was dressed in a black hoodie and cut-off denim shorts. Her hair fell over her face, and she didn't look up as Isabel approached.

"Hey, there. Need a refill?"

The girl rolled her shoulders over what appeared to be a journal in front of her. She didn't make eye contact, but with the hand not clutching a pen, she nudged her coffee mug toward Isabel. "I guess."

Isabel stepped forward and filled the mug.

"Thanks." The girl took a quick sip before setting the drink down and scribbling something on the page.

Isabel lingered, glancing between the food table and the girl. Something drew her to the teen. The way she sat off by herself, poring over the page, made Isabel wonder if they weren't a little like kindred spirits.

Or maybe Grace—and her canoodling nature—was rubbing off on Isabel.

"Mind if I sit?" Isabel plunked down in a chair one away from the teen before she could object.

"I guess not." The girl spoke quietly, but she didn't seem horrified by the company.

"I'm Isabel, by the way."

The girl peeked up at her. Recognition flashed across her face, and her eyes widened before she dropped her head and scratched something else out in her journal. "I'm Kylie."

"It's nice to meet you, Kylie." The girl didn't really invite much conversation, and Isabel didn't know what else to say, so she decided she'd just be honest. "This is my first time at one of these events. I don't really know what to do with myself. What are you working on there?"

Kylie shifted and pressed the journal shut, looking up at Isabel. "Nothing. It's nothing."

"Okay. If you say so." What Isabel had seen hadn't looked like nothing. It looked like some amazing hand drawings.

Kylie fidgeted with the tip of her pen. "What are you even doing here?"

"Right now? Right now I'm pouring coffee and sitting with you. Good times."

Kylie's lips quirked. "No. I mean, why are you here? Like *here* here. Serving us at this dinky little brunch."

"I'm helping out a friend." Her eyes found Daniel across the room where Mable Glasheen was bending his ear about something. He still wore his white apron, and the smile on his face as he listened to the woman prattle on made Isabel's insides melt. She glanced back at Kylie, who had followed Isabel's gaze.

"Daniel?" The teen nodded her head in his direction.

"Yup. Do you know him?"

Kylie shrugged. "Sort of."

"Do you come here often?"

Kylie's face darkened, and she flipped her journal open, doodling something on the corner of the page. She gave a bitter nod—one that, if Isabel wasn't mistaken, was also laced with sadness. "For the past six months, we haven't missed a Sunday."

"That's not a bad thing. It seems like the food is really good."

"Oh yeah, believe me. It's much better than anything my dad can whip up." She motioned to a middle-aged man who sat a table over, talking to some other brunch-goers. Kylie sighed then, some of the fight dissipating with her breath. "That's why he drags me here."

"You don't want to be here?"

"Not really. It's another reminder of how different my life is than how it was supposed to be. It's a reminder of what we lost." Kylie's voice cracked, and Isabel's heart lurched.

"I'm so sorry. I'm afraid I'm not from around here—I mean, I am, but not lately." Isabel fumbled over her words. "Never mind. This isn't about me. What I mean is, I don't know what's brought you here, even though everybody else in the room probably does, but I'm here if you want to talk about it."

Kylie pulled her lip into her mouth, and when she looked up and met Isabel's gaze, her eyes were glossy. "We lost my mom earlier this year. It was sudden. Ovarian cancer."

Tears sprung into Isabel's eyes. "Oh, Kylie. I'm so sorry." She reached across the table and placed her hand on the girl's arm. It wasn't enough to convey how sorry she felt, but right now, it was all she could do.

"Yeah." Kylie kept her eyes on her journal. "My dad's a mess, and he says he can barely toast bread, so we've been relying on charity from people bringing us meals and events like this one. It's sort of embarrassing, actually. But the worst part is it reminds me that my mom is gone."

Isabel nodded. "I can only imagine."

They sat in silence for a minute. Isabel's own mom was wiping down a table across the hall. She felt sick at the thought of losing her, and doubly sick at how she'd taken her for granted these past four years.

Isabel watched as Kylie sketched something onto the page. From her vantage point, Isabel still couldn't make out exactly what it was, but she was curious. She wondered if it had something to do with the girl's late mother, or if it was a way to cope with her grief. After a couple moments of silence, Isabel asked her about it again.

"Do you want to tell me what you're working on?"

"It's really nothing." She shot Isabel a sheepish look. "Nothing important, anyway."

Isabel frowned. "I wouldn't say that. I think journaling is very important. I journal a lot."

"You do?"

Isabel nodded.

Kylie put her pen down and took a sip of coffee before she met Isabel's eye again. "I'm actually writing a graphic novel. But it's really bad."

Isabel's mouth parted. She wasn't expecting that. "That's amazing. I'm sure it's not that bad. We're always our own worst critics."

Kylie shook her head. "No. I'm pretty sure it's really bad."

Kylie was a straight-shooter, and Isabel liked that. "Well, that's okay. I can relate, actually."

"Really? You?"

Isabel nodded. "Yeah. I'm supposed to write a book for work, and it's really bad, too."

Kylie's forehead creased with disbelief. "But you're Isabel Marshall."

"Yep. And my book is terrible right now. I can tell you that it doesn't matter who you are, when it comes to creating, it's always hard. But I won't give up on it if you promise not to give up on your graphic novel. Someday, I want to walk into a bookstore and see your name on the front cover of a bestseller. Deal?"

Kylie smiled at that. "My mom was a writer. I want to do it for her. So, yeah. Deal."

Isabel fought renewed tears that pricked at the backs of her eyes as she picked up the pen Kylie had dropped and scrawled her number on a napkin. "Good. Here's my phone number. Text me if you get stuck or if you ever need someone to talk to. I'll be here to cheer you on."

Kylie looked stunned, but not displeased. She nodded.

Isabel smiled and pressed her hands against the table, standing up and grabbing the coffee carafe. "I should get going before I get scolded for sitting down on the job."

Kylie raised her mug in a toast, sitting up straighter in her chair. "Thanks for the coffee. And for stopping to chat."

"You got it. Keep writing." Isabel waited for Kylie to nod before turning to the front of the hall.

Chapter 13

DANIEL

AFTER BRUNCH CONCLUDED, DANIEL sent all of the volunteers home, saying he would handle cleanup. His motives for tidying the space on his own weren't entirely altruistic. He wanted to be alone to try to figure out his feelings where Isabel was concerned.

Actually, he didn't need to try too hard to figure out his feelings—they were pretty obvious to him.

Daniel was as gone for Isabel as he had been four years ago when she'd left town. He'd danced with her, for crying out loud. Scooping Isabel into his arms and pulling her close was the most natural thing in the world—like eating ice cream on a hot summer night.

So, what he needed to figure out was what to do about how he was feeling, especially since he was still keeping something from Isabel. Something that, if she found out, would likely change her opinion of him. He hated that—hated thinking about that—but it was the truth.

Daniel sagged against the counter he'd finished wiping down. He'd been bowled over when he observed Isabel talking to Kylie. Kylie, who had been reluctant to talk to anyone for the past few weeks, peeling off from her dad the second they arrived at Sunday brunch and keeping to herself. She'd barely said two words to any of the other volunteers. Daniel didn't blame her. She'd lost her mom as an eighth grader. The poor thing was now facing down high school while her world was in tumult.

Daniel had tried to talk to her a couple times, always making a point to stop by her table and see if she needed anything. He could relate to her in a way, though he was much younger when his parents had passed away. But she clammed up around him. She was respectful and grateful, but distant, and Daniel hadn't pushed.

But Isabel sat down and put the girl at ease, made her feel less alone. He had no idea what inspired Isabel to strike up a conversation with Kylie. He doubted she knew the family's history. Which meant she had merely seen a young girl all alone in a church basement and sat down to keep her company—not for any other reason than because it was a good, kind thing to do.

He'd never doubted Isabel's goodness, but seeing it first hand, up close and personal, made it almost impossible to ignore the feelings he had for her.

The ones he'd stuffed down over the years.

The ones he told himself to forget.

They had all spilled out and scattered all over the floor of his heart, cluttering his mind and demanding his attention.

If he could put a little space between them, maybe he could check the longing in his gut to tug Isabel close and never let her go.

Daniel's phone jingled in his pocket with the sound of an email alert. He yanked it out, grateful for something—anything—to focus on that wasn't Isabel or his feelings for her.

In his inbox, he saw a new message from the editor of the local paper in Mapleton, *The Villager Tattler.*

To: Daniel Smith daniel.smith@gmail.com
From: Gerald Mahoney gmahoney@thetattler.com
Subject: Isabel Marshall Interview

Daniel,
As I'm sure you know, Isabel Marshall is in town. Her PR team has agreed to allow *The Tattler* an interview with her while she's here. They suggested

we coordinate it for early in the filming schedule,
as her days will fill up quickly. I'd like you to
conduct the interview. Let me know if this is going
to be an issue. I can always assign the interview
to someone else, but I'd rather it be you. A list
of questions that have been okayed by her team is
attached. Stick to the script, please.

    Regards,
    Gerald

Daniel gritted his teeth. So much for putting some distance
between himself and Isabel. From the looks of it, he'd be seeking
her out again in the not-so-distant future, whether or not his
heart would be pummeled in the process.

Daniel reread the email before clicking on the attachment and
skimming the questions.

Another email popped up from Gerald before Daniel finished
reading the interview outline. He opened it and had to read it
twice through to make sure he understood what his editor was
saying.

    To: Daniel Smith daniel.smith@gmail.com
    From: Gerald Mahoney gmahoney@thetattler.com
    Subject: Job Opportunity

    Daniel,
    While this isn't public knowledge yet, I want to
    get out in front of it where you're concerned.
    I've decided to retire, which means that *The
    Tattler* is going to be in need of an editor
    before the end of the year. You're my choice for
    successor. Obviously, you'll have to go through the
    application process, but my referral will go a long
    way. Let's set up a time to discuss your thoughts on

the position. I'd be happy to answer any questions
you have. Thanks for considering it.

    Regards,
    Gerald

A surge of excitement shot up in Daniel's chest like crisp
stalks of corn along the side of the road. To be the editor of his
hometown paper was the stuff his dreams were made of. He'd
always considered himself a little old school. He was a fan of
print papers that crinkled with each turn of the page and left ink
marks on the fingertips of loyal readers. He had countless ideas
for keeping the small-town paper relevant, and now, if everything
worked out, he'd be in a position to put them into practice, to
leave a legacy doing work he was passionate about and could be
proud of.

Daniel smiled to himself, typing a quick message back to Gerald
and setting up a meeting to discuss the job further. He couldn't
wait until he could share the news.

It felt like he took an arrow to the heart when he realized the
person he was most excited to tell was Isabel.

Chapter 14

ISABEL

"YOU CAN SEE WE tied in the richness of the restored hardwoods with period-appropriate furniture pieces. The whole room comes together seamlessly, and it's both beautifully designed and completely livable." Isabel stopped walking and clasped her hands together, waiting for Samson to stand next to her as Horatio instructed him to do. They were positioned in the front sitting room of the Dutch Colonial home. The cameras could pan out and see them, the shelf she refinished to look like a built-in, and all the natural light streaming in from the bay window.

"You're absolutely right. We can't thank you enough for your work here, Isabel. Mapleton is lucky to have you back in town." Samson shook her hand as they'd practiced.

"I'm happy to be here. Now, let's get to work on the next house!" Isabel delivered her final line, and they smiled at each other.

"Cut!" Horatio hollered. "Excellent, you two."

"Thanks, H." Turning to Samson, Isabel added, "You're a natural."

"I don't know about that." Samson tugged on his collar. "You work in a nerve-racking business."

"I tell you what," Horatio cut in as he walked over to them. "I'm toying with the idea of hiring all y'all. You Mapletonians sure add some spark to our filming. First Daniel, and now you, Samson."

Samson raised a singular brow. "You filmed with Daniel?"

Isabel nodded, swallowing down a familiar rush of...*feeling* at Daniel's name. The truth was, she hadn't been able to get him out of her head all week. "He found the mantel we have in the back room."

"You're kidding!"

"Nope. True story."

"Wow. I'm impressed," Samson said. "Who knew Daniel had design expertise. I might have to add that to the list of things I tease him about, right along with being the star writer of a wedding magazine."

Isabel fought dueling urges, the first to defend Daniel, and the second to picture him in a tux at the end of the aisle. She told herself she was being ridiculous on both counts. One, Samson was obviously just teasing. Two, marriage was not on her radar—even if Daniel had remained the only man she could ever imagine building a life with.

Horatio's phone went off, interrupting Isabel's runaway thoughts. He retrieved it from his pocket and frowned at the caller ID. "Excuse me. I'm going to have to take this."

Grace joined Isabel and Samson. "I'm starving."

Isabel checked her phone. It was nearing twelve-thirty. "Okay, then. How about a sandwich at the café?"

Grace's stomach rumbled in agreement, and they laughed.

Samson retrieved his cell phone from the back pocket of his jeans, glancing at the screen. "I'm heading that way, too. I'll see you guys there. Thanks again for showing me the ropes."

Isabel returned his smile as she hoisted her bag over her shoulder and walked out the front door with Grace. She spotted Ford coming out of a house across the street. Their eyes connected for a split second before he put his head down and stalked in the opposite direction.

Isabel's heart sank. She was starting to feel like she'd lost her brother for good. The thought dampened her mood as she trailed Grace to their rental car.

"I told H I would be in touch and let him know your plans. He'll want to develop a film schedule for the next few houses," Grace said, angling into the passenger seat.

Isabel forced a smile. "Thanks for coordinating all that. Have I told you lately you're very good at your job?"

Grace tapped her chin. "No, you haven't. In fact, I was starting to think you didn't like my, um, meddling."

"You? Meddle? Never!" Isabel's spirits rose and she smirked as she turned onto Mapleton Avenue and drove to On Deck Café.

"It was pretty obvious, wasn't it?" Grace had enough self-awareness to look sheepish.

"Not sure what was more blatant: you conspiring to get me back to Mapleton, or your attempts to thrust me back into the heart of town since we've arrived."

"Has it been so bad?" Grace asked.

"No," she said after a second. The village as a whole was a far cry from the deadbeat, anti-creative monster she'd turned it into in her head. She was finding inspiration everywhere she turned. "I guess it's true that absence makes the heart grow fonder. Unfortunately, I burned a lot of bridges with my family and those whom I was closest to." Her mind flashed to the hurt and distant look she'd seen in her parents' eyes when she first arrived. To Ford's constant dismissal of her. To Daniel.

"I'd argue your bridges aren't so much burned as they are, let's say, under construction."

Isabel just shrugged. She locked the car and walked to the front door of the café. Grace opened it and walked in first, the trademark bell jingling overhead. In front of her, Samson leaned over the counter to give Julia a peck on the lips.

Julia looked to the door, her cheeks glowing. "Hey, you guys." She waved at them from behind the bar. "Congrats on wrapping house number one!"

"Here, here!" Cheers went up from around the small dining room, and Isabel smiled in spite of herself. Nowhere in LA could she have gone and received this type of welcome. She was beginning to wonder what had made her so adamant about leaving Mapleton in the first place.

Grace pointed to the counter. "Do you want your usual? I can order if you want to grab a table."

"Sounds good. Thanks." Isabel took a seat and got out her spec sheet on house number two, making notes in the margins until Grace joined her.

"Julia said she'd deliver the sandwiches when they're ready."

"That's nice of her." Isabel glanced up at the barista, who was chatting with an older gentleman. Isabel recognized him from her childhood. Charlie was his name, if she recalled correctly. Julia beamed at something he said, and she gave his arm a pat. She was so good and wholesome. Like she truly cared about all those who came into her coffee shop. The world needed a little more of that, Isabel decided.

"So, talk to me." Grace clasped her hands in front of her, resting her wrists on the edge of the table. "What do we think? Bridges burned or just in need of your attention?"

"Are we still on that?" Isabel winced.

"Meddlers gotta meddle," Grace quipped.

"You're impossible," Isabel tsked before she bit her cheek, thinking. "I don't know. I'd like to think I can repair what I haven't tended to in the past few years, but it's all so far gone. And I'm a different person than I was when I left."

"Are you that different?" Grace asked, her voice turning quiet, all traces of teasing gone.

"Well, I'm famous now, for one." Isabel was only being half serious, but in a way, it was the truth. She didn't know how to relate to her family. Their worlds were so different.

"Even famous people have real lives—and pasts," Grace said pointedly. "Besides, you and Daniel looked pretty comfortable with each other on Saturday. Your *fame*"—she made air quotes—"didn't get in the way there. And I hear you spent time with him on Sunday, too."

Isabel wasn't even going to ask how Grace knew that. If her friend had somehow plugged herself into the Mapleton intelligence network, Isabel was officially done for. "Daniel is different."

"I can see that."

Isabel opened her mouth to say something—anything—to try to steer Grace away from prying into her relationship, or lack thereof, with Daniel. She wasn't ready to go there yet. Grace plowed ahead before she got the chance.

"For the record, I think you need to table the idea of being famous. Yes, you *are* famous, but I don't believe that's *who* you are, you know?"

Isabel frowned. She'd been so preoccupied with building her name and her brand that she hadn't stopped to think about the person she'd become in the process and how that compared to who she was and who she wanted to be.

Julia bustled up to the table. "Here are your sandwiches. Sorry for the wait. These are on the house."

"You don't have to do that," Isabel said, thankful for the distraction. Grace's point made her skin itch in a way that told her she needed to take a good, hard look at her life. But not right now, sitting in the middle of the café.

"I insist. Samson said the first house is gorgeous, by the way. I can't wait to see it!"

"It couldn't have turned out better," Isabel said, and Grace nodded.

"I'm so glad you're both here. I could pinch myself with how this all came together. Hey!" Julia's eyes lit up. "I'm not sure what you're doing on Friday night, but we're having a bonfire out at McGregor Farm. You remember, Isabel?"

Isabel nodded. The McGregor family owned property south of the village. Their farm was a Mapleton institution. It's where everyone got their Christmas trees each holiday season, and townsfolk had been convening there for local gatherings since before Isabel was born.

"You guys should join us."

"Oh, I don't know. I wouldn't want to intrude—"

"We can definitely check the schedule and see if we can make it work." Grace widened her eyes and smiled at Isabel meaningfully. "Thanks for the invite, Julia. I've never been to a bonfire in the country before."

"Then you don't know what you're missing! S'mores, star gazing, truth or dare, music, and the occasional ghost story. All the good stuff of summer and small-town living happens at a village bonfire."

Grace rubbed her hands together. "Sounds like my kind of good time."

"Well, I hope to see you both there. Isabel, you would be anything but an intrusion." Julia gave her a look that was full of welcome and warmth before squinting at her wristwatch. "I've gotta run. Shift change in fifteen minutes, and I hate to leave the counter and kitchen a mess for the guys. Let me know if I can get you anything else."

She hustled off, and Grace stared Isabel down.

"What?" Isabel postured. "You know I have a ton of work to do, and if I don't start working on my book sometime soon, it's never going to get done."

Grace crossed her arms. "We're going. You don't get to deny me this joy. Besides, it'll be good for you."

Isabel clicked her tongue. "We'll see," she compromised.

"I'm going with or without you. These are my people." Grace raised both arms to the side as if she wanted to wrap everyone in the café in a giant hug, and Isabel couldn't help but laugh.

The bell over the café's door jingled again, and Grace peeked over Isabel's shoulder before looking back at her, a Cheshire grin curling at her lips. "Speaking of something that'll be good for you."

"What?" Isabel turned around in the booth and spied Daniel, who had stopped to talk to a group of older gentlemen.

Grace grasped for the rental car keys that Isabel had set on the table.

"Grace," Isabel said her name with warning. "What are you doing?"

"I, uh…have to talk to Horatio about something. I should go do that right now. Someone else can give you a ride, can't they?"

"Don't you dare." Isabel all but hissed the words across the table as Grace stood and slung her bag over her shoulder.

"Oh, I do dare. Have Julia box up my lunch, and I'll get it from you later. We'll chat then, okay? Toodles!" With that, she made her way toward the exit.

Isabel turned and scowled at her retreating figure for long enough to see Grace halt briefly and talk to Daniel.

It was official. Grace fit in perfectly in Mapleton, where everyone made it a point to have their hands in everyone else's business.

Isabel whirled back around, sweat pooling along the dimples of her back as if she'd just gone for a five-mile run. It wasn't that she didn't want to see Daniel. Her issue was that she *did* want to see him, and she still hadn't figured out how to handle that.

"Hey, there." Daniel let his hand rest on her shoulder, grabbing her attention. His fingers didn't linger. If it wasn't for the sparks singeing her skin where his fingers had grazed, she would have questioned whether he'd touched her at all.

Isabel plastered on a smile, afraid he could see her chest heaving. "Hi."

"Grace said I could have her seat. It's packed in here."

Isabel peered around the café and found there was standing room only.

As if sensing her hesitation, Daniel added, "But if you don't want to share a table, I can grab my drink to-go."

"No, no." Isabel waved to the open spot across from her. "Sit, I insist."

A tentative smile opened up on Daniel's face. "Okay." He set his bag down against the chair. "I'm going to order."

Isabel nodded and looked to the counter, where Julia was already holding up a drink. "Daniel, I've got your coffee for you."

Daniel's lips hitched up. "The perks of small-town living, I suppose." He hurried to retrieve the mug from Julia.

Isabel fiddled with the centerpiece on the table, straightening the twine on the Mason jar Julia had filled with fresh flowers. She had nothing to get worked up about. It was merely a drink across the table from a friend.

As Daniel sat down and took a sip of his coffee, she smiled. "Is your drink of choice still black coffee with sugar, no cream?"

"Old habits die hard, as they say. And I can't seem to kick the sugar habit," Daniel admitted.

"What's life without a little sugar?" Isabel asked the question rhetorically, but Daniel grinned back at her.

"What's that look for?"

"I'm recalling our shared sweet tooth." Daniel leaned closer and drew her gaze. "Remember that time we climbed the water tower?"

Isabel couldn't help but smile as the memory resurfaced. They'd been hopped up on sugar and the unflappable nerves of young love when they'd climbed the ladder up to the water tower in town the summer after their freshman year of college.

"Shhhh. My parents still don't know that was me!"

Daniel smirked as he sat back. "No one guessed it was us—a pair of goody two-shoes—who left the spray-painted message. Do you remember what you told me to write?"

"Extra, extra, read all about it!" She smacked her palm against her forehead. "I thought that was such a clever play on the fact that this is a town literally known for paper, with the old mill and all. Gosh, we were so dumb. I'm going to blame it on the pixie sticks we'd downed before climbing up there."

They had been slap happy as they challenged each other to see how many of the candy sticks they could both eat.

Daniel's eyes danced, and Isabel's body warmed at the memory—at the ease of their reminiscing. It felt like the sun was rising in her soul, coloring the sky between them with a hint of a long-forgotten hue.

"That was fun."

"You're right. And we climbed up there again to paint over our work a few days later."

Daniel crossed his arms, showing off the muscles of his forearms and making Isabel feel buzzed in a way that had nothing to do with sugar, or pixie sticks, or the memories of days gone by.

"Well, I wasn't about to let you get arrested for vandalism. Your parents would never have forgiven me."

She mirrored his posture and stuck up her nose. "Me? It was your idea. You would have taken the fall for that one."

Daniel laughed and held up his hands in surrender. "The details are wishy-washy."

Isabel smiled, and they lapsed into silence, Daniel sipping his drink and Isabel moving the leftover crust of her sandwich around on her plate.

"Hey, speaking of the paper—"

Isabel's phone chimed, signaling an incoming text message and cutting Daniel off.

"Sorry." Isabel looked down at the screen to find a message from Tad Darling.

Miss you, gorgeous! When will you be back in town?

Isabel's neck tingled with embarrassment as she snatched her phone off the table, saying a silent prayer Daniel hadn't seen the message.

"You can answer if you need to." Daniel's tone was flat, and he stared beyond her, out toward the rest of the café patrons.

Isabel silenced her phone and stowed it in her purse. "It's nothing."

Daniel met her gaze, but the spark she'd seen flickering in his green eyes not a minute before was extinguished. In its place was a pile of ash. "If you say so."

"I do. It's just this guy from LA."

Daniel held up a hand, and the agonized expression on his face said he would rather not know. "Seriously, Isabel. You don't have to explain yourself to me. You don't owe me anything. We're friends now."

"No, that's just it. I've told Tad that I don't want a relationship. He's a nice guy, and we've seen each other a couple times, mostly for work events. But that's all there is to it."

Daniel blew out a breath across the table, though she caught him trying to mask it with a cough. His shaky reaction did something to Isabel's insides. A lightness swelled up in her stomach, like the fizzy foam of a soda poured over ice.

"Well, that's that, then." He gave her a glimmer of a smile before looking away again. "I should get going, though. I have meetings this afternoon. Thank you for letting me share the table. And for indulging me in some good memories." He stood up and was about to walk away when he stopped and turned to her.

Isabel's pulse kicked up, waiting to see what he would do next. As it had on Sunday, that crazy part of her brain hoped he'd lean in and kiss her, but she checked it—checked it *real* hard.

"Actually, I have another favor to ask."

"Sure. What is it?"

"It's for the paper. I need to set up an interview with you."

The paper. Right. That was what he had started to tell her about before Tad texted. Isabel told herself she was being silly for feeling let down that he needed a professional favor and not a personal one.

"Of course," she said, pleased with her breezy tone. She reached for her cell phone so she could check her calendar. "When were you thinking?"

"Whenever you're free. We could come here for coffee tomorrow morning—early. I know you have a lot of work to do."

"Sure. Let's say six-thirty tomorrow morning? It'll be like old times." Isabel clamped her mouth shut. Their senior year of college, when their days were packed with classes and internships and other commitments, the two of them used to meet up at six-thirty every morning for a breakfast date. It was their only consistent chance to spend time together.

But this wasn't a date. She would do well to remember that.

"Just like old times." Daniel winked.

Isabel's pulse snapped as he walked away.

Crazy or not, it might have been time to admit how much she longed for what used to be.

Chapter 15

DANIEL

DANIEL HAD AN EXTRA hop in his step as he walked to the old office of *The Village Tattler*. He didn't want to admit to himself it was because he found out Isabel was unattached. But he couldn't deny that the memories they shared were curling around his heart, making his blood flow as sweet as pure maple syrup. He was in such a good mood he'd almost convinced himself that the mistakes of his past where Isabel was concerned weren't as significant as he'd made them out to be. If he didn't dwell on them, he could practically forget them. And that felt amazing.

Everything was so easy with Isabel, and that had to count for something. Granted, he was doing a terrible job of distancing himself from her, but he could hardly bring himself to care.

He opened the door to the cramped newspaper office, and the scent of stale coffee and printer ink assaulted him. He entered, and the hardwood floors squeaked and groaned under his weight.

Overhead, the local radio talking heads blared from the speakers affixed in the upper corners of the room. On either side of him, the walls were paneled and painted white. They were lined with framed articles from past newspaper editions.

Daniel loved this place.

Gerald Mahoney, the longtime editor of the paper and an institution in Mapleton, emerged from his office at the back of the small building. "Why, hello there, Daniel. Glad you could make it."

Daniel stepped forward and pumped Gerald's outstretched hand. The man was almost sixty-five years old with a rotund belly that hung over his belt and thinning light-brown hair. Gerald was still as sharp as a tack—he had been for the decade he and Daniel had been working together.

The editor had taken Daniel on as an intern when Daniel was still in high school, showing him the journalistic ropes. Daniel had spent many an afternoon after school in these cramped quarters, listening as Gerald talked distribution numbers and ways to keep the print paper relevant.

Gerald was a shrewd businessman. Daniel had learned a ton from him, and he'd be forever grateful to Gerald for managing to keep Mapleton's small-town paper afloat when, all around them, newspaper presses were closing up shop. If it wasn't for Gerald's work for the past thirty years, Daniel wouldn't have the opportunity he had now. He did not take that lightly.

"Glad to be here, sir."

"Follow me. We can talk more in here." Gerald led Daniel back into the office.

It was a crowded space with only enough room for a desk and a visitor's chair. Gerald had a filing cabinet wedged into the corner, and pale-yellow curtains hung on either side of a small window, open to let in fresh air, on the back wall.

"Well, let's cut to the chase." Gerald settled himself behind the desk, realigning a framed photo of him and his wife, Tess, on the desk's corner before pinning Daniel with a no-nonsense look. "I take it you're interested in the role of editor, correct?"

"Yes, sir. Very much."

Gerald nodded, studying Daniel over the top of his glasses, which always seemed two sizes too small for his face, in Daniel's opinion. "Good. Good. I had hoped to hear that. Let me tell you. It takes work, keeping this paper in print. It's a big job. I realize you have other writing commitments, and I'm not saying you should give those up. Honestly, the paper probably pays me a part-time salary as it is, so you'll want to keep your other lines of income open."

Daniel nodded, and Gerald launched into an explanation of what his day-to-day work efforts consisted of.

Daniel was able to ask his questions, and after twenty minutes, he was more excited about the prospect of running the paper than he had been when he walked in.

He shot Gerald a smile. "You've sold me on it, Gerald. Where do I apply?"

Gerald rocked back in his chair and crossed his arms over his belly, the corners of his mouth hitching up. "We'll get to that. One more thing I will say, Daniel. This cannot be a remote position. You'll have to hold office hours at least three days a week. Here. In person. You'd be amazed at the foot traffic I get. I've found folks are more willing to purchase ad space or to ask for a feature article on a community event if there's a person who they can talk to about it available, in the flesh."

"Of course. I get that."

"And it won't be a problem?" Gerald arched his wiry brows.

Daniel inclined his head. He was puzzled that Gerald was emphasizing this aspect of the role. Sure, it would be a bummer not to get to work at the café every day, but he could still frequent Julia's place when he wasn't here. The two buildings were less than a five-minute drive from each other. "I don't see why it would be."

Gerald worked his jaw, and Daniel suddenly felt like he was being scrutinized. He sat up straighter, hoping he passed whatever silent, unknown test he was taking.

Finally, Gerald smiled at him, a full-blown toothy grin. "Good. To tell you the truth, I am thrilled you are excited about this, Daniel. I'm not sure I could have parted with the paper to anyone who was less worthy of it. And that would have been a problem for the missus."

He nodded to the photo of Tess.

Daniel's cheeks grew warm under the praise, but then his smile faltered, an image of Isabel popping into his mind. And in a blink,

Daniel knew exactly why Gerald wanted to make sure he was okay with being in Mapleton—at the office—three days a week.

Daniel would be putting down more roots in Mapleton with this gig, so technically, he no longer could say he could work from anywhere.

Which meant he was once again choosing to put states between himself and Isabel.

Gerald had a front-row seat to the fallout of Isabel and Daniel's break-up after college. He, of all people, probably gathered what having her back in town was doing to Daniel. But what did Gerald think? That Daniel was going to want to follow her back to California?

He wasn't planning on that.

Was he?

Daniel replayed the conversation he and Isabel had had not an hour before—the same interaction that had him feeling like he was walking on sunshine when he arrived at the newspaper office. Every moment with Isabel was good. So good, in fact, that it scared him.

Because Isabel hadn't said anything about wanting him back in her life in *that* way, even if their time together since she returned to Mapleton had been better than he could have hoped for. She'd only asked for his friendship. So, at the moment, there wasn't a *Daniel and Isabel* to consider.

And he could hardly decide to apply or not apply for this position based on her and what could be. After all, this was the job he'd always wanted.

And Isabel?

She was only a dream.

Daniel brought his focus back to the man sitting across the desk and ignored the slight roiling going on in his stomach. "I have big shoes to fill, Gerald, but if I get this chance, I won't let you down."

Chapter 16

ISABEL

ISABEL SAT ACROSS THE table from Daniel and squeezed her coffee mug until her knuckles turned white. She worried that if she let go, her hands might tremble, and she didn't want to face the proof that Daniel affected her so much. Two days in a row now she'd been face to face with him at the café, and as it turned out, she had completely lost her chill where he was concerned.

They were tucked in a booth in a small alcove off to the right of the ordering counter. It was far too intimate for Isabel's comfort—especially since this was a non-date.

"Is it okay if I record our conversation?" Daniel held up his cell phone. "It'll help me in case I need to reference something when I'm writing up the article."

See. Not a date.

"Of course. Whatever you need to do."

"Great. Give me one second."

Isabel nodded as Daniel got organized. He was in his element, and the furrow of concentration between his brows as he scanned his computer screen made him all the more attractive.

As Daniel bent to grab something from his messenger bag, Isabel caught a whiff of his cologne. The scent of him—a mix of pine and old books—was an intoxicating combination, one that, if she wasn't careful, would render her incapable of thinking of anything else.

She stifled a groan. The fingertip hold she had on her composure was slipping, and if she lost her grip, she was afraid she'd fall head-first in love with Daniel right in front of the whole dang town.

Why was the café so packed, anyway? It wasn't even seven o'clock in the morning.

"Are you sure you don't mind doing this now? I know you have a full morning of work." Daniel wore his most professional expression, and his tone was all business.

A strange desire to reach across the table and ruffle his hair or bop him on the nose to get him to crack a smile zipped through Isabel's mind, but she told it to take a hike.

"It's no problem." Isabel waved a hand across the space between them, proud of her friendly tone and thankful he couldn't read her mind.

"I appreciate it. I'll try to be quick." He set his phone on the table in between them, clicked a button, and spoke directly into the microphone. "Isabel Marshall, Village Tattler Interview."

His deep, matter-of-fact voice saying her name made her toes curl.

Since when had interviews turned her on? Since never. Except she'd never been interviewed by Daniel.

Isabel mentally chastised herself for being ridiculous and took another drink of her latte, giving herself something to focus on.

You can do this. You are Isabel Marshall. A strong, confident, independent design maven and style icon. You can handle a small-town interview.

Daniel typed something into his computer and spoke without looking at her. "That's a nice ride you've got out there."

She glanced out the window to where she'd parked the rental car the network had provided her before returning her gaze to Daniel. This wasn't how she expected him to start the interview.

"I guess." She shrugged. "I don't drive much anymore. I walk, or call for a ride, or use public transportation. It's way easier than trying to figure out parking or navigating the busy freeways. Drivers in California are a little different than drivers in Wisconsin."

"Is that right?" Daniel peered up from his computer and wiggled his eyebrows. "I can't imagine why."

Isabel loosened the grip on her mug and felt the pinch from where she was holding her back stiff slacken. Daniel had sensed her nerves, and he was joking with her, trying to put her at ease. Isabel's heart stumbled on its ascent up her throat and back down into her chest cavity. Somehow—after all these years—he still knew exactly what she needed, when she needed it.

Right now, she needed to not think too much about that.

"Let's just say, when I drove into town the other day, I got stuck behind a tractor. That doesn't usually happen in LA. That, and I was driving the speed limit and didn't feel like I was going to get run off the road."

"You sound like you speak from experience." Daniel chuckled. Then, after a pause, he asked, "What happened to your little red car, anyway?" He focused on his computer screen again, avoiding her eye.

"I sold it when I made it to LA. It helped cover my first bit of rent." It was the first step she had taken in shedding her past life in favor of a new beginning. The first step of many.

Daniel looked up and studied her for a minute.

She held his gaze, unsure what to make of the clouds in his eyes, until it dawned on her: the red Honda was his last memory of her, of them together—at least until she arrived in town earlier this month.

She'd spent the last four years not letting her mind rehash the day she left. Driving away from him with her whole life packed into that tiny red car was one of the most challenging things she'd ever done. She hadn't wanted to leave him, but she knew she had to go. And he wouldn't come with her.

Staring at him now, for the first time in a long time, she wondered if it had been worth it to leave him behind. She wondered if he'd ever thought he made the wrong decision.

If she asked him to, would he come with her now?

Isabel pressed her lips together. Where had *that* thought come from?

Across the table, Daniel blinked a couple of times in quick succession, erasing any trace of lingering sentimentality from his eyes. "Okay, enough about cars. Let's get started. Can you tell me about your life in LA? What does a typical day look like for Isabel Marshall?"

Daniel lobbed a softball for the first question. She could answer this one in her sleep, and she was glad it kept the conversation professional. She didn't trust herself with anything that directed her focus to Daniel himself, their shared history, or how endearing he looked when he typed his notes, biting his tongue between his teeth.

"My days are full of work and design. When we're filming episodes for *Inspired Interiors*, I'm at the houses we're working on for five or six hours a day. When I'm not there, I'm at furniture stores or home improvement stores, getting the materials we need, or I'm meeting with clients. At home, I like to dream up new design ideas and try out new recipes to share on my blog. And in the evenings, I'm out on the town, networking."

"Can you tell me a little bit about your blog?"

"Sure," Isabel said, smiling. She gave him the rundown of the blog's history and her hopes for it going forward.

"And what about Grace? Has she been with your show from the beginning?" Daniel asked. "You two seem like good friends."

"We are. I've never met anyone like Grace." Isabel couldn't help gushing over her assistant. Grace had become a friend over the years. Really, if Isabel thought about it, she was her only friend out in LA—at least her only true friend. Everyone else was more of an acquaintance. She didn't want to think about what that said about the life she'd made for herself. All she knew was that she was so lucky to have Grace in her corner.

"When I started at the network, I was terrified." Isabel laughed, and Daniel smiled at her. "Grace was a life saver. She gives the best pep talks of anyone I know. Over time, we bonded over a shared love of home and design. And Harry Potter," Isabel added with a smile.

"Let me guess. You're both Gryffindors?"

Isabel gasped, shaking her head. "How did you know?"

"Just had a hunch." Daniel winked.

Isabel chuckled. "Well, we spent a lot of time with each other working on the show. One weekend, we hit up The Wizarding World of Harry Potter at Universal Studios together, and that sealed the deal of a real friendship. She's been with me every inch of the climb. Honestly, I don't know what I'd do without her."

Daniel dropped his chin and typed away on the laptop in front of him. "I'm glad to know you have a friend like her." His voice was so low she almost didn't hear him.

When his words registered, a flicker of warmth licked its way up Isabel's spine. After all these years, he was still looking out for her. Was he even conscious of what he was doing—making sure she was taken care of?

It had been so long since someone had taken care of her. After falling out with her family, she'd convinced herself she didn't need it. But the emotion his declaration stirred in her chest told a different story. The independent streak in her should have shirked at his chivalry, but she couldn't. This was Daniel, and his intentions were always pure.

"And what about for fun? What do you do in your free time?" he asked, interrupting her thoughts.

Isabel froze. "Pardon me?"

"Free time. When you're not working?" Daniel clarified.

What free time?

Her whole life was bound up in her work. She gave a nervous laugh, which she hoped came out sounding less tight than it felt. "Right. Well, you know LA never sleeps, so there's always something to do."

"Such as?"

Isabel shifted in her seat, racking her brain for a suitable answer. "Let's see..." she stalled. Why couldn't she think of anything remotely interesting to say? Was her life so pathetic that she didn't do anything for fun? Other than Harry Potter World, which she'd already brought up, nothing came to mind that held a candle to the good times she and Daniel used to have, spending summer days at the swim lake or going for long bike rides through the Sunrise Park trails.

"Well, I dabble in the kitchen, trying to come up with new recipes. Mostly baked goods. For my sweet tooth."

Daniel's eyes crinkled with a smile as he typed something out on his computer.

"Oh, and I've taken up photography. Or at least I'm trying to teach myself how to take good photos."

It wasn't much, but at least she'd come up with some things that resembled hobbies, even if she was mostly cooking and taking photos for her blog. She made a note to herself to try to relax and get out more when she went back to California.

At the thought, unease coated her stomach, and Isabel crossed and uncrossed her legs under the table, trying to shake off the sudden queasiness.

If Daniel noticed her discomfort, he didn't draw attention to it. "What's your favorite project to date?"

Isabel took a steadying breath and thought for a moment, happy to be on to the next question. She described a particularly massive redesign she did for an older couple, Mr. and Mrs. Sinclair. They'd purchased a smaller home after the kids moved out, and she helped them make it their own.

"I loved integrating the family heirlooms in the Sinclair project. It made that one really special. But as I've said before, all of my clients are a joy to work with."

Isabel looked down. That was sort of a lie. Some of the people she did business with were a handful. Like the guy who called her up at two in the morning to ask her to come over so she could see how the moon shone in through his living room window. He wanted to match his paint color to the hue of the light hitting his wall at that exact moment.

For real.

Or the couple who would not stop arguing over every little design detail she proposed. It took double the time to finish the job because every time one of them would agree to something, the other one would change his or her mind. They divorced a month after filming on their house was complete.

"Anything else to add?"

Isabel glanced up to find Daniel staring at her, one half of the pair of lips she used to kiss hitched up.

Maybe he actually *could* read her mind.

She plastered on an airy smile. "Nope. I'm lucky to do what I do."

"Alright, then. What are some of your future business plans? You've built quite the empire with Inspired™."

"Thank you." Isabel told herself he was just doing his job, offering her that bit of praise. It didn't mean anything. Still, the glow she felt in her chest made its way up to her cheeks, which felt pleasantly warm all of a sudden. "We're hard at work on new episodes of *Inspired Interiors*, as you know." She smiled at him across the booth, and the other corner of his lips rose.

Gosh he had a nice smile. Then again, maybe *nice* wasn't the right word for it—not when every time he flashed a happy look in her direction, all her lucid thoughts fled and her world felt like it got turned on its head. No. In that way, Daniel's smile was better described as being earthshattering.

Isabel looked toward the counter in an attempt to get ahold of herself. Julia waved, and she held up her hand before returning her focus to Daniel. "My blog following has also grown exponentially in the past year, so I hope to keep fostering relationships with my readers. And I'm excited about the book I have in the works."

"Can you tell me a little bit about that project?"

Isabel's face fell despite her best efforts to keep her composure. Daniel was kind enough to look down at his computer and give her a second to recover.

She summoned her most chipper voice. "The book will include my thoughts on design and what I've learned from working on the TV show and with clients. My first draft is due in September, so I have my work cut out for me if I'm going to get that done while also handling all the work around here."

Daniel glanced up and held her gaze for a beat, studying her before—mercifully—moving on. "That brings up another good point. Can you talk about the projects here? What are you most excited about?"

Isabel rattled off details about the homes she was working on in Mapleton. She made a point to praise Samson—he deserved it—and she threw in a shout-out to Julia for her design assistance. That got a smile out of Daniel, but it froze in place as his eyes scanned the next question on his list.

Isabel chewed on the inside of her cheek, afraid of what his stoic expression might mean.

Daniel massaged his temple with his pointer finger. "Uh, what do you miss the most about Mapleton?"

"The people," she heard herself say. "Definitely the people."

Daniel dropped his hand from his head and stared at her, a blizzard of inquiry swirling in his green eyes, turning them from summer to winter.

They sat looking at each other until Isabel was certain her lips were starting to quiver. So, she rambled. "Everyone has been so kind since I've returned, welcoming me back with open arms. Well, almost everyone. My family has been distant and none too thrilled with me, but I expected that."

Isabel slammed her hand over her mouth. "I can't believe I said that out loud. Can you please strike that from the record?"

Daniel looked sideways at her, holding up his hands in the universal *stop* sign. "Isabel. Relax. I won't print that. Don't worry."

She inhaled through her nose and blew out from her mouth in an attempt to drag her blood pressure down from where it had flown up and through the roof. "Thank you. It's just that...well, I

GOOD TO BE HOME

don't know. Things at home have been rocky. I don't need to stir the pot by saying something like that for all the world to read."

Daniel shook his head. "It's fine. Really. I won't write a thing about it."

"Thanks." Isabel slumped down in her seat. "Sorry. I have a love-hate relationship with the press. I can get a little sensitive at the thought of a news outlet printing anything that could paint me in a bad light. You probably don't know this, but one of my first reviews ever ripped me apart, calling me a phony, saying my show wasn't inspired, it was insipid." Isabel's mouth contorted into a scowl as she said it, hating that she still had the article memorized. "It made me want to quit. So, yeah. There are enough of those anonymous sleazebag journalists out there, spouting off nonsense, and enough readers and fans who are willing to pass judgment. I don't need that from my hometown paper."

When she finished her rant, Daniel was staring back at her like he'd seen a ghost.

She quickly replayed what she'd said, and then wished she could yank the words back.

Daniel *was* a journalist, and now she'd gone and insulted his profession. It wasn't a good look. What was wrong with her? She didn't usually fail so miserably at reading the room.

She leaned forward against the table in an effort to shrink the gap that had opened up between them. "I'm so sorry. I didn't mean to go off on a tirade. I-I'm really grateful I can trust you not to publish dirt on my family and me."

Daniel clenched his jaw before offering her a small smile, but it didn't reach his eyes. "Right. Okay, moving on. Last question. And let me preface this by saying these are the newspaper's questions, not mine." He took a fortifying breath and spit out the words so quickly it was as if they burned the roof of his mouth. "Are you dating anyone?"

Isabel scrunched up her nose and scoffed. "I was wondering when that was going to come up."

Daniel laughed a tight laugh, running a hand behind his neck. "You know it's called *The Tattler* for a reason."

"I know, I know. Small-town gossip disguised as hard-hitting news."

Daniel grinned, looking more like himself. "Some may say small-town gossip *is* hard-hitting news."

Isabel dipped her chin in acknowledgement. "Touché."

The type of understanding that only comes with a shared history danced across the table between them, and Isabel lapped it up, grateful that they'd moved past her outburst about her family. She didn't want to dwell on that, and she was thankful she could trust Daniel not to make a big deal about it.

"So, are you seeing anyone?" Daniel broke into the comfortable silence they'd fallen into, jolting Isabel back to reality.

"Oh! Right." She sat up in her seat. "No. Let it be known I am single. Have been for quite a while." She prayed he wouldn't press her for specifics, because she didn't want to admit that she'd been single the entire time she was in LA. And he was a big reason why.

Perhaps the sole reason why.

Fortunately, Daniel seemed as ready to be done with that question—and the interview—as she was. "I'll make sure the record shows you're single, then. Even though you know folks would love to hear about you and Tad Darling."

Isabel rolled her eyes. "I hate to disappoint the people, but yeah. No."

"Fair enough." Daniel grasped for his cell phone and turned off the microphone. "Thanks for this." He wiggled the phone before shoving it in his bag and standing. "*The Village Tattler* appreciates your time, and so do I."

"Like I said, it was no problem at all. And thank you again. For being understanding about my family." His discretion meant a lot to her.

"You're welcome." Daniel nodded, shoving his computer into his messenger bag. "I hate to cut our visit short, but I've got to run. See you around, Isabel."

Without giving her a chance to say goodbye, Daniel walked past her and out the front door.

Isabel sat still for a second before slumping forward in her chair and resting her forehead on her thumb and pointer finger, shielding her face from the rest of the café. She and Daniel had covered a lot of ground—at least she felt like they had. And she wasn't sure what she expected, but Daniel fleeing the scene of their date—er, non-date—and leaving her with a serious case of emotional whiplash wasn't it. It would have been nice to debrief with him after the interview was over.

Then again, maybe that was just her heart trying to lobby for more time with Daniel, however she could get it.

Chapter 17

DANIEL

THERE WAS NO WAY to describe how Daniel had left Isabel except to say that he straight up bolted. He could have given Julia Roberts in *Runaway Bride* a run for her money. And the fact that *that* was the analogy he came up with only confirmed that all the wedding writing he was doing was rubbing off on him, which wasn't helping his cause. At all.

After he stalked from the café, he drove directly to Colony Elms. His guilt-ridden mind and muddled heart called for a heavy dose of Grandpa Gus.

Arriving in the parking lot, Daniel locked his car and kept his head down as he hurried into the building. He wasn't in the mood to make small talk with any of the residents milling about, chatting over their morning coffees.

He was frustrated. By Isabel. By his feelings for her. And by the mistakes of his past—the ones that he couldn't, and shouldn't, bury. He had been a fool to think he could shove aside his secret. It wasn't in him to be dishonest, especially when he had caused someone else pain.

He nudged open the door to his grandfather's apartment.

Gus looked up from where he was reading a book in his recliner. "Hi, Son."

"Hey, Grandpa." Daniel sunk into an open chair.

"What have you been up to this morning?" Gus eyed him.

Daniel closed his eyes, collecting his thoughts. "I've been with Isabel."

"Oh? Is that right?" Intrigue crept into Gus's voice, and he snapped his book closed.

Daniel stared straight ahead, unsure what to say or where to begin. Finally, he turned to face his grandpa, whose eyes were soft and understanding behind his glasses. "You were right. I have feelings for her."

"I figured as much." Gus rocked back, observing him.

Daniel scrubbed his hands over his face. He had four years' worth of regrets ricocheting around in his mind, colliding with the new emotions that being with Isabel over the past two weeks had stirred up.

"Are you ever going to tell me what really held you back from going with her to California?" Gus's wizened gaze bore into him like a laser. "And don't say it was me. At least, I can't be the only reason, Danny. Your grandmother and I always taught you to go after what you want, and I know you would have done that four years ago if there hadn't been something else in the way. All these years I've wondered, but I've never asked. Well, now I'm asking."

Daniel looked out the window. Voicing his cowardice was embarrassing, so he spoke to the sky. "I told her—and myself—it was you who needed me, but really I was scared to leave. I guess it was me who needed you. I was afraid I wasn't going to be good enough for her. I was sure if I went to LA, we'd get out there, and Isabel would be swept up in the glitter of the big city. Everyone would love her because...well, everyone loves her. Isabel is hypnotic. And soon, she'd realize I was yesterday's news, and I would be left all alone. There was no way I could compete with the allure of LA. Or with the droves of men I was sure would be banging down her door. So I didn't even try. And she proved me right. She hasn't had any time for any of us from Mapleton for the past four years."

Daniel thought of her off-handed comment about *The Village Tattler* during their interview. He'd gone along with the joke about the paper being small potatoes. In a way, it was, and Isabel didn't mean anything by what she'd said. But it was his work, and it *was* small in comparison to what she was doing. She was out there with big production crews and million-dollar budgets, and he was simply gunning to become a one-man editing show for the local print newspaper. As far as their lives and work were concerned, it felt like not only were they not on the same playing field, but they weren't even playing the same sport.

Gus frowned, and Daniel figured he may as well lay the rest of his secrets bare.

"And I made a mistake, Grandpa." When he met Gus's eyes, he saw care and concern. God bless the man.

"Do you want to talk about it?"

"No, but I should." His voice sounded weaker than usual, but Daniel summoned the courage to say what he needed to say. "I wrote a nasty review of her show when it first launched."

Gus's frown deepened. "Why? That doesn't sound like you."

"I know." Daniel let his head fall back. "I wrote that piece from a position of pain. I'm not proud of it. It's one of the only times I ever let something personal affect my writing in such a direct way—and cloud my judgment."

Gus remained quiet, so Daniel went on.

"She doesn't know I wrote it. *Entertainment Magazine* published it anonymously, and a part of me always held out the faintest bit of hope that maybe she hadn't seen the article at all. I had started to think that it was buried so deep in the archives I wouldn't ever have to face having written it. But that would never have worked. And today, I found out not only has she seen it, but it nearly destroyed her resolve to pursue her dreams." He sighed. "I've been ashamed of myself for writing it since the day it hit newsstands, but hearing how it affected Isabel is eating me up inside."

His grandfather leaned forward in his chair, resting his arms on his thighs. After a minute, he offered Daniel a slight smile. "You have to tell her you wrote it. I know you know that."

"I know." Daniel grimaced. "I'm dreading it."

"I don't blame you, but you wouldn't be the man I raised you to be if you didn't speak up. You may have acted cowardly once, but now you have a chance to rectify it."

"My conscience won't let me sleep until it's out in the open."

"And perhaps you can rekindle your relationship, as well." Gus's eyes twinkled. "Maybe she'll decide to stay in Mapleton."

Daniel choked out a strangled breath. "I don't know about that." After a minute, he added, "Maybe."

He'd be lying if he said he didn't want that. Because despite the differences in what they did, he couldn't help but believe that he and Isabel were still a good fit. Who he was aligned with who she was.

"It's weird. After seeing her and getting a taste of what her life is like these days, I sense she's insecure about her fame—like LA isn't all it's cracked up to be. I don't think she's really that happy, Grandpa."

It was the assessment he'd come to during their interview. She talked about her life in California in such a superficial way. All she did was work and eat and think about working some more. She didn't light up while talking about any of it the way she had when her eyes landed on the blue buffet at Vintage Market. Sure, she had Grace—and Daniel was thankful for that—but everything else about Isabel's chirpy treatment of her life in LA fell a little flat.

"Her happiness isn't your responsibility at this point, Son."

It was a gentle reminder, and Daniel recognized it for what it was. He couldn't control other people's feelings or decisions. He could only control his own actions. And with his actions—the words he'd written—he'd caused unnecessary harm.

Daniel exhaled. "I know, but telling her what I did is only going to make her upset, and I hate that. What if she refuses to talk to me? What if she doesn't care for me like I care for her, and by speaking up, I break her heart for nothing? What if—"

"That is the consequence of your choice, Daniel. And there would be no one to blame but yourself."

Daniel frowned, but it was the tough love he needed.

"But if I may say"—Gus's tone was gentler as he went on—"I think you're getting too far ahead of yourself."

"What do you mean?"

"You can't let the what-ifs consume you. Focus on the what-about-nows. If you live looking ahead at all the pain the future may hold, you won't be living at all. Seems to me that's what got you into this whole mess four years ago. You were thinking too far down the road. There's enough struggle in each day to last for each day."

Daniel heaved a sigh. "I know you're right."

Gus nodded and, satisfied that he'd made his point, switched on the television.

Daniel settled in to watch the morning show with his grandpa. He was surprised to find his spirits improved the moment he got his secret off his chest, even if the worst was yet to come.

He had to tell Isabel the truth.

Chapter 18

Isabel

Isabel sat tucked in her childhood bedroom, snuggled up on her bed under the faded pink quilt, with her computer on her lap. After her early-morning interview, she'd put in a full day of planning between houses two and three. She'd texted Kylie to see if she wanted to stop by, and Isabel was delighted when the teen rode her bike over and joined her on set for an hour. Kylie was shy, but she was opening up. They'd been communicating on and off all week, and Isabel was happy to be there for her.

She wished there was more she could do for Kylie and her dad, but she didn't want to insult them by offering some sort of financial handout. Still, getting to know Kylie was triggering an idea of a way she could use her position, connections, and income for good. It was a fledgling notion for now, but Isabel was excited about what it could become.

She couldn't daydream too much more tonight, though. She was beat, and she still had her blog to tend to.

She opened a blank post on her blogging platform and buried herself further under the covers, allowing them to blanket her from the chill of the air conditioning her parents had cranked up. She tapped a finger on her chin, trying to summon a new idea for her post. Her eyes roamed around the room and landed on the lava lamp on her desk in the corner.

It screamed 1970s. It was an original Lava Lite Lamp that was her mother's growing up. Isabel thought about it for a minute, and her mind drifted to the different styles and eras of houses she was working on. The time periods for each of the five were so unique, and each had so much to offer. After another minute, she started typing.

Isn't it amazing how times change? When I am working on a house, I like to take into account the stories of its past. If it was built in a specific time period, I ask myself, "How can that era inform my design?"

I'm hard at work on several new projects, and while I can't share the specifics with you now, I will say I'm learning to let the house or room I'm working on speak to me. I want to hear its history and shine a light on it. You may benefit from the same practice.

I think we get so caught up in chasing the latest design trends that we run the risk of everyone's homes ending up looking the same. I can't tell you the number of times I get asked to design a white-on-white kitchen with a bling-y chandelier. Of course, that's a beautiful style, but it may not be the style that fits with the home you're living in.

If you have, say, a 1920s Tudor home, why not use that as your starting point and design from there? Or if your property has mid-century modern lines, let them guide your decision-making when it comes to décor. Less is more, and trying to cram a square peg into a round hole, or a 1950s bungalow into a modern-day ranch-style home, will prove impossible.

Work with what you have, and you may be surprised at how great the result is. You never know, maybe you'll discover a little bit of the past you want to take with you into the future. Until next time, dear readers, happy designing.

Love, Inspired

Isabel read through her post and chuckled to herself.

All that from a lava lamp.

But as she sat in silence, nibbling her lip, she realized her inspiration was from more than the lava lamp. It was

Mapleton—this town and these people. Julia and Samson. Kylie. Marge. Daniel.

Isabel spell-checked her post and scheduled it to publish the next morning. She shut down her computer, closed her eyes, and rested her head against the headboard.

A cupboard door slammed downstairs, and the faucet turned on. Through the cold air return vent, the muffled sound of the evening news floated upstairs to her room. The noises of her family's home were so much a fixture of her days growing up she hardly noticed them then, but now, they startled her. She was used to the silence of her condo.

"What's on tap for tomorrow, hun?"

Isabel barely made out her mom's voice.

She'd lamented to Daniel about being estranged from her family, but she wasn't doing anything proactive to patch things up between them—to build a bridge, as Grace suggested.

That was on her, but it didn't have to stay that way.

Before she could think twice, she pushed herself out of bed and tiptoed to the stairs. On the bottom tread, Isabel hesitated before peeking into the living room.

Her dad sat facing the TV, reclined in his chair. Her mom sat with her feet up on the couch, a glass of ice water in her hands. The weatherman on the screen was the same one she remembered, with a few hints of gray in his hair.

The bottom step creaked, and her mom glanced at her, swinging her feet down and off the couch. "Izzy, what a pleasant surprise! Come on and join us." She patted the cushion next to her.

"Thanks." Isabel crossed the room and sat by her mom, clasping her hands together in her lap.

There was no reason to feel awkward. These were her parents, and this was her home, yet she felt like she'd made herself an outsider, and she wasn't sure how to rejoin the family club. Fortunately, her mom was never at a loss for words.

"I was talking to your father about our weekend plans. We're thinking about driving over to Turner to take in the regional baseball games. You know, if Mapleton wins, they'll play in the state finals next weekend."

Isabel arched a brow. "I hadn't realized they were that far into their summer season."

"It is amazing," Val prattled on. "You know, the other day I was talking to Marge about how soon it'll be back-to-school time, and then the Halloween costumes will be out in all the stores. It's too early for that hooey if you ask me, but I've always been a little more old-fashioned than most."

Her dad shot Isabel a knowing grin from where he sat listening to his wife's diatribe, and Isabel returned the smile. The wonderful thing about her mom was, Val owned all her idiosyncrasies, and they became part of her own unique charm. Isn't that what Isabel had just written about? Embracing that sort of charm?

"Sure is nice to have you here, pumpkin," her dad said.

Isabel's heart warmed. "Thanks, Dad. I'm glad to hear you say that."

Her dad sat back in his chair, a small smile on his face as he turned his attention to the news.

Isabel's chest glowed warm with relief. It was a definite step in the right direction. Could it really be that all her parents needed was this—for her to make the effort to spend time with them—in order to re-establish their trust in her? To patch up their relationship? This she could do. This she *wanted* to do.

"Anyway, dear. What are you up to this weekend?"

"Work," Isabel said without thinking. At the sight of her mom's instant frown, she went on. "And Julia Derks invited me to a bonfire at McGregor Farm."

"Biscuits and gravy, that sounds fine, now doesn't it? Just like old times."

Isabel nodded.

"Ford will be there," her dad said. "He and the McGregor's youngest kid were in school together, remember? What's her name?"

"Laney," Val supplied.

"Right, Laney. I heard she's home from Madison at the moment. Anyway, maybe you and Ford could drive out there together."

"I don't know, Dad. I don't think Ford wants anything to do with me."

"Now, now. I wouldn't go that far," her mom said. "You haven't given each other much of a chance, have you?"

"No, I guess not." Isabel would give Ford a hundred chances, but she doubted he would give her even one at this point.

"Try to talk to him. It'll go a long way. I'm sure you'll be glad you did."

"Maybe you could put in a good word for me." Isabel's voice rose in question. She was not above begging.

Val clicked her tongue. "I'm afraid it's going to have to come from you, dear. You wounded Ford's feelings when you abandoned him. No one can fix that but you. If I try to interfere, it might make things worse."

"Okay." Isabel heaved a sigh, some of the happiness at the strides she'd made with her parents tonight dissipating at the thought of what a tough nut to crack Ford would be. Still, she vowed to try her best.

The ten o'clock news wrapped up on the TV, which she knew from past experience was her parents' cue to head to bed.

"I'm going to go back up." Isabel stood, and her mom rose to hug her.

"This was nice," Val whispered into her ear.

"It was," Isabel agreed, squeezing her mom extra tight.

"See you in the morning, pumpkin."

"Night, Dad."

Isabel walked up the stairs to her room. She flipped off the lava lamp, climbed into bed, and perked up her ears. Sure enough, two minutes later, she heard the lock on the front door click and the creak of the stairs. Then, her parents shuffled past her room, down the hall to the master bedroom, and closed the door. In another five minutes, all was quiet.

All except Isabel's brain.

Because, for the first time in a long time, she had a head full of the past and a heart hopeful for the future.

Chapter 19

DANIEL

DANIEL PARKED HIS CAR a half mile down South Road from McGregor Farm. The dusky air held the faint tinge of campfire smoke, and the orange August sun dipped down to the horizon, making the firm line ripple. Daniel walked along the ditch to the farm before cutting across the gravel drive and the front yard of the house and making his way to the barn.

Chatter and country music were coming from the south side of the structure as he approached. He turned the corner around the barn, and a crowd was sitting around the large in-ground fire pit, with old stumps serving as chairs. Daniel spotted Amanda and her fiancé, Seth, standing with Julia and Samson across the yard. Isabel's brother, Ford, stood off to one side of the bonfire pit near Laney, the McGregor's youngest child, who was around his age. Daniel walked in that direction to greet her.

"Daniel! Welcome!" Laney gave him a hug.

"It's good to see you, Laney. Thanks to you and your family for having us," Daniel said. "Hey, Ford."

The two men shook hands.

"It's a great night for a party." Laney took in the scene before glancing down at her phone, which had just buzzed in her hand. "I'm going to go check on the drink and snack supply and take care of this." She waved her cell. "You guys help yourself to anything. Bathroom is in the house. You know the drill."

"Thanks, Laney." Daniel turned to Ford, who watched Laney retreat with a look in his eyes that Daniel hadn't seen before.

Huh.

As he was about to mention it, Ford blinked, and whatever Daniel thought he saw was gone.

"How's it going, man?" Ford asked Daniel. The two made small talk about work and life in Mapleton, catching up and setting a date for their next cribbage match.

"I can host," Daniel said.

Ford poked him in the chest. "I can't wait to skunk you again."

Daniel knocked his hand away and narrowed his eyes. "That happened *one* time. I don't plan on making a habit of losing to your sorry butt."

"But I plan on making it a habit to beat you, and beat you bad." Ford's gaze flitted up and over Daniel's shoulder, and his mirth-filled expression vanished. "What's she doing here?"

Daniel turned to see Isabel walking to the fire pit with Grace.

His breath caught. She looked so much like the Izzy of old. She had on a faded Mapleton Paper Shredders hooded sweatshirt, and her long hair was tied up in a high ponytail. Her worn jeans hugged her hips and thighs before flaring out over a pair of white sneakers.

A pit of dread formed in Daniel's stomach, competing for space with the ball of burning attraction that was rattling around, pinging off of each of his ribs.

When he left Gus's apartment, following his interview with Isabel, Daniel promised himself he would tell her the truth about the article he wrote the next time he saw her. He hadn't expected that to be tonight.

"Julia must've mentioned it to her."

"Still. Why is she *here*?" Ford asked. "Hasn't she proven she doesn't want anything to do with Mapleton?"

"Maybe things have changed."

Ford's eyes turned to slits. "She thinks she's too good for us."

"How do you know that? Have you talked to her?"

"Not since our parents forced us into a family dinner the first week she was here."

"You should give her a chance."

Ford arched a brow. "Have *you* given her a chance?"

Daniel hesitated, finally shrugging. "Maybe."

"What does that mean?" Ford accused.

"Hey, guys."

The two men swung around to face Isabel. The hair on the back of Daniel's neck stood up, and he felt weirdly winded.

"Hi," he said at the same time as Ford muttered, "Unbelievable."

Isabel offered them a tentative smile. "This is such a great setup. Ford, Laney was in your grade, wasn't she?"

Ford grunted in response.

"Right." Isabel's cheeks turned pink, and she dropped her head and studied the ground.

Seeing the siblings so at odds made Daniel feel all sorts of helpless, but he had no clue what to say to diffuse the tension between them. Fortunately, Grace approached from the picnic table on the far side of the fire pit.

"Isabel! Look at this. Have you had one of these? Delicious." Grace took a bite of her graham cracker, chocolate, and marshmallow sandwich.

Isabel snorted. "Don't tell me you've never had a s'more."

"Well, yeah, but not one cooked over a real, live bonfire in the woods. The smokiness of the marshmallow makes this to die for. Go and get one!"

Grace's enthusiasm made Isabel laugh, and Daniel's stomach pitched at the sound of it.

"Excuse me." Ford walked off.

Grace stared after him before turning to face Isabel with wide eyes. "Is he allergic to s'mores?"

"I think he's allergic to me." Isabel looked like someone popped her birthday balloon.

"No, he's not." Daniel gave her what he hoped was a reassuring smile.

She returned an appreciative look, but her eyes still looked sad.

He pointed to the campfire. "Come on. You need a s'more. You probably haven't had one in a couple of years yourself."

"That would be true."

The three of them walked up to the fire pit. Daniel found two sticks that appeared to have been yanked out of the woods at the back of the property and gave one to Isabel while Grace went off to fetch marshmallows.

Isabel studied the twig Daniel handed over. "You know they make actual s'more-roasting sticks. I've seen them online."

"Where's the fun in that?" he asked. "Besides, half of the experience of roasting a marshmallow is doing so with an old, whittled-down stick."

Isabel screwed her mouth to the side. "Think of all the germs."

Daniel tsked. "Living in LA has made you softer than one of these marshmallows."

"It has not. I'll have you know I've had to be pretty tough living in a big city on my own."

"Then I think you can handle a little dirt with your s'more." Daniel nudged her shoulder with his. "Builds character."

Grace returned and handed him the bag she'd procured before immediately heading off to talk to Samson.

Daniel took two marshmallows out for Isabel and skewered them for her before doing the same for himself.

Isabel stuck her stick directly in the fire pit.

"Careful, you'll burn it," Daniel scolded as he assessed the fire to find the perfect clump of coals for roasting.

"Burnt is best." Isabel's eyes met his in a silent challenge.

"I remember."

They used to have this sort of playful marshmallow argument every time they were at a bonfire. He preferred his marshmallows tastefully toasted, and Isabel preferred hers charred to a crisp.

The orange firelight made Isabel's hair glow redder than usual, and the heat caused her cheeks to turn a deeper shade of pink. She was striking. A few loose tendrils fell from her ponytail and framed her face. Daniel's fingers tingled with a desire to reach out and tuck them behind her ear.

In an effort to avoid doing something rash, Daniel directed his gaze to where he propped his marshmallow up on a fieldstone, turning his stick ninety degrees to apply the proper amount of warmth on every side of the marshmallow.

He gestured to his setup. "Suit yourself. But you know I'm right. An evenly toasted golden marshmallow is the way to go."

In response, Isabel drew a flaming marshmallow from the fire pit and blew it out. "Perfection."

Daniel scoffed and shook his head. While he finished toasting his marshmallows to his version of flawless, Isabel went off in search of graham crackers and chocolate.

Someone across the fire got out a guitar and was strumming "Me and Julio Down by the Schoolyard" by Simon and Garfunkel. Grace was deep in conversation with Julia and Samson. Ford was by the food table, talking to a couple whose house he sold last month. As Daniel observed the trio, he saw Ford's eyes drift to Laney more often than not.

Interesting. Very interesting.

Before he could think more about it, Isabel returned and held two graham crackers for him. As soon as he made his s'more, they clinked them together in a toast before enjoying the first gooey bite.

"You know," Isabel said around her mouthful. "It feels good to relax here. To just *be*. I haven't done anything like this in years. Grace keeps telling me it's beneficial for my creativity, and I think she's right. I've got to try to channel it into the draft of my book, though."

"What's the deal with your book?"

Isabel stared into the fire. "What do you mean?"

"You know what I mean."

She didn't say anything for a minute but then heaved her shoulders up and down. "Writer's block, I guess."

Daniel tipped his chin up. "Huh. That's never been an issue for me."

Isabel flung her head around. Her jaw hung open, and she tossed him a look of disbelief. "You write for a living, and you're telling me you've never gotten stuck? No way."

"Oh, I've gotten stuck many times, but I haven't used it as an excuse to stop—or worse, not get started." Daniel held her gaze, daring her to dispute his reasoning. The Isabel he once knew needed to be pushed every so often, and he was glad to lay a challenge down if it would help her in the long run.

She sat staring at him. He could tell she was chewing on his words as she munched on her s'more. When she finally spoke, her voice was barely above a whisper. "I wish it were that easy for me."

"How so?"

"I want this book to be this masterpiece on style and design and life and lessons learned, and I don't know how to deliver all that." Isabel pulled in a breath. "And no one knows this, but I'm donating part of my proceeds, and I just really don't want to let down the charity I'm supporting. I feel like I'm drowning under all the pressure."

Isabel's shoulders slumped as if the weight of the world was pressing upon her.

No wonder she was extra worried about the book—there was a lot more riding on it than just her own personal success. Finding these sorts of details out about her behind-the-scenes work only cemented his admiration for her. Most people would look at Isabel and think it wasn't possible for her to be more beautiful on the inside than she was on the outside, but Daniel knew it to be true.

"Hey. Look at me." He angled his head toward Isabel and waited for her to meet his eye. "You're not going to deliver everything you hope to deliver in the first line—or even in the first chapter. But you've got to start somewhere."

"That's just it. I can't figure out where to begin. Every time I start, what I write seems so...so...I don't know. It seems like it's been done before. I don't want to come across as mechanical."

Daniel instantly recalled the *Entertainment Magazine* article, hating himself anew for planting seeds of doubt in Isabel's head by using words like "mechanical" to describe her. He swallowed against his discomfort. He had to tell her the truth...but not quite yet. Right now, he would do anything to unburden her from some of the weight she was carrying.

"Just be you. Tell your story. If you're true to yourself and your style, that'll be what shines through. And don't worry. People love you."

Isabel shot him a dubious look, but she was sitting up straighter. His words seemed to have strengthened her resolve. "Thanks, Daniel. You give a good pep talk."

"I'll be sure to add that to my resume." Daniel winked and then turned serious again. "While we're covering tough subjects, though, what's up with you and Ford?"

Isabel winced. "You saw how he responded to me, didn't you?"

"Yeah. He took it hard when you left."

"I know." Isabel was silent for a moment. "But I'd like to reconcile. Do you think he'll give me a chance? You guys seem like you've gotten close?"

Daniel nodded, not admitting out loud that they bonded over their shared anger at her. "You'll have to give him some time to come around."

"I don't have the luxury of a whole lot of time."

The reminder that she was leaving town snuck up on Daniel, even though it shouldn't have surprised him. That was always the plan, but he'd be lying if he said that he hadn't gotten used to having her around again.

He hadn't even realized he was doing it, but he looked for her around town now. The thought that she might be at Hal's Diner, or at the café, or at the same weekend mass had him on edge in the best possible way. He wasn't thrilled about the prospect of giving that up.

Then again, she might not give him a choice when he told her the truth.

"I wanted to thank you again for being understanding during my interview." Isabel leaned against him for a beat. "Saying anything about my family dynamics would have only made things worse with Ford."

Daniel nodded, inhaling the lingering aroma of honey that wafted off of her. "I hope you guys can make it right."

She gave him a soft smile. "I hope so, too."

They talked a little longer about everything and nothing. Daniel tried to enjoy himself. How many times had he dreamed of sitting shoulder to shoulder with Isabel at a community bonfire? Too many to count.

Eventually, she popped the last bite of s'more into her mouth, closing her eyes to relish it. "I forgot how good these are."

So had he. The s'mores, sure, but mostly, he and Isabel. They were really good together. He wondered if she thought so, too.

"You've got something there." Daniel used the pad of his finger to gently scrape some marshmallow goo from the corner of Isabel's mouth. Their gazes locked, and the rest of the activity around the bonfire faded away.

"Thanks," Isabel whispered. Her russet eyes burned with firelight and something else...something Daniel couldn't quite place.

He let his fingers linger against her cheek. He couldn't help it. Isabel's skin was so soft under his touch it drew him in like a magnet. But then he dropped his hand to his lap, the flame of desire in his chest doused with the dread of having to admit what he'd done. He would gain absolutely nothing by pining over her when what he needed to do was come clean with her. The least he could do was be honest about the review before he tried to explore what might still remain of the relationship they once had—or could have.

Daniel looked down and then up again. He'd better get it over with. "Do you want to go for a walk?"

Isabel's eyes widened before she smiled. "Yeah. Let's do it."

The sky was black overhead as they took off in the direction of the back of the property, but the McGregors had tiki torches around the clearing and along the line of trees behind the barn.

"I never forgot about the stars in Mapleton." Isabel stopped a distance from the fire and stared up, a look of awe washing over her features. "There's nothing like them."

Daniel tore his gaze from the smooth line of her neck and looked upward. Above them, the sky was covered in twinkling stars. There were swathes of white that reminded him of the whipped cream topping on one of Julia's coffee concoctions.

"We used to do this a lot, didn't we?" She directed her question to the sky.

"Yeah, I guess we did." Daniel scuffed his feet against the pressed dirt ground. Reminiscing about the times they used to spend together—the good times—was not going to make what he had to say any easier.

"I loved that. Look, Daniel." She fumbled for his hand. When she grabbed it, her grip was warm against his. Could she tell his hands were clammy with nerves? "I haven't given you an appropriate apology for how things ended between us."

He should have pulled away, but he couldn't. It was like he was tethered to her, and there was nowhere else he'd rather be. Daniel pressed his lips together. This was awful. She was apologizing when it was him who was in the wrong. He shook his head. "You don't have to do this."

"Yes, I do." Her eyes were set with a determined gleam. "I want to say I'm truly sorry for leaving the way I did. I won't apologize for going. It's what I needed to do at the time. But I could have gone about it better, and I apologize. And I—"

"I have to tell you something." Daniel's heart punched the walls of his chest, and he squeezed her hand before dropping it.

Isabel's eyes bore into his, and the corners of her lips drooped. "What is it?"

"That review from *Entertainment Magazine*. The one you told me about during our interview?"

Isabel nodded, frowning deeper. Her whole aura turned cold at the mere mention of it. "I know the one."

Daniel grimaced. "I wrote it."

Her brows creased. "What?"

"It was me. I wrote the article about your pilot episode for *Entertainment Magazine.*"

As his words hit her, the emotions flashing in Isabel's eyes were like dominos, one colliding with the next until everything landed in a heap: shock, hurt, and then anger. She started shaking her head. "No. You wouldn't have done that."

Her disbelief eviscerated him. She trusted him. She expected better of him. More of him. He'd failed her. It was what he'd always been afraid of doing, and he'd brought it completely on himself.

"I've regretted it since the moment it was published. I'm so, so sorry, Isabel." Daniel went to take her hand, but she backed away from him.

"I don't believe this." Her mouth hung open on a dazed gasp until she snapped her jaw shut and tightened her gaze. All the warmth that had been building up between them evaporated. "How could you? Were you trying to ruin me?"

"No! Of course not. I was upset, and I let my personal feelings get in the way of an honest critique of the show. It was wrong, and—"

"I almost quit because of that. Because of you! But you probably would have liked that." She turned and marched in the direction of the bonfire.

Daniel jogged to catch up with her. "You have to know I didn't mean it. What can I do to make it up to you? Izzy, please. I'm sorry."

She whirled around and faced him. "Don't call me Izzy." She pointed her finger at him as if to put physical space between them before putting her hand on her forehead, flexing her fingers and looking up at the sky.

Daniel knew better than to try to say anything else. Instead, he stared at her helplessly, waiting to see what she'd do.

After a minute, she glared at him again, her eyes glistening with unshed, angry tears. "I never, *ever* expected this from you, Daniel. I've got to go, and I need you to leave me alone."

Her lips trembling, she shook her head like it was all too much and walked away from him. She wove in and out of the villagers around the fire pit until she found Grace. She leaned down and whispered into her ear. Grace's head jerked up, and she gave Isabel a quick nod before rising and following her around the barn.

As soon as they disappeared from sight, Daniel trudged forward. His feet felt like bricks. He didn't want to risk running into Isabel as he left the bonfire—not after she expressly asked him to leave her be—so he sat down on an empty log, a little removed from the nearest group, and stared into the orange and red flames.

The heat of the fire on his face was nothing compared to the heat of shame licking at his heart. Daniel sat staring into the embers—lost in thought of all he would do differently if only he could—until he was sure that Isabel and Grace were gone. Then, he rose and snuck away from the firepit circle before cutting to the house and making his way to his car.

Sometimes, doing the right thing felt terribly wrong.

Chapter 20

DANIEL

"YOU DID THE RIGHT thing." Julia gave him a kind smile as she slid a mug of On Deck Café's house roast across the counter to him.

Daniel mustered up a wry, weary smile of his own, but he was dead tired. The memory of the hurt he'd seen etched into each of Isabel's features had made it impossible for him to sleep last night. He had all but resigned himself to never sleeping again. How could he?

Daniel took a fortifying sip and plunked down across from Grandpa Gus at the table nearest to the front counter. The Saturday morning rush had quieted, and now it was just Daniel, Gus, and a select few village residents at the café.

Once a month, Daniel took Gus out on a morning coffee date. Today happened to be that day, and no matter how crummy Daniel was feeling after everything that went down the night before, he didn't want to cancel on his grandfather.

So, here he sat, rehashing the events of the bonfire and dissecting his decision to tell Isabel the truth about the *Entertainment Magazine* article.

"Julia's right." Amanda fixed a drink for a drive-thru customer. "I know it doesn't feel like it right now, but you're better off being honest upfront. It'll save you a lot of hurt down the road. Look at Julia and Samson."

Samson angled his chin up thoughtfully. "Yeah. If I would have told Julia the truth, we could have avoided a whole lot of trouble with the café and the village."

Gus nodded as he sipped a double-caramel frozen cappuccino with chocolate sprinkles. "Communication is everything in a relationship, both real-life ones and literary ones. I get so annoyed when the heroes and heroines in the stories I read keep things to themselves. Just say how you feel and tell the truth! Everything else will fall into place. Do you know how many books would have gone so much smoother if folks would have been up front about their feelings? Every romance novel in history, for starters."

Daniel couldn't help but roll his eyes. "And yet you've read all of them."

Gus took it in stride and lifted his chin. "What can I say? I'm a sucker for a happy ending, communication miscues aside. And I sense a happy ending in your future." He twirled his finger around in a circle in front of Daniel's face, as if to emphasize his point.

Daniel slumped into his chair. "Happy endings are all well and good in books, but real life doesn't always end in a perfectly tied-up story. I don't have the first clue whether or not Isabel will ever forgive me."

"What would have been the alternative, though, Son?"

Daniel didn't answer. The alternative would have been sitting on his secret and never disclosing that he was the anonymous writer. He knew he couldn't have done that. Not if he wanted to pursue some sort of a relationship with Isabel.

Julia interrupted his thoughts. "What I want to know is what's going on between you and Isabel. Obviously something, or you both wouldn't be reacting so viscerally."

Daniel bent to tighten the laces on his Oxfords, trying to ignore her, but when he sat upright again, Julia had crossed her arms and was staring him down.

"Don't think you're getting out of this one, Daniel Smith. You live in Mapleton. Your relationship status is fair game."

"Besides, it comes from a place of love," Amanda shouted while grinding ice for a frozen coffee drink. "And I want to know, too."

She lifted a shoulder as if to say she wasn't going to apologize for her interest.

"I don't see why it matters at this point. Even if I wanted to give a relationship with Isabel a go, she'd have to talk to me again first."

"She'll talk to you again," Gus said in between slurps of coffee.

Samson nodded. "I'm with Gus on this one."

"Well, she was pretty clear last night that she didn't want anything to do with me, so..." Daniel scrubbed his hands over his face. "This is so dang hard."

"Nothing worthwhile ever comes easy." His grandpa took another swig of his drink.

Julia clasped her hands, holding them in front of her chest. She was practically shooting rainbows and sunshine from her eyes. "Well, at least now we know where *you* stand. You want to make a go of it with Isabel! You wouldn't be so torn up if you didn't! If you ask me, your story is romance novel material. A second chance at love, if you will. Gosh, you two are such a cute couple. Grace told me Isabel has never glowed so much on camera *or* in real life as she did when you filmed with her. She said there was something so effortless between you guys. The cameras ate it up."

"Can you imagine if they become an item?" Amanda said on a gasp.

"That would be so great," Julia all but squealed.

"Okay, ladies." Samson held up his hands and tried to temper the pair. "Let's give Daniel a little reprieve from hypotheticals and your match-making efforts."

Samson shot him an apologetic look, but Daniel didn't miss the indulgent glance he spared for his fiancée. The man was enamored.

The vise around Daniel's heart squeezed. He wanted *that*—what Samson and Julia had—with Isabel. Too bad he'd blown his chance with her...twice now. He wished he could be as optimistic as Julia and Amanda, but they didn't see Isabel's face last night.

If only he could rewind two years. He would tear up the article. Fry his hard drive. Hack his email account. Anything to prevent himself from submitting the review.

If only Isabel had never left.

If only he'd gone with her.

Gus snapped his fingers from across the table, drawing Daniel's attention. "Stop it, Son."

"Stop what?"

"I can see the wheels in your head spinning, and I'm guessing you haven't gotten any traction."

Daniel ran his teeth over his bottom lip. "You really think I did the right thing telling her, Grandpa? I know it was the right thing in theory, but...it gutted her. I feel like the worst sort of scoundrel."

Gus looked thoughtful. "If anything, you telling the truth proves that you aren't a scoundrel, Danny. This is a case of things having to worsen before they improve. You had to be honest, and now the ball is in Isabel's court. If she comes around, then it'll be good for both of you, I'd say. If she can't forgive you, or if she refuses to do so, then that's on her. You've done all you can do."

Somehow that wasn't good enough for Daniel. He stared into his coffee, as if the black liquid was a cauldron and he could conjure the answers he sought with the swirl of his spoon.

Daniel looked up when the bell over the door jingled, and Grace strolled into the café.

"Morning, Mapleton!" Grace beamed. Isabel's assistant certainly fit in around here, and the town took to her like a fly to a hamburger.

"Good morning, Grace." Julia waved from behind the counter.

Grace approached the front of the café, and when her gaze landed on Daniel, her mouth flattened into a thin line. It was the first time Daniel had seen her anything but chipper.

He half-rose from his chair. "Is Isabel okay?"

Grace paused in front of him, a wary look in her eye. "I'm not sure why you'd care."

Daniel's head kicked back at her cold tone, and he dropped into his seat.

Gus raised a bushy eyebrow and shoved his glasses up his nose, studying Grace. "And who might you be?"

"Grandpa, this is Grace Bartal, Isabel's design assistant and friend from LA. Grace, my grandfather, Gus."

Grace held out her hand, and Gus shook it, surveying her with interest, as Daniel tried again, desperate to make Grace understand.

"Grace, I never meant to hurt her."

Grace's retort was swift and firm. "Well, you wrote the *Entertainment Magazine* review. *That* hurt her."

Gus held up his hand. "Now, now. You listen here. There's no need to guilt Daniel into feeling any worse than he already does."

"It's okay, Grandpa. I deserve it."

"No, no. This has to be said." Gus dismissed Daniel's pity party before turning his full attention to Grace. "It took a lot of courage for Daniel to tell the truth last night. I imagine once the initial shock wears off, Isabel will realize that. As I was saying to Daniel, there really wasn't another option. If he wants to build any sort of relationship with Isabel going forward, it needs to have a foundation of honesty. You can't have a solid relationship with secrets, now can you?"

Grace gazed at Gus with an unreadable expression on her face before turning to Daniel. "He's a wise man, your grandfather. I'm going to give you the benefit of the doubt and hope you've learned from him and from your mistakes. Isabel deserves someone great. She hasn't found that in LA. I'll admit I was rooting for the two of you, and I'd like to see if you can recover from this. But I've got to ask you not to trifle with her. If you hurt her again, I don't know if she'll be able to recover."

"And I'd say the same to you regarding Isabel," Gus spoke up before Daniel could, drawing Grace's attention back to him. "If Isabel is considering a relationship with my grandson, then she would do well not to break his heart again. I don't imagine he'd want to take many more chances, either."

Gus leveled Grace with a glare. It was as if they were opposing lawyers, each representing their sides of Daniel and Isabel's case.

Maybe Daniel should have been embarrassed to let his grandfather do the talking for him. He was a grown man, after all. But Grace and Gus seemed to be coming to some sort of silent understanding, piled high with mutual respect, so Daniel stayed quiet and sat there with his head swiveling back and forth between the unlikely duo.

Finally, Grace held out her hand for Gus to shake.

Gus smiled his crinkly eyed smile at her. "We're speaking the same language, my friend."

Grace nodded. "Couldn't agree more."

"Let's hope these two can work this out." Gus hooked his thumb toward Daniel.

"Fingers crossed."

"Guys, I'm sitting right here," Daniel said dryly.

The two turned to him with identical innocent looks on their faces.

"So?" his grandpa asked.

Daniel just shook his head.

"I'll see you around, Gus. And I'm trusting you, Daniel. Don't make me regret that." Grace bounced her way to the counter to order a drink, undoubtedly filling Julia in on all that she didn't overhear.

Across the table, Gus finished the final sip of his coffee. "I'm ready to head out if you are, Son." He set his mug down. "This has been an exciting morning, I'd say."

If Daniel didn't know his grandfather, he'd say he was enjoying all this drama. But Gus wouldn't wish him pain. Then again, he sure acted like he knew something Daniel didn't know.

If only Daniel could channel his grandfather's confidence in a happy ending.

Chapter 21

ISABEL

ISABEL SLAMMED THE CABINET door in her parents' small kitchen and banged her cereal bowl down on the counter. Bending over, she wrenched the cupboard open and retrieved a box of oatmeal squares. She spilled several and huffed as she stopped to toss them into the bowl.

She'd spent the night wallowing in self-pity, watching P.S. I Love You and sobbing herself dry. How dare Daniel do what he did? How dare he? Thank goodness she found out about it when she did. Isabel was inches away from letting him in and falling for him all over again. The silver lining in all of this—if she could call it that—was that she was spared the heartache that the start-and-stop relationship would have caused her.

But still. Her heart was already shredded to a pulp.

"I think it's best to keep our distance," her mom whispered to her dad. The pair sat at the dining table, eating breakfast and reading The Village Tattler.

Isabel rolled her eyes. "I'm fine, guys."

"You don't care to share what's making you so crabby you're about to pour orange juice on your cereal?"

Isabel stopped and looked at the container in her hand. Sure enough, it was orange and not white.

She shoved the cap on the juice and got out the milk. "I went to the bonfire last night."

"Was it that bad?" her dad asked, looking pensive. "We thought you'd have a good time."

"The bonfire itself was lovely," Isabel assured him. "The McGregors are such gracious hosts, and the farm looks as magnificent as ever. But I saw Daniel there."

"Oh?" Her mother feigned indifference, but Isabel didn't miss the look Val shot Dave.

"I found something out about him that made me physically sick," Isabel spat.

Her dad closed the paper and looked up at her.

Her mom inhaled, pressing her lips together. "Oh dear. Dare I ask?"

Isabel slammed the spoon down next to the bowl and pressed her hands into the bar-height counter, leaning forward to draw them in to the horror.

"He wrote an article about me, about my show, when it first came out. He gave me an awful review. He called me stiff and said my show wasn't inspired, it was insipid." Isabel stood up straight and crossed her arms, waiting for her parents to be indignant on her behalf.

Her father looked at her mother, then at her.

Val batted her eyes, nibbling her lip.

What was wrong with them?

Isabel held out her arms, palms up, in an exaggerated shrug. "A little support would be nice, guys."

"Of course, dear." Val folded her hands and rested them on the table. "That must not have been very pleasant."

"Not very pleasant?" Isabel reeled. "Walking to work in the rain is not very pleasant. A root canal is not very pleasant. This. This was nearly career-ending."

Her mom frowned. "I understand that you must be upset about this, dear, and I'm sorry for not being as upset myself. But famous people get chewed up in the press all the time, don't they?"

Isabel opened her mouth, then shut it without saying a word. Her mother had a point.

"Well, yes," she said after a beat. Recovering herself, she added, "But not by friends! This was personal. This is Daniel we're talking about. He wrote this. About *me*."

Her dad cocked his head to the side. "And why is it only bothering you now?"

"Because I just found out it was him. The review was published anonymously. Do you know the reach of *Entertainment Magazine*? I thought it was going to ruin me. It could have derailed everything."

"But it didn't?" her mom asked.

"Obviously not, Mom." Isabel tossed up her arms and let them fall to her sides with a slap. "I'm here, aren't I? Filming my TV show two years later."

"Now, no need to be snippy," Val scolded. "I'm trying to understand where you're coming from. What I've gathered is that Daniel wrote an article about you and critiqued your show—quite heavily. He told you about the review a couple years after the fact, and now you're upset. Am I missing anything?"

Isabel frowned. When her mother said it like that, it seemed inconsequential. "No, that covers everything. But don't you think it's awful what Daniel did?"

"At least he told you about it," her dad said offhandedly.

Isabel narrowed her gaze. "What do you mean?"

"Well, he wouldn't have had to, would he? I mean, you didn't know any different. The fact that he addressed it up front demonstrates that he cares about being honest in your relationship."

"We don't have a relationship."

"Such a shame," Val said into her coffee cup.

"What?"

"Nothing, dear."

"I can't believe you guys don't see what a big deal this is." Isabel crossed her arms. She fought the urge to stamp her foot like she used to do when she was a teenager and her parents had restricted her phone access.

Her dad set down his coffee mug and looked her in the eye. "Maybe you're making it a bigger deal than it is," he challenged. "Maybe you're focusing on the wrong thing here. Were you perfect when you filmed your pilot episode?"

"Well, no. But—"

"Have you gotten better with time?"

"Of course I have!" Isabel said, affronted.

"And has Daniel done anything since writing that article to dis you or your career?"

"Not that I know of," Isabel scoffed. "But I didn't know about this until now, either."

"And you wouldn't have known about it at all if he hadn't had the integrity to tell you. Think about *that*." Her dad pushed back his chair and stood from the table. "I'm off to the home improvement store. Gotta fix the gutters out back."

With that, he marched upstairs, and Isabel was left in the kitchen with her mother.

"Sweet baby rays, your dad sure is hunky when he gets on a roll like that."

Isabel smacked her face with her palm. "Mom! Gross."

She dug into her soggy cereal, and her mother left her alone with her thoughts, disappearing into the living room. But a couple minutes later, the doorbell rang, and Val led Grace back into the kitchen.

"For you," Grace said to Isabel with a smile, handing over a to-go cup of coffee from On Deck Café. "Figured you needed this. How're you doing?"

"I'd be doing better if I'd gotten a little support from my mom and dad this morning," Isabel complained, reaching for the coffee and taking a deep, sustaining sip. "But I'm okay. This is so good."

"Best coffee I've ever had. I'm trying to convince Julia to move to LA and start a satellite café there." Grace made prayer hands.

"Grace Bartal, don't you even think about it. You won't be stealing Julia from us. You already get Isabel," Val reprimanded her.

Grace held up her hands in defense. "I mean no harm, Mrs. Marshall. Maybe I can convince her to start selling her grounds so we can stock up." She winked at Isabel. Grace was probably only half kidding. Good coffee made the world go around, and Isabel would be lying if she said she wouldn't miss Julia's when she resumed her real life.

At the thought of *real life*, Isabel felt a twinge of panic tugging at the bottom of her belly. She ignored it. She had enough on her mind right now without dealing with *that*.

"What's this I hear about you not taking Isabel's side?" Grace asked Val.

Isabel's mother hugged herself and looked at the floor. "Isabel's father and I were trying to understand the situation with Daniel's article, mostly."

"They think I'm overreacting," Isabel cut in. "And that I'm in Daniel's debt since he went out of his way and told me the truth," she said dramatically. "Never mind what he did in the first place."

Isabel expected Grace to rush to her defense, but she only stood there looking thoughtful.

Isabel frowned. "You think they're right, don't you?"

Grace shifted her jaw, hesitating before she spoke. "I don't know if this will make you feel better or worse, but I ran into Daniel at the café. He's miserable."

"Good." Isabel bent over and shoveled a bite of cereal in her mouth. "I hope he feews tewwible."

"Isabel, mind your manners." Val let out an exasperated breath.

"Sowwee," she said, swallowing.

Val shook her head but stayed silent as Grace covered her mouth to hide a laugh before schooling her features.

"You know," she said, "as an outsider looking in here, I'm not privy to your history with Daniel. All I know is what I've observed since we got here. And what I've gathered is you two still have feelings for each other. You got your feelings hurt last night. Rightly so," Grace placated her before she could defend herself. "But he *did* tell you the truth."

Grace turned away and struck up a conversation with Val, who launched into a discussion of the baseball games she watched yesterday, once again leaving Isabel to her thoughts.

Last night, she'd been willing to write Daniel off as a man who hurt her and who would surely do it again. But now, her parents and Grace had given her another side of the story to consider, and when she thought about what they said, she couldn't deny that she was being more than a little self-centered.

Chapter 22

ISABEL

AFTER SEEING GRACE OUT, Isabel's mom stood in the entryway to the kitchen, looking timid.

Her mother *never* looked timid.

"What's up, Mom?"

"I know you're busy, dear, but I thought if you didn't have any plans, maybe you'd like to help me out back in the garden."

Isabel's heart split. Her own mother was intimidated to ask her to spend time together. Talk about a reality check.

She put as much reassurance into her smile as she could. "I'd like that."

Val's face lit up. "Dungeon my dragons! That's great. Let's get to it."

Fifteen minutes later, breakfast dishes put up and pajamas shed for gardening clothes, Isabel walked with her mom to the shed on the back of the property. Val rummaged around and piled Isabel's arms high with garden gloves, a couple of shovels, a bucket, and two watering cans.

"That should be everything." Val stared into the near-empty shed, brushing her hands together.

Isabel's grip on the items was precarious, and she had to peek around the pile to navigate the backyard. When she made it to the flower bed, she let the tools spill onto the ground.

"I'm sweating already." Isabel wiped her brow and assessed the tumbled mess of gardening supplies spread before her. She couldn't remember the last time she did yard work. Her condo didn't have any green space unless you counted the plants that surrounded the in-ground pool. And when she was designing homes for her clients, she spent most of her time indoors, leaving the landscaping work to her crew.

"I know. It's great, isn't it?" Her mother adjusted the wide-brimmed sun hat on top of her head. "I love getting my hands dirty."

"Your garden is amazing." Isabel followed her mom's lead, and the two set to work weeding in and around the daylilies and blanket flowers. Her mother had a line of bird feeders hanging from the branch of an elm tree that shaded half of the deck. A hummingbird was currently having a bite to eat.

"I remember when you planted these black-eyed Susans." Isabel stood and walked over to the full, yellow-and-black flowers planted along the south side of her parents' house. She took one in her hand and felt the velvety petals between her fingers. "I was little. Only ten or eleven. Look at how hearty they are now."

"I like these ladies." Her mom joined her. "Low maintenance. I haven't had to do much with them since I planted them all those years ago. They just bloom every summer. It's my kind of flower." Her mom winked, and Isabel smiled.

She looked around at the backyard. It was an oasis. Birds flew to and from rustic feeders and baths positioned in different corners of the space. Oversized trees swayed in the breeze, shading the patches of bright-pink, purple, and red flowers and lush green ground cover. It was evident her mother cared for her garden and took pride in maintaining it. Isabel hadn't bothered to look when they'd been out on the deck for the family dinner the first week she was here, so she'd missed the beauty right in front of her. She was so caught up in herself and her issues.

And wasn't that the problem? The past four years had been all about her. *Her* job. *Her* rise to fame. How busy *she* was. Isabel had used her career as an excuse. She had been so concerned with how well she was being received by the public that she'd failed to consider her private life. She'd been selfish, and her relationships—the area of her life she should have prioritized—suffered the most.

As she stood among her mother's flowers, tears threatened to spill from Isabel's eyes as, suddenly, the long trail of pain her self-absorption had left in its wake became crystal clear.

"Mom, I'm really sorry."

Val turned to her with concern draping her features. "Whatever for, dear?"

"For everything. I've been the worst since I left town. I'm so sorry if I made you feel like I was too good for you."

Val's mud-smudged face softened. "You're not the worst, Izzy. And you're forgiven. Consider it all forgotten. You know we love you, and we're proud of the woman you've become. But thank you for apologizing. It hasn't been easy feeling like we don't matter to you. We just want to be here for you, but we can't do that if you don't let us." Her mother reached over and gave her a hug.

"Well, don't get too close right now. I'm all sweaty," Isabel said.

"It's not sweat. It's a summer sheen." Her mom threw her another wink.

Isabel laughed through her tears before turning serious. "I'm going to be better about prioritizing what really matters. Who really matters. And that's you, Mom."

"I like the sound of that." Val beamed at her.

Isabel kept her arm around her mom's shoulder as they turned to assess the garden.

Fortunately, her mom was like a black-eyed Susan. Low maintenance. And though Isabel had been neglectful the past few years, she hadn't stomped out Val's spirit completely. She swore she'd be more attentive going forward.

Her mind shifted to Daniel and his review of her show. When he'd tried to apologize to her for writing it at the bonfire, she hadn't let him get a word out. She'd been too blinded by her hurt. But once again, she'd made things all about herself. Daniel had admitted he'd messed up. Yes, his words had caused her pain, but like her parents pointed out, that was a long time ago.

She'd grown and changed since then, hadn't she? For the better, she'd like to believe. She was more confident in who she was as a designer, and on top of that, she was rediscovering who she wanted to be as a human, as well.

What she didn't want to be was the type of person who was too *in her own head* to let go of an old grudge. And wasn't it unfair to define anyone by so narrow a scope so as to miss the true, underlying goodness of their character? The least she could do was let him know she didn't hold it against him. After all, none of the things she knew and knew well about Daniel before last night had changed. He was kind and humble and loyal.

"He's a really good man," Isabel mused on an exhale.

"What's that, dear?"

Isabel hadn't realized she'd spoken out loud. She smiled over at her mom. "Nothing. What can I do to help tidy up?"

Val scurried about, collecting pots and shovels. She loaded Isabel down with equipment to put back in the shed, but even under the physical weight, Isabel felt lighter than she had in ages—like a hot air balloon when the ropes holding it on the ground are released and it can finally soar.

·♥·♥·♥·♥·♥·

Later that night, Isabel sat on her bed, music turned on and lava lamp glowing in the corner. She stared at her computer screen, trying to figure out what to write. A lot had happened in the past two days, and she didn't know where to begin.

Downstairs, her mom was belting out the lyrics to a song by ABBA, singing in perfect pitch about being a dancing queen and having the time of her life.

Isabel smiled, suddenly inspired.

Many of you have followed me for four, almost five years in my little corner of the internet. Thank you for being here! I don't take you for granted. But there is someone who I have taken for granted, and that ends today. You see, up until this point, I've kept my personal life, well, personal. When I left home at the age of 22, I set out to make a new name for myself as a designer. In the process, I'm sad to admit I wasn't the daughter, sister, or friend I should have been to those who got me to that point.

Today, I want to talk about my mother and introduce you to the stunning woman she is. I haven't given her enough credit over the years for forming me into the person and the designer I am.

I used to think my mom and I couldn't be more opposite. She's not what I would consider high fashion. I can say that because she'd agree with me! The woman marches to the beat of her own drum and has a distinct style. The more I learned about style and design, the more I became embarrassed by her and her trademark disregard for the latest trends. But lately, I've realized it was my mom's confidence in who she is that gave me the confidence to follow my dreams and become who I wanted to be.

So, this one's for you, Mom. Thank you for being you, and for loving me in spite of all my mistakes. You inspire me, and I promise to do a better job of showing you how much I admire you from here on out.

That's all I've got, friends. I realize this blog post doesn't have much to do with design, but I hope it encourages you to take a closer look at a person or a moment in your life, someone or something you've brushed aside until now. I speak from experience when I say, doing a reassessment of what matters may open up more doors than you expect. Like me, you might be surprised what you learn about yourself and be inspired anew in the process. Until next time, dear readers, happy designing.

Love, Inspired

Isabel searched the folders in her cloud storage and found an old picture of her and her mom. They were in the garden, and Isabel must've been in high school. She added it to the blog post next to the selfie she'd insisted they take together this morning.

Isabel marveled at how so much had changed since she was a kid, yet how much was the same. Her mother wore her old straw hat in both images, and the black-eyed Susans still smiled up at the sun.

Isabel clicked *schedule* on her draft so it would publish on Monday morning. She sat still for a moment, waiting for the anxiety she expected she'd feel about letting her online fan base into her private life to set in. But she was at peace. She shut her computer, hopped out of her bed, and went downstairs to see if her mom needed any help with dinner. She could learn a thing or two from her in the kitchen, too.

Chapter 23

ISABEL

WHEN MONDAY ROLLED AROUND, Isabel was ready to work. She arrived at the second house early and stood on the sidewalk, taking it all in. Samson's choice to paint the house a deep, vibrant blue was spot on—or rather, Julia's choice. Isabel smiled. The color reminded Isabel of the writing on the village's water tower. She wondered if that was intentional. Julia always did love Mapleton.

Isabel walked up to the front stoop and took a seat, wiggling the sketchbook out from her bag. She let her mind loose and doodled ideas as they came to her. After a weekend of heartache and a lot of self-study, it was therapeutic to fall into doing what she loved.

In no time, the house was filled with production crew members and cameramen. Isabel huddled up with Horatio and Grace to discuss what they wanted to accomplish. Horatio was frowning.

"What is it?" she asked him.

"It's the network. They're putting on the pressure, and we're getting some pushback about being here."

"What do you mean?" Isabel asked. "I thought we were here to please them."

Horatio shot her a guilty look. "Well, that's only half the truth. I told them we were coming here. I promised them it would infuse the show with new life, but they never officially signed off on our plans. And now the network is getting more and more restless because the reviews of the episodes of season two that are airing continue to be subpar."

Grace's and Isabel's gazes met, and her friend's face was lined with concern, but the news of poor reviews didn't send Isabel spiraling like it would have in the past. After all, the reviews were right.

Isabel shrugged. "And we know why that is. Unlimited budgets and lavish lifestyles aren't relatable to our viewers, and I've lost some of the personalized feel of the show."

"You've regained that here, though," Grace pointed out. She turned to Horatio. "Can't you tell the network that?"

"That's what I've been trying to convince them of. I'm not sure how long I can hold them off, though." Horatio laced his fingers together behind his neck and let out a stream of breath. "I wasn't blowing smoke up your skirt when I told you the footage we filmed at the Dutch Colonial and some of the early shots we got of you at the other houses was some of your best work to date. But it's been a challenge to get the powers that be at HoSt to buy in without having the finished product ready for them."

"We should accelerate the filming schedule so we have something to show for ourselves, then," Isabel said.

"That's not a bad idea." Horatio nodded. "Don't worry about this, though, Isabel. You focus on doing your work, and I'll deal with the network."

"You got it, boss. Grace, let's go." Isabel strode into the kitchen. She was eager to get started.

"What's gotten into you?" Grace jogged to keep up with her. "You're like a new woman. I was expecting a panic attack at the mention of bad press."

Isabel bobbed a shoulder. "I guess Daniel did me a favor by outing himself as the writer of that first bad review. I mean, it can't get worse than that, right? Someone I used to love thinking I've amounted to a robotic pile of garbage? We can only go up from there!"

Isabel was going for self-deprecating, and she felt like she nailed it.

"You're not a robot or a pile of garbage." Grace put her hand on Isabel's elbow, pulling her to a stop. "And you know Daniel doesn't think that, either."

"Honestly, at this point, if he did, I couldn't really blame him. But I'm good. I promise."

Grace was sweet to worry and to come to her defense, but Isabel needed to take ownership of her life, including the mistakes she'd made. She recognized that now.

"Besides, deep down, I feel the same way the network does. What I've been doing has become rote. It's boring. I've been going through the motions because that's what I was told to do. But that's not why I went to LA, and that's not how I want to operate. I've been so concerned with what other people think of me that I've failed to consider what I think about myself. So, let's give HoSt a show they don't even know they need yet, one with originality and design flair."

Grace gave Isabel a onceover, and a smile blossomed on her face. "That's the spirit!" She held up a hand and high-fived Isabel.

They turned to get to work, but Grace paused. "Hey, by the way, I read your blog this morning."

"Oh yeah?"

"It was excellent."

"I'm waiting for you to say, 'I told you so.'"

"Nah. I'm not going to rub being right in your face. I will tell you I think you should apply that same spirit in your book, though."

"You think so?"

Grace gave her an exaggerated nod.

"I think you might be right." She dipped her head and picked at her fingernails. "Daniel told me the same thing—before everything blew up between us."

Grace swung her head to the side, an unreadable look on her face as she turned her attention to her tablet, checking the to-do list. "Well, I don't know about Daniel, but I'm usually right."

Isabel rolled her eyes. Leave it to Grace.

·♥·♥·♥·♥·♥·

That evening, Isabel was the last one left at the house. They'd made good progress, and now she was enjoying some time to herself. These were the quiet moments in the design process when she did some of her best dreaming.

After putting a final coat of paint on the walls inside the front door, she took the paintbrush and roller and rinsed them in the kitchen sink until the water ran clear. She walked outside through the back door and bent to set them on the small stoop to dry. As she stood up, her eyes landed on two wood beams laying in the dirt to the left of the storage shed on the property's lot line.

"What do we have here?" Isabel wandered through the yard to the shed and stopped to look at the four-by-six planks. They were old and worn, and immediately, she knew exactly what she wanted to do with them.

She'd been hung up on the front entrance of this house. Fresh paint was a good start, but it was still missing something. And these. *These* she could work with. The beams were the exact size she needed to create custom shelves. They'd make the perfect statement in the front entrance and bridge the outside and the inside.

The wind whipped her hair and the trees overhead as Isabel hoisted up one of the beams. She yelped when several roly-poly bugs came crawling out.

"Gross," Isabel whimpered.

She turned the piece of wood from side to side. If she had to guess, she'd say it measured about six feet, and it was caked with a deep layer of dirt and grime.

And probably some more bugs.

She shuddered before telling herself to woman-up. These beams would fit the house and outshine anything they could have bought from the store.

She dragged the first one to the center of the yard and went inside in search of some of Samson's sawhorses.

Finding what she needed, she set them up outside and hoisted the beam up onto them so it was waist-high. She ran inside for a bucket and filled it with soap and water. She snagged a scrub brush from the kitchen and got to work.

Twenty minutes later, she was covered with splattered dirt, and pieces of her hair were stuck to her face with sweat, but she felt alive and energized by the project.

The wind increased in intensity, swirling around her, and Isabel peered up at the darkening sky. A storm was brewing. She glanced to the shed and decided she'd chance it. She wanted to get the other beam scrubbed before she left for the night. Given the thunder rumbling in the distance, she needed to work fast.

Isabel focused on scrubbing her soon-to-be shelf as lightning illuminated the dusky sky. She was almost done when the first raindrops fell.

She hugged her arms to her chest in an attempt to protect herself from the sprinkles, but the rain started to fall in sheets. No attempt to shield herself from the elements was going to matter.

Instead, she savored the coolness of the rain on her hot skin, not caring that she was fast becoming a sopping-wet, muddy mess. She threw her head back, content to stand in the storm, letting the rain pelt her upturned face.

Until the tornado siren came blaring through the night air.

"Crap." She needed to get inside, but she didn't want to risk leaving the shelves to the elements. Hurrying, she hauled the first one down off the sawhorses and carried it to the house. She laid it inside the back door and ran into the storm for the second board. The wind blew her sideways, and she could barely see. When she got to the center of the yard, she found the sawhorses toppled over and her beam on the ground. She half carried, half dragged it inside as the tornado warning siren shrieked.

She grunted, heaving the beam inside the back door with her and letting it fall to the ground. Outside, the trees bent under the power of the wind. It wasn't safe to be near the windows, so Isabel bolted downstairs. When she got into the dimly lit basement, she patted her pockets.

"Double crap." She'd left her cell phone in the living room. She didn't dare go upstairs. Not in this weather. She may have been removed from the storms of the Midwest for several years, but that didn't mean she had forgotten all the drills she was subject to in elementary school each year during Tornado Awareness Week. All she could do now was pray the storm would blow over quickly without causing any significant damage to the home.

Isabel peeked around and shivered. She was freezing cold from her sacramental moment in the backyard. She was also sure there were all sorts of creepy-crawlies down there with her. She spotted cobwebs upon cobwebs in the corner and lunged to the center of the small, damp space.

"I'm fine. Everything's fine." Isabel breathed in through her nose before blowing it out of her mouth, trying to calm her racing heart. Just then, the small, one-bulb light flickered overhead and went out.

"Crap on a stick."

A door slammed above her, and Isabel screamed.

Chapter 24

DANIEL

THE OUTDOOR COURTYARD AT Gus's assistant living facility was packed with old people and humidity. It was bingo night. Daniel always made it a point to come by for the monthly event, and this week, he was grateful for the diversion.

Occasionally, things grew heated between the seniors—once he'd seen a tennis ball plucked from the bottom leg of a walker and hurled across the room—but most of the time, it was a good dose of friendly banter. He'd gotten to know the men and women who lived on either side of his grandfather over the past decade. Now, Daniel considered them his extended family.

"B – 18!" Marge Wilson shouted out. Marge always volunteered to emcee the bingo nights at Colony Elms. No one in town had her same knack for organization or commanding a room. The residents were lucky to have her, and they all knew it.

"BINGO!"

Daniel looked up from Gus's card to see Cheryl waving her hand in the air. Several groans went up from the crowd as Marge hurried over to check Cheryl's numbers.

"We'll see if she has bingo or not," Gus muttered.

"What do you mean?"

Gus furrowed his brow. "You know Cheryl. Sometimes she tries to be fancy with her marker and slips up."

Daniel suppressed a grin. His grandfather and Cheryl were always bickering, trying to one-up each other.

"We have a winner! Congratulations to Cheryl, and thank you all for playing. We'll see you back in September for another Bingo Bash," Marge's voice boomed from the other side of the courtyard.

Several nurses rose from their seats among the residents. Daniel stood and waved to LeRoy before turning to help Gus out of his chair.

A gust of wind blew up from the west, scattering bingo cards.

"Looks like a storm's brewing," Gus commented to Daniel, who hustled to collect the strewn papers.

Cheryl wandered over, pointing up to the sky. "Going to be a big one tonight, boys."

"I'll say." Daniel checked the weather app on his phone and half listened as Gus and Cheryl squabbled.

"Your card must be rigged, Cheryl. Let me see it so I can make sure you won fair and square."

"Oh, Gus, you big baby. What good would it do for you to look at my card? Your eyesight is almost as bad as your hearing. And besides, Marge already checked it!"

Daniel figured he should cut them off before they came to blows, though he had a sneaking suspicion Gus and Cheryl's teasing was kind of like when a little boy liked a little girl, so he tugged her pigtails.

Or like how he liked Isabel, so he wrote that mean article about her.

Daniel gave himself a mental shake, forcing his attention back to Gus and Cheryl and shooing them in the direction of the assisted living complex. "A nasty-looking storm cell over the central part of the state is moving in our direction. We'd better get inside."

Daniel stopped at the front desk to hand off the bingo sheets he collected before trailing Gus and Cheryl down the hallway.

"Sleep tight, Cheryl. Don't let the storms keep you up, now."

"I can sleep through anything. Except your radio," Cheryl retorted as she turned into her room. "Night, Gus. Daniel."

Daniel waved and followed his grandpa into his room two doors down.

"The news better not cut into the game with severe weather coverage." Gus eased into his recliner and pressed power on his remote. The Brewers were playing the Dodgers in LA, so it was a late start. Daniel fully expected his grandpa to fall asleep in his chair by the third inning.

"Well, Grandpa, they have to make sure everyone is safe. Promise you'll listen to the nurses, okay?" Daniel gathered his bag. "I should go before it gets bad out there. We might get a tornado."

"Don't worry about me. I'll be fine here. I'm sure it'll blow over, anyway." Gus had half an eye on the pregame.

"Do you want me to turn the radio on?" Daniel asked.

"That would be great, Son. And could you pop me some popcorn, too? My hip is acting poorly, or I'd get it myself."

"It's no problem." Daniel flicked the radio on and turned the volume down two notches. Although, maybe if he left it loud, Cheryl would come by, and she and Gus could have a cozy night together while the storm raged outside.

Daniel rolled his eyes at himself. That settled it. He *was* too close to the wedding magazine scene.

He got a bag of microwave popcorn out and set the timer. He stood and waited, listening as the pops mirrored the rolls of thunder outside. Through the window, the night sky turned hazy. It looked like it was going to be a bad one.

When the popcorn was ready, he poured it into a large bowl for his grandpa. He set it in his lap and went to the sink to fill a glass of water.

"There you go," Daniel said. "Looks like a tasty way to watch the storm roll through."

"Sure does. Thanks, Danny. You go on." Gus shoveled in a mouthful of popcorn.

"Alright. I'll talk to you soon, Grandpa."

Daniel slung his bag across his body and ventured out to the courtyard. It was now abandoned except for a nurse who was fighting the wind in her attempt to move tables against the building. Daniel stopped to help her before walking to his car.

The air was so humid Daniel thought he might have been able to drink the moisture. The wind tossed leaves and dirt around, and he opened his car door only to have it whip from his hand. He managed to climb inside and slam it shut as the first drop of rain fell.

Easing out of the parking lot, Daniel gripped the steering wheel to ensure his car stayed on the road. The wind worked against him, and the rain coming down in waves made visibility nonexistent. At least he knew the way through Mapleton by heart.

Daniel took his foot off the gas pedal and hovered over the brake in case he came upon another car, but he didn't see anyone else. He circled around the old mill property and crept down Mapleton Avenue. The tall trees on either side of the road swirled like beaters being thrust around a mixing bowl. At the mercy of the wind, they bent this way and that.

"Please don't fall on my car. Please don't fall on my car," Daniel chanted. All he wanted was to make it to his house on Spruce Street in one piece. It was only about a half mile away, but that was farther than he liked, given the situation.

Mapleton was a ghost town. It was only a few minutes before eight o'clock, but every door was shut. The car radio boomed a message from the National Weather Service. A tornado touched down in Apple Creek and was moving toward Mapleton, and wind speeds were upwards of 80 miles per hour.

"Residents should seek immediate shelter in basements or interior rooms. Stay off the roads and away from windows."

"Peachy," Daniel muttered. He peered out his windshield at one of the houses Samson was in the process of restoring. "What in the world?"

The front door was open, light streamed out, and the storm door was banging against the exterior wall, like it had failed to lock. Had someone forgotten to secure it before leaving for the day? That didn't explain why lights were still on. Unless someone was working inside? Daniel slowed and strained to get a better look at the property. He didn't see a car.

Daniel ran through his options. He couldn't leave the house wide open. If the wind shifted, rain would splatter in and cause significant damage to the wood floors and the drywall.

Making a split-second decision, Daniel wrenched his car over to the side of the road. He would lock up the house and ride out the storm there. It was safer than trying to make it home, even if it did mean leaving his car out in the elements. He opened the driver's side door and made a dash for the front stoop. The wind howled as he hurtled himself inside, clutching the edge of the storm door and yanking it shut before closing the front door and throwing the deadbolt lock for good measure.

Daniel slumped against the door frame when he was plunged into darkness.

A scream rang out from somewhere in the house, propelling Daniel forward.

"Hello!" he shouted. "Is someone here? Are you okay?" Daniel felt his way along the wall of the front hallway. "What the—" He ripped his hand away. He'd stuck his palm in fresh paint.

"Down here!"

"Izzy? Is that you?"

"Daniel? I'm in the basement. I can't see anything."

Daniel returned his hand to the wall to keep his balance and feel his way around. They were going to have to repaint the stains he was making, but that was the least of his concerns at the moment. With his other hand, he dug into his pocket and cursed. He left his cell phone in his car, so he was without a flashlight.

"Hold on. I'm coming," he yelled. Following her voice, he felt his way to the back of the house. The thunder in Daniel's heart rivaled that of the storm. Turning a corner, his foot connected with something on the ground, and his momentum flung him forward. He landed on his knees in front of the open door to the basement.

Graceful. Real graceful.

Daniel tried to make out what he'd run into but didn't dawdle. He needed to get downstairs. Outside, the storm raged.

"What was that? Are you okay?"

"I'm fine." Daniel took one step at a time. It was pitch black. "Where are you?" His foot made contact with the earthen basement floor, and Daniel turned and held out his hands in front of him.

"I'm right here." Isabel reached out and gripped his shirt, pulling him nearer.

Her knuckles dug into his chest, each one feeling like a bolt of lightning to his heart, shocking him back to life. She clung to him like a security blanket, and Daniel inhaled, drawing in the scent of late-summer rain and honeysuckle.

"I see that—er, feel that," Daniel stuttered. "What in the world are you doing here?"

"I was working, and the storm came up. What are *you* doing here?"

"I was driving home from my grandpa's, and I saw the front door banging open."

"Oh no!" Isabel's voice sank. "I was in the backyard working on a project. When I heard the sirens, I panicked and came down here without thinking. Then, I didn't dare go upstairs. I don't even have my phone. And there're all sorts of spiders down here. I'm completely squeamish right now."

"You somehow managed to work up a booby trap at the top of the stairs, though?" Daniel kidded, trying to keep the mood light and take her mind off her discomfort in their surroundings. Although, if it meant she was going to keep a tight hold on him, Daniel would have to figure out a way to keep Isabel squeamish forever.

"What? Oh, the shelves!"

"Come again?"

"My project. I found these wood beams in the backyard and scrubbed them down. I'm going to use invisible brackets to hang them up as shelves inside the front door. I couldn't leave them in the backyard, so I lugged them inside and dropped them there."

"I noticed," Daniel said wryly. "Could've used a head's up."

Isabel let out a nervous snicker before turning serious. "I'm sorry. Are you hurt?" She ran her hand along his chest and over his arms, blindly checking for injury.

The feel of her fingers seared his skin, and Daniel's heart kicked into overdrive.

"I'm okay." His voice came out sounding husky, a surge of desire jamming his throat.

Isabel clutched at his wet shirt as if guaranteeing for herself that he wasn't going to go anywhere. He wondered if she had any idea what she was doing to him.

"I'm so thankful you're here. I was scared. I didn't know who was up there when I heard you come in, and of course the lights went out. It's like the making of a horror film."

Isabel shivered, and Daniel drew her into a hug. It was the most natural thing. Her head still fit under his chin like it belonged there. He let the scent of her shampoo and the feel of her in his arms invigorate his senses. "You don't have to be scared anymore."

"I know." Her voice was muffled as she spoke into his chest.

Daniel leaned away, trying to make out Isabel's eyes and the frame of her face in the darkness, but he couldn't see her. All he could do was feel her firm grip on him and the way her body had melted into his arms.

Daniel wanted to kiss her. Wow, did he ever want to kiss her. Judging from the soft breath he felt puffing against his chin, her lips were so close. Knowing that was pure torture, but he held himself in check, working to keep his voice under control as he sought her forgiveness. "Isabel. I'm so sorry...for everything. I— "

"Shhh." Isabel rested a finger over his lips.

His heart rocketed to his mouth at the unexpected touch, pressing forward as if on a single-minded quest to feel more of Isabel's skin on his—to be even closer to her.

Isabel let her hand fall down, tracing a line with her finger over his chin and down to his heart, where she rested her palm flat. Daniel swore their heartbeats started pounding as one. The basement may have been without power, but Daniel was pretty sure the electricity pulsing back and forth from him to Isabel could light up the whole town.

"You don't have to apologize any more. I'm sorry, too—for a lot of things," Isabel whispered.

Instinctively, he moved to cup her face and gently stroke her cheek with the inside of his thumb. Her skin was soft to his touch, and Isabel shuddered—from the cold or something else entirely, Daniel wasn't sure. He waited for her to think better of what they were doing and step away. When she didn't, he trailed his other hand up to her forehead, feeling a strand of her silky hair. He tucked it behind her ear, and she sighed.

Blindly exploring Isabel's features felt incredibly intimate. Daniel moved slowly, with a reverence he'd only ever had for her, and inch by inch, he closed the distance between them. He was a breath away from kissing Isabel—his entire being aching to do just that—when the bulb overhead flickered on, coating the basement in a dull, yellow light.

Isabel's eyes flung open, their deep, brown depths tinged with the wisps of longing, and Daniel's entire world fit into the tunnel of vision between the two of them in that moment. But she fluttered her eyelids, and the moment was lost. They each took a step back and squinted to adjust their eyes to the brightness.

Isabel's mouth curved upward. "Yikes, you look rough."

Daniel glanced down at his soaked shirt and muddy shoes, giving himself a moment to collect himself. He held out his paint-covered palms, and Isabel clasped her hands over her mouth, trying to hold in her laughter.

"I'm telling you. You were like Macaulay Culkin in *Home Alone* with all your booby traps. I'm sorry you'll have to repaint, though."

Isabel giggled. "There are worse things."

"You want to go upstairs and assess the damage? It sounds like the worst of it is over."

Isabel nodded, and Daniel held out his hand. When she took it, he felt invincible. Daniel still yearned to kiss her, but his heart strummed, hoping it would come later.

For now, he led her up the steep staircase. "Watch out for the, ahem, *shelves.*"

Isabel huffed. "Hey, I'll have you know those are going to be exceptional pieces of design in this house. They will be worth your bruised knees, I promise."

This whole night was worth my bruised knees.

They walked to the living room, and Isabel retrieved her phone from the window sill.

"I've missed, like, ten calls." She grimaced. "Everyone is worried about me."

"Of course they are," Daniel said. "Hey." He lowered his voice and moved closer toward her when he saw tears glistening in her eyes. "What's wrong?"

"It's really nice to know people care."

Daniel smiled at her. "Well, you know Mapleton. Sometimes people care *too* much."

"I know." Isabel's sniffle turned into a slight laugh. "I used to think it was annoying. But now I'm realizing I kind of love it. I'm going to call my mom. Excuse me."

"I should get my phone, too." Daniel opened the front door to find the rain had turned to a light drizzle.

The street looked like a war zone. Whole trees were uprooted, and some had snapped in half. A giant maple tree had fallen on the post office. Daniel had never seen anything like it. He jogged to his car, which was covered with leaves and twigs but otherwise unharmed, and retrieved his cell phone so he could touch base with his grandpa. Daniel called the number for Gus's room first, but the answering machine kicked on. He hung up and dialed the front desk at Colony Elms.

"Hello," a harried voice answered.

"Hi, this is Daniel Smith. I'm calling to check in on my grandfather, Gus Keller, and the other residents."

"Hi, Daniel. Everyone here is fine. We moved them all into the activities room the second we heard the sirens. Even had the Brewers game on until we lost power. It's back now, though, thank goodness. We're getting everyone tucked into bed—or trying to. Lots of excitement around here for a Monday night."

Daniel ran a hand over his wet hair and blew out a sigh of relief. "Great. Thank you."

"All good?" Isabel's voice startled him as he ended the call.

Daniel whirled around to find her standing just behind him, biting her lip. "Yes. Grandpa and the rest of the residents are fine."

She nodded. "Thank goodness. Look at this mess," she said, her voice forlorn. "What are we going to do?"

Up and down Mapleton Avenue and along the side streets, neighbors were emerging to survey the damage. A truck turned toward them from the street where Julia lived. The driver honked, and Daniel recognized Samson. He parked in front of the house where Daniel and Isabel had taken cover, and Julia hopped out of the front passenger seat.

"You guys okay?" She rushed forward and enveloped Isabel in a hug.

"We're fine."

"Were you here?" Samson asked, eyes widening in question.

Daniel explained what happened, leaving out the near-kiss they shared in the basement. "I am sorry about the paint job in the front hallway, though."

"That's the least of my concerns. I'm glad you guys are alright. Looks like we have a lot of work ahead."

As he said it, they all turned at the whir of a chainsaw being fired up down the street. The community was showing up.

"That's the wonderful thing about Mapleton," Daniel said. "We may get knocked down, but we're never out. Come on. Let's move these branches to the terrace."

Chapter 25

ISABEL

AFTER TIDYING UP AS much as they could before they lost daylight, Isabel left Daniel, Samson, and Julia and made the quick walk to her parents' house. Val and Dave were waiting for her outside, and they embraced her with tight hugs, grateful she was in one piece. Isabel was a whole bundle of emotion, so she excused herself, slipped upstairs, and took a steaming-hot shower to try to get her head and heart in order.

Now, even as she donned her pajamas and unwrapped the towel from her hair, she couldn't stop her racing mind.

If someone would have told her a month ago that she would be heartbroken over a tornado tearing through Mapleton, she wouldn't have believed it. Yet, here she was, completely invested in the community she had convinced herself she was better off without. If she'd been in Los Angeles when this storm hit, she wouldn't have even known about it because she hadn't bothered to keep in touch with her family. This was yet another reminder that, in her quest to find herself and make it big, she'd lost sight of what mattered most—the people and the place that made her who she was.

With that thought, inspiration hit her like a lightning bolt. She rushed to open her computer to a blank page and started typing.

The words for her book poured out of her: words of community and staying true to yourself in life and design, of first loves and second chances, of transformation and finding the rainbow after the storm, of goodness and truth and beauty.

Three hours later, Isabel was more tired than she'd ever been, but she was also supremely satisfied with her progress. For the first time since getting her book deal, she believed she had something worthwhile to say.

No, that wasn't it.

She believed her town had something worthwhile to say, and she could be the messenger to share it with the world. Her notes on design and tips for décor would fit into the outline of the book about life and love and home. She scrolled up to her first page and wrote the title for her book across the top: FEELS LIKE HOME.

Isabel climbed into bed, letting her ideas and what she'd written sink in. As she drifted off to sleep, she eased into a sweet dream of a basement room awash in candlelight and the image of a knight in shining armor who'd come to rescue her from giant spiders and their tangled webs.

·♥·♥·♥·♥·♥·

When Isabel went downstairs the next morning, her dad was gone, helping to haul branches to the designated drop-off site in the parking lot by the swim lake.

"The village posted a message online this morning saying crews would be out to clean up branches, but if anyone was able, they could drop them off there. Ford and your dad were off early," her mother explained.

"Makes sense." Isabel scooted onto a stool at the kitchen counter. "Anything I can do before I head back for filming?"

"Don't think so, dear. I'm going to spend the morning trying to salvage my garden. It withstood the storm pretty well. Only a few casualties."

"Good, because I have a proposition for you. If you'll let me, I want to film here, in your garden."

Her mom froze with her coffee mug halfway to her mouth. "Come again?"

"For my show. You, me, the garden. What do you think?"

Val shot her a skeptical look. "When you got to town, you made it seem like filming here would be about as pleasant to you as having a colonoscopy."

Isabel screwed up her mouth. "Changed my mind."

She hid her smile behind her own mug as her mom narrowed her eyes and stared her down.

"You don't have to do this, Izzy. I told you, all was forgiven. "

Isabel set her mug down and gave her mom her most earnest look. "I believe you, but I'm not filming here to get on your good side, Mom. Your garden really is spectacular, and it's part of my home, so I told Grace we should film it as part of our show—but only if you want to."

Isabel explained her idea to transplant some of the plants from her mom's house to the newly renovated homes around town. "That way, it's like a little piece of the past will be carried forward to the future."

Her mom looked thoughtful. "Huh. There's a definite metaphor there, that's for sure."

"So, what do you say?" Isabel crossed her fingers behind her back.

"Yes!" Val squealed and clapped her hands together, her eyes shooting out of their sockets. "Jumping jellyfish. I'm going to be on TV! Oh my heavens, when? I should really start working out." She stood up straight and tried to suck her gut in.

"Mom, stop. You're perfect exactly the way you are."

As she said it, Isabel realized she meant it. Whether she fit in with the image of Isabel's brand or not, Isabel wouldn't change a thing about her mom. And that was the way it should be. "Look, I've got to run. We'll talk details tonight, okay?"

Val came over and gave her a squeeze. "Have I told you how wonderful it is having you home?"

Isabel hugged her back. "It's pretty wonderful to be here."

Chapter 26

ISABEL

ISABEL WALKED UP THE street and over on Mapleton Avenue to the bungalow. The production crew was there, and she greeted Grace and Horatio with a hug.

"Glad to see you survived the storm," Grace said, letting her go.

"My shelves survived, too, thanks to some heroic effort." Isabel explained her night.

"You have to tell that story on camera. Viewers will eat it up. You, risking your life to save the project. Hey, what happened to our paint job?" Grace gasped as they walked through the front door.

Isabel rolled her eyes at Grace's dramatics. "First of all, I didn't risk my life. Daniel did, when he tripped over the beams I dropped inside the door."

The thought of it made her snicker, and she could tell Grace was on to her by the arched brow and twinkle in her eye. Getting Grace's matchmaking Spidey-sense firing so early in the morning would spell disaster, so Isabel coughed.

"Anyway, the paint got smudged because it was dark, and Daniel was feeling his way along the wall when he came inside. Nothing a little touching up can't fix, right?"

Grace opened her mouth, certainly about to interrogate her about Daniel, but Horatio cut her off, clapping his hands.

"Let's get on that. Filming starts in thirty minutes."

Hilde bustled over and sat Isabel down. She let the woman work her makeup magic while Horatio talked production details with Grace. Isabel was eager to install the shelves, certain doing so would make for an impressive segment. The story of the storm would add a personal touch, one Isabel hoped would inspire her viewers to get out and help out the community where they lived.

They cruised through filming, and by noon, Horatio suggested Grace call Samson and Julia to see if they could come by so they could film the "reveal." Isabel shot a quick text to Daniel to see if he wanted to check out the finished product as well.

He responded immediately that he would be right over, and Isabel wondered if the cameras would be able to pick up on the glow of happiness she swore was emanating from every pore of her body.

She scanned the house. It was as darling as she dreamed it would be. They didn't spend a fortune to make it cozy, and they were able to keep the design in line with the period of the original home. She hoped she did Julia proud with this one.

When the coffee shop owner walked in an hour later, Isabel knew they hit it out of the park.

Julia's jaw hung open, and her eyes shone with admiration. "I can't believe how amazing it looks in here."

Grace walked over with Samson and Daniel.

Isabel's eyes found Daniel's immediately, and they shared a smile that held with it an entire story. It was this house and the moments they shared here last night.

Isabel rotated her smile to Julia. "That's what staged furniture will do for a place."

"That, yes, but also, look at all the personal touches." Julia pointed to the front hall. "Those beams are amazing, and are those family photos on the fireplace?"

Isabel nodded, pleasure swelling in her chest over her efforts. "We enlarged several photos I found stashed in my childhood bedroom. They make the room really approachable. Like it can be lived in. Everyone has memories captured in pictures. Hopefully, with these as an example, folks will be able to see themselves coming home here."

"That's so touching. You're so good at this." She hugged Isabel, and Isabel laughed. Over Julia's shoulder, Daniel was grinning at her. Grace looked on like a proud parent. Isabel wanted to freeze time so she could mentally catalog every emotion swirling around in this house and tattoo them all on her heart.

"Hey now, hey now." Horatio sashayed over. "Don't be using up all your good lines before the cameras roll."

Julia pulled back. "Oh, he's right! You have to say what you just said on film. It was perfect."

"I'll try," Isabel said.

Horatio waved his hand around in a circle. "Alrighty then. Let's get to it!"

A couple hours later, Isabel and Grace followed Samson and Julia to On Deck Café for a celebratory drink. Daniel begged off. He had a meeting with his editor at the paper. Isabel tried not to be too disappointed. She was consoled when he said he would catch up with her later.

"Two houses down, three to go! Here's to you, my friends!" Isabel clinked her coffee mug with Julia, Samson, and Grace. She froze in the booth. *Friends.* Saying that felt right.

"You're like Wonder Woman," Samson told her. "I knew the houses looked good when we were finishing them, but the way you take them from renovated to move-in ready is truly remarkable."

Isabel ducked her head at the compliment. "Thank you. I'm glad to do Mapleton proud."

The bell over the door jingled, and they all looked up. Ford strode into the café. Isabel's nerves jolted.

Though she was feeling more and more at home, Ford was the last remaining holdout in welcoming her back into the fold. She was starting to think he'd never forgive her for leaving and losing touch. She looked up, and their eyes met. Ford turned in the opposite direction, keeping his attention focused on the counter where Amanda was working with Seth.

"Well, we better be going." Julia nudged Samson, who moved out of the booth. "Wedding planning waits for no one."

Samson blanched but recovered when Julia put her arm around his waist. He smiled down at Julia, and not for the first time did Isabel envy the mutual affection and admiration between the two.

"Is this the part when I say, 'Yes, dear'?" Samson teased.

Julia swatted him playfully. "Don't act like you're not excited. We've got to call your parents and finalize a date." She stomped her feet in a happy jig, her face aglow.

"That is exciting." Grace smiled, and Isabel nodded.

"We'll see you guys," Isabel said. "Thanks for being willing to film today."

"Are you kidding me? Dream come true. For real. Bye now." Julia waved and strolled off with Samson.

"I love them," Grace said after they left. "I have to go, too. I'm going to connect with Horatio at the hotel to talk through the game plan for the rest of the week."

"Do you need me there?" Isabel asked.

"I don't think so. I'll figure out logistics and bring you in so you can work your magic."

Isabel stood to hug Grace. "Thanks for everything. Thanks for bringing me here."

Grace gave her a tight squeeze. "Happy to be of service."

As Grace left, Ford turned away from the counter with his drink. Isabel smiled tentatively. He didn't so much smile in return as grumble.

She motioned to her now empty booth. "Do you want to sit?"

Her brother scanned the half full café, and Isabel watched as he weighed whether or not it was worth it to make a scene. The eyes of the village were on them, and she recognized the moment he decided against a public spectacle and agreed.

"I can only stay for a minute."

"That's fine." Isabel was relieved to have any time with him. She took in his slick, black business suit and the briefcase he stashed on the seat of the booth. "What are you up to today?"

"In between showings." Ford sipped his coffee. "There's a huge house for sale along the river in Turner."

Isabel sat up straighter. "Not the Kinney Manor?"

Ford shot her a look. "Actually, yes."

"Gosh, I loved that house growing up. I always wanted to see the inside of it." Isabel's eyes widened. "Hey!"

Ford took another sip of his coffee. "I know what you're going to ask, and my answer is going to be no."

"Oh, come on! You have keys to the manor. You could show me around! That house is like a designer's dream."

"No," Ford said staunchly.

"Pleeeeeease," Isabel begged.

"Still no."

"Pretty please with a cherry on top." Isabel batted her eyelashes at him. When his mouth twitched, she wanted to jump up and cheer. She used to say that to get what she wanted from their dad growing up.

"Fine, but we won't be able to linger because I'm meeting a potential buyer there at four-thirty. And I'll have to call and see if it's even okay."

"Yes! Thank you, Ford!" Isabel went to give him a hug but thought better of it.

Baby steps.

They took their drinks, and she followed him out to his BMW. He held the door for her, and she got in. "This really is an amazing car. I wasn't kidding when I said that at Mom and Dad's."

Ford opened the door to the backseat and tossed his briefcase in before getting in the driver's seat and starting the engine. "Yeah, but you didn't think it was mine."

He had her there. "Well, when I left town, you were driving Dad's hand-me-down Oldsmobile."

Ford smirked. "Not anymore. Man, that thing was a hunk of junk."

"Remember how we couldn't fill the gas tank with more than five dollars' worth of gas because it had a leak?"

Ford nodded. "The gauge was always on E. It was a car, though."

The two lapsed into silence as Ford drove in the direction of Turner.

"So…" Isabel readjusted her position in her seat. "Tell me what's new with you."

"Nothing. I sell houses, mostly. Don't have much time for anything else."

"You must be good at your job. Do you like it?" She looked out the window at the fields of gold on either side of the road.

"I do. I interact with a lot of interesting people, and I enjoy finding them the right house to fit their needs."

"Good for you. I'm proud of you."

"You don't have to say that."

Isabel's heart sank. She thought they were making progress, reminiscing and spending time together, but Ford's tone had turned hostile.

"Say what? That I'm proud of you? Sorry, but I am."

"Well, don't be. You can't prance in here and act like you have any claim to my life, Izzy. You cut me out. And yeah, I went and made something of myself, no thanks to my absent sister—who, by the way, I could have really used the past few years, since, you know, houses are sort of your thing. But you couldn't be bothered to return my calls. How do you expect me to feel?"

Isabel bit her lip to stop herself from crying. She kept her eyes on the landscape out the window. She deserved Ford's anger—and his hurt.

After getting her emotions in check and waiting a minute to formulate her thoughts, she spoke quietly into the space between them. "Remember the nicknames you used to have for me when we were little?"

Ford's gaze darted in her direction. A puzzled look crossed his face and revealed his confusion at her subject change. "I guess."

"Isadore. Dory. Doorbell."

Ford's lips twitched. "Ding Dong."

"Oh gosh, I forgot about that one." Isabel made an *ick* face. "But you always had my back. Like that time I was in sixth grade and Missy Jenkins told everyone my outfit for the spring choir concert was trashy, even though she knew I sewed it myself."

"Missy was not a likable person."

"Yeah, but you put her in her place for me, right in front of half the school. Do you remember what you said?"

"Not really." Ford looked uncomfortable.

"*Isabel is the most creative person I know. Probably the most creative person any of us will ever know.*" Isabel's eyes welled up with fresh tears. "You were my hero that day. I've never forgotten your words. They're what encouraged me when I felt like my dream of making it big in LA was going to implode. Your confidence in me was worth more than you'll ever know."

When she said it out loud, she realized she'd been clinging to her home and her family all the way in LA, whether or not she was conscious of it.

Isabel had to work to get words out around the knob of emotion clogging her windpipe. "Ford, I am so sorry."

Ford stayed silent, so the only sound in the car was the purr of the engine and Isabel's sniffles. Finally, he spoke up. "Don't think your tears are going to work on me. I'm your brother, not your boyfriend."

Isabel snorted out a wet laugh. "I don't mean to cry. But it's been a lot, coming home and realizing how much I lost when I left and stayed gone. I don't know. Mom and I had a total come-to-Jesus moment, and the community has welcomed me with open arms. And..." She thought of Daniel, but she didn't say anything. "Yeah. It's been a lot."

Ford's eyes narrowed. "That's Mapleton for you—and Mom and Dad, for that matter. Nobody around here holds a grudge."

"Except for you." Isabel poked his shoulder with her finger.

"True." Ford nodded.

She punched him, and he smirked.

"Listen, I know a couple kind words aren't going to make up for my absence, but I mean it. I'm proud of what you've accomplished. And I hope you'll let me prove that to you going forward." Isabel rolled her lips into her mouth, waiting to see if Ford would give her a chance.

Chapter 27

Isabel

Ford kept his eyes on the road as they stopped in front of the sprawling Kinney Manor. Throwing the car into park, he turned in his seat. He studied her for a minute before his face softened.

"I missed you, Izzy. And you know you rocked that outfit in sixth grade. Missy Jenkins was eating her words."

Isabel launched herself across the console and wrapped her brother in a hug. She sobbed into his shoulder. "Thank you. I missed you, too."

He stiffened for a second before relaxing and giving her a squeeze.

"Alright. Alright. You've made your point. Do you want to see the house or not?" Ford asked, extracting himself from her grip.

"Yes, please!" She wiped her face and got out of the car, feeling ten times better.

Ford plugged in the code on the lockbox hanging from the front door handle and retrieved the key, letting them in. Isabel entered the giant foyer, and her jaw dropped. The Kinney Manor was a masterpiece. A giant staircase rose up in front of her, splitting in both directions, like the kind she always loved in *Beauty and the Beast* and *The Sound of Music*.

Isabel's gaze zipped this way and that, trying to take it all in. Her design senses were so stimulated she didn't know where to look first. She listened as Ford walked around with her, detailing the different features the house boasted. They walked up the stairs and saw five huge bedrooms, two of them with en suites.

"This house would be great for someone who wants to have lots of kids," Ford quipped.

Isabel touched her face absently, her breath suddenly shallow as an image of Daniel flashed before her eyes. What was that all about? She knew she wanted a family, but she hadn't let herself think much about it, and she certainly hadn't visualized it with a certain someone...at least not for several years.

"Are you okay? You look sort of flushed?" Ford interrupted her thoughts.

"What? Yeah. Fine." Isabel walked over and peered into the walk-in closet to give herself something to do. When she turned to walk into the hallway, Ford was staring at her intently.

Isabel clapped her hands once. "Where to next?"

"Well, usually, now I'd show people the basement and the backyard."

At the thought of a basement, Isabel's heart did a three-sixty flip in her chest. "No basements for me, please." She gummed on a casual smile, though her thoughts were anything but casual.

Casual was not Daniel Smith in a rain-drenched t-shirt, hovering with his lips an inch away from her, his tickling breath warm and his presence filling the damp air of the basement with something that felt an awful lot like a soft place to land. Nope. Definitely not casual.

"I know all about that," Ford said on a snort.

"What?" Isabel shot him a look, panic tinged with mortification making her voice sound all screechy. How did Ford know about her and Daniel? Sure, the town talked, but she hadn't told anyone about their basement encounter.

"You've hated spiders since the day you were born."

"Oh, right." Isabel let loose a strangled giggle. "Yuck."

"What did you think I was talking about?"

"Nothing," Isabel said too quickly.

"You know I'm going to find out somehow, right?" he said, cocky as only a big brother could be.

"There's nothing to find out." Isabel hurried after him outside and onto the lawn. The Squirrel River meandered by. "This is exquisite."

Ford caught her by the arm as she tried to walk away from him. "You're changing the subject."

Isabel ignored him, shook off his grip, and walked closer to the river, pretending to be enamored with the scenery.

"You know I can ask Mom and Dad and they'll tell me. Or Daniel," he said.

Isabel stumbled.

"Ha! I knew it!" Ford reached out a hand and steadied her. "What's going on with you two?"

Isabel put her hands on her hips. "For as stoic and stubborn as you pretend to be, Brother, you sure do care an awful lot about my relationship with Daniel."

"So you're saying there's a relationship?"

"What? No! Nothing's going on." Isabel groaned. "Well, there was almost something. But still nothing. I don't know. It's a lot, remember?"

He studied her for a minute, a solemn look on his angular face. "Daniel and I are good friends, so let me just say, Izzy, you need to be careful with him. And not because he's a bad guy. Actually, he's one of the good ones. But if you're going to mess with him again—leave town and break his heart—you shouldn't. He doesn't deserve that."

Ford turned abruptly then. "I've got to lock up and get you to Mapleton so I can get back here in time to meet my client."

Isabel walked to Ford's car, her mind reeling. They drove in silence, and Isabel was glad to have the time to sort through her thoughts. Her heart wanted to explore a relationship with Daniel. Their chemistry was off the charts, and he made her feel safe and taken care of. How could she not run straight into Daniel's arms?

But Ford was right. She'd known it from the second she stepped foot in town. It was selfish of her to consider a relationship with him when she'd built her life in LA. The position they were in now wasn't any different than the position they were in all those years ago. As the realization of a dead-end with Daniel dawned on Isabel, her stomach bottomed out, and fresh tears pressed at the backs of her eyes.

When Ford pulled up in front of their parents' house, Isabel was drowning in emotions, but as Ford hopped out of the car and jogged around to open her door, she pasted a smile on her face.

"Thanks for making one of my childhood dreams come true. I have so many ideas from the manor that I want to implement in my designs now," Isabel told him.

"I'm glad we went." Ford smiled down at her, and Isabel's heart grew. "Listen. Promise you'll consider what I said about Daniel." He waited for her to nod before going on. "You should think about what you want your life to look like, the big picture, and decide if he's part of that."

"Wow, do you double as a relationship therapist?" Isabel tried to make a joke so she wouldn't burst into tears in front of her brother, but Ford didn't buy her nonchalance.

He swung his head back and forth in a solemn motion. "No, but I've been reflecting on what I want from my life a lot lately, too." Before Isabel could press him for more information, he leaned forward and kissed her cheek. "Gotta go, Sis. See you later."

With that, he was off, his vulnerability masked, and Isabel was left with a lot of questions.

For now, though, at least she had her brother back.

Chapter 28

DANIEL

THE NOON SUN WAS high in the pale-blue sky when Daniel and Gus arrived at Sunrise Park on Saturday, geared up for a full day at the ballfields. Gus had peppered Daniel with stats and predictions the entire drive to the park. He kept up with box scores and stats over the course of the season and was not shy about making his predictions known.

"Mapleton has a chance, Son. They haven't won since the summer before your senior year."

"I remember." Daniel smiled. He'd played on the team throughout high school. The day they won the summer state championship was one of his happiest memories. Gus had been there with his grandma Cathy, too, and the whole town held the team up as heroes. After their victory, he and his teammates had gotten to ride in firetrucks down Mapleton Avenue, hoisting high their state trophy while village residents lined the road and cheered them on.

He bent to peek out the top of his windshield at the fluffy white clouds that filled the sky like mounds of cotton candy. "It's a good day to play ball."

"Sure is." Gus kept his eye on the field as Daniel parked along the third base line. The green grass was shaved to perfection, and the white foul ball lines were painted with an unflinching hand. Blue flags flew from the fence in the outfield, reminding visitors this was home of the Mapleton Paper Shredders.

Since Monday night's storm, the Mapleton faithful had banded together, and Sunrise Park was in tip-top shape for the tournament. A pile of tree limbs and branches was stacked neatly beyond right field, but the walking path around the diamond was clear, and the infield and outfield were free from the storm's debris.

Undoubtedly, the entire village would be on hand to cheer on their team during the Division Two game later this afternoon. Daniel found one of the last parking stalls that wasn't in foul-ball territory and gave himself an imaginary pat on the back.

"Let's find you a seat, Grandpa." Daniel walked around the car to help Gus out.

They eased their way to the bleachers, and all at once, Daniel was struck by Gus's fragility. In his head, he always pictured him as the spitfire of a man he grew up with—the one who leapt up and down in celebration at that state championship they'd brought home over a decade ago. But Daniel had to face the fact that Gus was getting older. His heart clenched at the thought that Gus wouldn't be around forever. And when he was gone, who would Daniel have?

Daniel stopped those thoughts in their tracks. Today was not the day to get melancholy. Today was a day to make memories.

He walked a half pace behind Gus as they made their way into the park, stopping to chat with friends and neighbors, who were happy to see them. They snagged two seats on the second row of bleachers behind home plate.

The sights and sounds of America's favorite pastime filled the air, and Daniel's thoughts of the future fled as his adrenaline kicked in. Kids screamed and ran in and out from underneath the stands. Folks chomped on sunflower seeds and Big League bubble gum, and the aroma of buttery popcorn permeated the sticky August air. The players of the team at bat stood leaning against the dugout fence, hollering encouragement to the man who was up. The crackling voice of the announcer came over the loudspeaker, calling out the count. The pitcher wound up and fired a pitch.

"Ball four!" the umpire hollered.

A mixture of groans and cheers rang out from the spectators while "Free Ride" played over the loudspeaker.

"The away team is in a bind." Gus's eyes glistened with excitement, and in that moment, he looked young again. "Bases loaded with nobody out."

Whoever was running the loudspeaker cued up "The Imperial March" from *Star Wars* as the pitching coach approached the mound. Daniel grinned as Gus hooted and hollered with the rest of the fans. "I'm going to buy us some snacks."

Gus nodded, and Daniel got up and wove his way to the concession stand.

Val Marshall was behind the counter, waving goodbye to a family with a couple young kids. As Daniel approached, she turned her beaming smile to him. "Daniel, hello!"

"Hi, Mrs. Marshall."

"Call me, Val, dear. We've known each other long enough to be on a first name basis, I'd say. You here with your grandfather?"

When Daniel nodded, Val craned her neck to try to see him through the crowds. "I'll have to come say hi when I'm done in here. Izzy is planning to come down. She should be here any minute."

She said it so casually Daniel was caught off guard. He wasn't expecting to see Isabel here, but then again, it was a Saturday, and this was about the only thing to do in Mapleton, so it made sense.

The thought of her coming to Sunrise Park to take in a ball game sent a rush of happiness surging through him. And not just because he'd been longing to see her since he watched her wrap house number two. Truthfully, it had felt like the longest week ever. They hadn't been able to connect. She'd been working hard to design houses three and four, and he'd been catching up on his writing assignments and shadowing Gerald to get a better sense for the editor's role.

Isabel had checked in a couple times via text—*like friends do*, he tried to reason with himself—but he hadn't seen her in person.

So yeah, that was part of his anticipation—a big part of it—but it was bigger than that, even. He was thrilled Isabel was embracing the community, for her sake and for her family's sake. He wanted to see them reconcile, and from the look of pleasure on Val's face, they were well on their way.

"That's great." Daniel ordered Skittles, licorice rope, and two bags of popcorn, fishing cash out of his wallet while Val collected the goods. "Thanks, Mrs. Marsh—I mean, Val."

Val gave him a thumbs up and winked. "You're a quick study, young man. I'll send Izzy over to see you when she gets here."

Daniel nodded, his pulse speeding up. He returned to his grandpa to distribute the candy, settling in next to him to watch the end of the game.

When it concluded, the players from the division three teams took the field to warm up, and Gus struck up a conversation with the gentleman to his left, leaving Daniel to his own thoughts. He wasn't sure how long he had let his mind wander when, as if he'd conjured her, he smelled a whiff of sweet honey and felt a soft hand on his shoulder that sent an immediate jump to his heart. He knew it was Isabel before he saw her.

"Hey." Daniel smiled.

"Hey," she said, nibbling on her lip and looking a little nervous. She glanced down at the packed row. "Is there any room to sit here with you? I'm all by myself until my mom's done in the concession stand."

Daniel followed her gaze and then turned to face her. "Want to walk instead?"

Isabel shifted on her feet. "Are you sure you don't mind missing the game?"

"Nah, Grandpa will catch me up, won't you?" Daniel tapped Gus on the shoulder to get his attention. His grandfather was staring intently at the program for the upcoming game.

"What? Oh!" Gus jerked his head upright. "Hello there, Isabel. Care to join us?"

Isabel gave Gus a winning smile, her nervous expression disappearing. "I'd love to, but there's not much space."

"We're going to go for a walk, Grandpa," Daniel said.

"Excellent. I'll save your seat, Son."

Daniel hopped down from the bleacher and gestured for Isabel to lead the way.

She snaked her way between the metal stands and into the open space along the first base line, and he followed. They cut over to the path and distanced themselves from the noise of the game and spectators.

As the atmosphere around them shifted from frenzied and loud to calm and quiet, Daniel felt a crackle of electricity zip between them. It was like they were both conscious that they were alone together for the first time since the basement incident. He didn't try to stop his fingers from brushing hers as their arms swung side by side.

"Did you get the third house finished?" he asked.

"We sure did. Grace convinced me to paint the front door chartreuse, and it actually turned out amazing."

Daniel chuckled. "I'll have to drive by and check it out."

Isabel nodded. "You should. Also, I owe you a thank you."

Daniel arched his brow. "What for?"

"I've been writing." Isabel stared straight ahead with a determined expression on her face.

"Your book?"

Isabel nodded.

"And it's going well?"

"Better than I could have hoped." Isabel smiled up at him, and his heart doubled in size. "I was trying to wedge my book into the hole I thought all design books should fit in, but like you suggested, when I started writing my story, the words flowed much more smoothly. I have a story to tell, and I'm doing it. It feels really good."

"I can't wait to read it."

"Thanks." Isabel ducked her head, shy again.

Daniel was struck by how good she looked in Mapleton. How comfortable. Over the course of the past month, she seemed to have shed a little of the big-city shell she'd returned to town with. Not that there was anything wrong with being from a big city, but relaxed, small-town life agreed with Isabel. From where he stood, the more she sank into it, the more lustrous she was.

Her eyes sparkled as she peered around the grounds as they walked together down the path. "I forgot how nice this park is."

Daniel looked at the Sunrise Park grounds, trying to see them through Isabel's fresh eyes. The maple trees swayed majestically in the warm summer breeze. The pastel sky above served as a muted backdrop to the energy and color of the park. Behind them, the Squirrel River meandered from east to west, bubbling over rocks near the shallow shoreline. Isabel was right. It was spectacular.

"We're lucky to have the park in town. Something is always going on. Grandpa is partial to the ball tournaments, so we're here often."

"Gus hasn't lost his interest in baseball, huh?"

"Nope. Bingo, baseball, and books are kind of his things. He's constantly telling me about one or the other."

"I want my brain to work like his when I'm as old as he is," Isabel said, and Daniel agreed.

A crack of the bat drew their attention. Daniel turned to the field to see the baseball soaring out to the centerfielder who was backpedaling. He leaped up with his glove outstretched, but the ball skipped off the top edge. The fans from the opposing team cheered as their player rounded second base. The centerfielder rocketed the ball to his cutoff man, holding the runner at third base, but the visiting team struck first blood.

Daniel squinted over his shoulder and could make out Gus in the crowd, clapping wildly.

"I'm glad you two have stayed close." Isabel hooked a thumb behind her and motioned to Daniel's grandpa.

Daniel faced her and studied her profile. She chewed on the inside of her cheek and didn't meet his eye. What sorts of thoughts were rattling around in her head?

"He's my father figure," Daniel said after a minute. "Everything I am I owe to his guidance."

"And to your own hard work." Isabel looked at him then. Her eyes were filled with something akin to admiration and—maybe—regret.

Daniel's insides liquefied. "Yeah, but he's the one who taught me to be the type of person who works hard."

Isabel sighed. "Yeah. You're right."

They fell into silence, and Daniel was content to stroll with Isabel at his side.

"You know, I was wrong to ask you to leave him. I'm sorry." Isabel's voice was low and nervy, like she was fighting for control of her emotions.

When Daniel met her gaze, Isabel's watery eyes couldn't have looked more sincere.

Daniel took hold of her hand, relishing the feel of her smooth skin on his. He ran his thumb over her knuckles like he had done so many times before. But this? This felt significant. It felt like another turning point for them.

"That was a long time ago, Izzy—Isabel," he corrected himself.

"Izzy's fine." She smiled, looking up at him through her damp eyelashes.

"Okay, then. Izzy it is." Daniel kept hold of her hand and was grateful she didn't pull away. There was no denying they fit well together. He was still more comfortable around Isabel than he was around anyone else. Which was why the next words out of his mouth shouldn't have surprised him. "I'm realizing Gus is getting older."

It was the first time Daniel had admitted that to anyone. He had a tough time admitting it to himself. But something about being with Isabel made him want to open up his heart, made him feel safe enough to unburden some of his thoughts and feelings. "It makes me sad, you know? Life won't be the same without him and all his quirks."

Isabel squeezed his hand twice. "You were right to stay close to home and be with him. You can't get time back once it's gone. I've learned that the hard way."

Daniel didn't say anything. Isabel, too, sounded like she was grappling with some big issues. Daniel tried to think of something profound and helpful to say to her. His mind spun with what it all meant, and they stared at each other, time suspended, with so many unspoken words hanging in between them, until Isabel broke eye contact.

"Okay, that's enough heavy business." She dropped his hand. "Tell me about this wedding writing you've been doing."

Daniel exhaled at her teasing tone. He allowed the change in subject, mostly because his own emotions would take some serious time to untangle. "Actually, after our Vintage Market shopping spree, I pitched another idea to the wedding magazine."

"Really? What's that?"

"I figured a lot of couples who put together their own reception space—outdoors, or in a barn, or wherever—would benefit from having a feature on antique shops and vintage markets around the state. Sort of like a roundup of places to buy pieces to furnish these one-of-a-kind venues." Daniel stopped explaining himself when Isabel stopped walking, her jaw coming unhinged. "What?"

"Are you kidding me? That's brilliant!"

Daniel's neck burst into flames under her praise. "You think so?"

"Of course. It's a really good idea." Isabel swatted at a fly that buzzed around them. "I would love to help couples design those spaces, too," she added offhandedly before posing another question to him. "What's been your favorite article you've written for the wedding scene?"

Daniel tipped his chin up. "Actually, I haven't written it yet, but I've been planning to write a series of stories from the groom's perspective. I'm thinking that'll be fun. And I'm hoping to glean some insight from right here in Mapleton."

Isabel arched her brows.

"I'm gearing up to interview Seth and Samson, but shhh..."—Daniel held his finger over his mouth—"they don't know it yet."

A giggle escaped from Isabel's lips before she made a show of locking her mouth with a figurative key. "Your secret is safe with me."

The path they were walking on had led them around the outfield and halfway up the third base line. Daniel was about to tell her about the editor position. She'd keep it in confidence, he was sure. But ahead, Isabel's mom was flagging them down.

"Izzy! There you are!" Val shouted, waving her hands at them from the near side of the bleachers.

"I want to hear how this wedding story develops. I would pay money to sit in on your interview with Samson and Seth," Isabel said to him before turning to her mother. "Hi, Mom."

"Dad's sitting over here if you want to join us." Val pointed to the bleachers behind her.

"Yeah, I would," Isabel said.

The expression on Val's face would have lit up a new moon night. Daniel was thrilled to see it and to see Isabel making an active effort to patch things up with her folks.

"Thanks for walking with me." Isabel smiled at him. "See you around?"

Daniel tipped his head to the side and quirked his brow. "Yeah. It's a small town."

Isabel giggled as she waved over her shoulder at him, walking with her mom to their seats.

Daniel's heart leapt. Isabel used to scoff at the size of Mapleton. Maybe, just maybe, she was coming around to the village as a whole, and she *would* choose to stay here.

Chapter 29

ISABEL

THE MAPLETON BASEBALL TEAM ended up losing in extra innings, but the mood of the villagers gathered at On Deck Café to rehash the game was still relatively upbeat. Isabel's mom had asked her if she wanted to join them there, and Isabel jumped at the opportunity.

Now, she sipped some sort of blended caramel-mocha frozen coffee that reminded her of the taste of Cracker Jacks. Kylie was at a table with several friends, and when the teen caught her eye, Isabel went over and said hi, but she didn't linger. She was thrilled to see Kylie having a fun night with her peers, and she didn't want to hinder that.

All around the café, villagers exchanged greetings and stopped to chat with each other. Julia was in her element, bustling back and forth from behind the counter to the dining area, topping off drinks. Her eyes and smile held a certain sparkle—the kind that glowed bright when a person was exactly where they were supposed to be.

As Isabel surveyed the café again, she couldn't deny that it felt good to be a part of it all: this town, its traditions, its people. She overheard Marge talking about how lovely the Dutch Colonial house was, and pride charged through her chest. She'd never given a second thought about having the approval of Mapleton. She'd all but taken it for granted when she left town. But now, being back among the people who knew her—really, deeply knew her—she was acutely aware that their positive opinion, their support, was invaluable.

A renewed wave of guilt crested in her chest, and she wondered if she would ever truly feel like she deserved Mapleton's good will.

"Fancy seeing you here."

She turned to find Daniel approaching, and everything inside of Isabel seemed to let out a deep, contented sigh. He had a way of relaxing her that was unparalleled.

"What's that you were saying about this being a small town?"

"Exactly this." His words came out on a smile as he tipped his chin to the crowded dining room, and Isabel nodded.

"It's nice, actually."

Daniel arched his brow. "You think so?"

"I do." Isabel meant it.

"Well, I was going to ask you if you wanted to get some fresh air, but if you're comfortable here, then don't let me disturb you."

A new bucket of nerves spilled over Isabel, and Ford's warning to be careful with Daniel blared in her ears, but she tuned it out. A man whom she cared deeply about was standing in front of her, wanting to spend time together. She'd be a fool not to do so. Besides, they were just two friends going outside to enjoy a pleasant summer evening.

"No. Let's go."

Daniel studied her face for a half second and gave her a small smile. "Follow me."

He took off, cutting across the dining room—or attempting to. It was standing room only, and he had to elbow his way through.

Isabel got jostled a couple of times as groups of baseball fans and villagers mingled, reliving the game and telling stories of days gone by. She fell a couple paces behind, caught up in a group of middle-aged dads who seemed to be reminiscing about the glory days of the early '90s.

Daniel stopped and waited for her to catch up before reaching for her hand and lightly looping his fingers with hers, tugging her gently along behind him.

Isabel's lungs seized, just as they had at the baseball field earlier today, and she had to talk herself down from the silly little ledge her mind had taken her to the brink of. Yes, Daniel was holding her hand, but he wasn't *holding* her hand. He was merely trying to get her from point A to point B without losing her in the masses.

And this afternoon, he'd merely been comforting her when she was apologizing to him. It was a friendly gesture. They were friends. That's what she wanted. That's all she should let herself want.

Then again, when their fingers were intertwined, it felt so good, so familiar, but so unexpected and new, too. Like a long-lost puzzle piece that, once pressed into place, brought into focus a breathtaking, happily-ever-after sort of scene. She loved that he'd reached for her, and if she was being honest with herself, she wasn't sure she wanted him to let go.

Whoa.

Daniel pushed open the door with a *woosh* that mimicked the contraction and subsequent release Isabel had just experienced within her own heart.

He led her out onto the deck, dropping her hand and motioning for her to go ahead of him down the stairs off to the side.

With the thoughts that had been swirling around in her head, Isabel should have been thankful to put a little distance between herself and Daniel, but all she felt was the loss of his touch. Her hand itched with desire to cling to him.

"Let's go this way. You've got to see the gazebo Samson built for Julia." Daniel turned to cut around the deck.

"It's so beautiful," Isabel said as they walked over to it. She'd seen the gazebo from afar, but up close, it was even more magical. The structure looked utterly whimsical. Dangling twinkle lights winked back at her, and the air was scented with the intoxicating, sweet aroma of the late-summer flowers that hung from baskets around the lip of the structure's ceiling.

"It is."

Isabel felt Daniel's eyes on her, and a blanket of heat worked its way up her neck. She shot him a sidelong glance, but he looked away and pointed to the center of the gazebo.

"This is where Samson proposed to Julia earlier this summer." Daniel filled her in on the night of the engagement.

"Why am I not surprised that Samson is so smooth?" Isabel climbed up onto the picnic table, taking a seat on the top of it and letting her feet rest on the bench.

Daniel chuckled. "Well, the year before, he almost accidentally ruined her business, so he wasn't so smooth then, but I'd say all is well now."

Isabel figured there was a story there, but she didn't ask. She liked Samson—and Julia, for that matter—but she was more interested in Daniel at the moment.

"So what else is new around here? I feel like I've missed a lot."

Daniel scooched up onto the table next to her. He left six inches of room between them, which was so like him. Always a gentleman.

"There's a lot that's changed. Do you want me to prepare a five-paragraph essay or something?"

Isabel giggled. "No. Not unless you want to. I know writing is sort of your thing." She nudged his shoulder. It wasn't really an attempt to get closer to him—at least not an intentional one. But the result was the same, which, to Isabel, wasn't terrible.

Daniel turned to face her, his features shadowed in the dim glow of the setting sun, but the remnants of a smile hung on his lips. He looked dangerously good out here in an obviously romantic spot in town. And if her heartbeat was an indication of the rate at which she wanted to throw herself into his arms, then she was in big trouble. She may as well toss her *friend*-card in the Squirrel River.

She picked at a sliver of wood on the picnic table's top. "Just tell me one thing."

Daniel leaned back, resting his palms on the table and staring out toward the now quiet grounds of Sunrise Park. "Let's see. We started the Merry Mapleton Ball."

Isabel pinched her brows together, cocking her head to look at Daniel again. Was he blushing? "The Merry Mapleton what?"

"Ball. As in a dance. It's a Christmas dance. It was my grandpa's idea, actually. He was lamenting how there used to be so many opportunities for the community to come together and dance. He and my grandma used to love it, and they'd go out dancing together all the time. It got me thinking that we should start a tradition like that again, so I pitched the idea to Marge."

"Smart."

"Yeah. It's always better to have her and her influence in town on your side"—Daniel lowered his voice, angling his head toward her—"if you know what I mean."

Isabel didn't know how a conversation about Marge had somehow made her feel all tingly, but she decided it had more to do with the way the words rolled off of Daniel's tongue and *not* what the words actually were. She couldn't help but focus on his mouth. She liked his mouth. She'd like it even more if his mouth was on hers...

"Anyway," he went on. "We got the event up and running at Heritage Hall. Seeing Grandpa Gus's face when he walked in was priceless. Probably one of my favorite memories from the past couple of years."

Isabel's heart kicked. Daniel was looking out straight again, not meeting her eye, so she stared at the side of his head, studying his profile.

Finally, after a couple moments, he glanced at her. "What?"

She let out of puff of disbelief. "You know what."

His forehead wrinkled as she squinted at her. "I'm afraid not. Care to spell it out for me?"

"That's the most endearing thing I've ever heard, Daniel. You planned and executed a village-wide Christmas dance to bring joy to your grandpa and, in the process, countless others. Surely you have to recognize that that's not something your average Joe would do. On top of that, you give up your weekends and volunteer your time to help those who need it most. And I'm sure I'm just scratching the surface here. Honestly, are you even real?"

Daniel shifted, obviously uncomfortable being on the receiving end of her praise. "It's not that big of a deal, Izzy."

"I bet Gus would say differently. And Kylie. And the families whom you help each week. I think it's a big deal, too. I should make sure I'm home this year so I can attend the ball and see it for myself."

Daniel opened his mouth and then shut it, nodding instead of making whatever comment he had thought about making.

"What?" She was dying to hear his thoughts, but he shook his head.

"Nothing. Never mind. Besides, in comparison to what we're doing around here, your life is much more exciting."

Isabel cleared her throat. "That's not how I see it at all."

Daniel held her gaze. "Well, thanks for saying that. And hey, if I haven't said it before now, I'm really proud of you. I know I don't have any claim to you, but it's remarkable what you've done. You're remarkable."

It was her turn to blush. "Thank *you* for saying that." She extended her legs, crossing them one over the other and letting her ankles rest on the bench. "It's been really good to be home. I didn't know how much I needed to make things right with my family, but it's like a dark cloud that was hanging over me has finally dissipated. And Mapleton—everyone here—has been nothing short of wonderful. I've been so inspired."

Daniel's eyes gleamed. "I'm so glad to hear that. Your family loves you, and hey, we Mapletonians are good for something!"

Daniel chortled at his own joke, but Isabel needed him to get one thing straight. She reached over and squeezed his upper arm.

Daniel's laughter puttered out as he glanced first down at her hand and then up into her eyes.

Isabel turned her shoulders so she was facing him. Daniel matched her position.

"You are *good*. Good for more than just something." She dropped her gaze, her own insecurities shoving their way forward and turning the heated blush of her cheeks from that of attraction to shame. "Honestly, it's me who's not good enough, or at least I don't feel good enough for this town anymore. Who leaves and doesn't even try to keep in touch with anyone from her past? It was so wrong of me. I still can't help but feel like I'm not worthy of the love that everyone here has been so willing to shower on me since coming back."

How could she ever live up to her parents, to people like Daniel and the members of this community, who were so willing to welcome her home after how negligent she'd been? She'd been selfish, and they were anything but.

Daniel took her hand from where she was still gripping his arm. He held it in his, forcing her to look up at him. "That's the great thing about forgiveness, isn't it? Once it's offered, you don't have to dwell on your past mistakes. It's like the slate is wiped clean...even when we feel unworthy or like we don't deserve it.

"I can't thank you enough, because that's what you've given me, Izzy. Grace in the wake of my mistakes. And that's what everyone here wants to give you."

He took a deep breath, and she couldn't look away. It was like every fiber of his being was willing her to hear him and believe what he was saying. The way his gaze was isolated on her made her soul flutter.

"You deserve every good thing, Iz. You are light and joy and hope for people. You're sharing your gifts with others, and that is so beautiful to witness. You are so beautiful."

Daniel said the last words in a whisper, almost as if they'd slipped out. But he didn't make any move to take them back. He stared straight at her, his gaze skimming back and forth between her eyes before locking in place.

Isabel's chest heaved up and down as he leaned his face closer to hers, never breaking eye contact. In the fringes of her vision, the twinkle lights blurred to shroud them in a golden haze.

Daniel gently laid the pad of his thumb on the center point of her bottom lip, rubbing it back and forth gently. "So beautiful."

His words came out hoarse, like he was trying to control himself. "Inside and out."

Chill bumps sprinted up and down Isabel's arms, but she wasn't cold. In fact, warmth spread out from her heart, coating the inside of her chest with a long-dormant sensation of belonging, of safety and security and peace.

Daniel swallowed hard across from her. His thumb was tantalizing her with the soft, swishing path it was making back and forth across her bottom lip. Suddenly, he stopped, and Isabel almost whimpered at him, but then he cupped her cheek, and she sunk into the gentle feel of his full hand on her skin. She'd forgotten how it felt to be taken care of, to have someone care for her like *this*. Not like Grace cared about her as her assistant and friend. Or like Horatio cared about the show. Or like her parents and brother cared about her as a member of their family. But to have someone care about the deepest parts of her. The parts that it felt like no one else knew and no one else saw until, one day, someone had the gumption to peel back the layers and look straight into her heart.

"Izzy, can I kiss you?"

Isabel stared back into Daniel's eyes. He cared, and she'd never trusted anyone like she trusted him.

"Yes."

One word. That was all it took. With that one word from her, Daniel closed the distance between them. He pressed his lips to hers in a soft, tender motion that filled her with such aching sweetness she thought her eyes might start leaking tears.

He didn't move to deepen the kiss. Time stood still, and they rested against each other for a moment, cherishing the connection that Isabel thought had been severed forever. Instead, with that one kiss, everything felt whole again.

Chapter 30

DANIEL

GUS MOVED SLOWLY DOWN the hallway at Colony Elms later that evening. "I'm beat."

"It's been a long day," Daniel agreed.

"I'll sleep well tonight. And what about you? Will you have some happy dreams about love, lost and found?" Gus asked.

Daniel shot him a look.

"Oh come on, Danny. Don't you play dumb with me. I was watching you and Isabel. I may be old and hard of hearing, but I'm not blind!"

Busted.

Daniel opened the door to Gus's room and followed him inside.

"Did you two have a nice time together?" Gus pressed.

"We did." Daniel shut the door behind him, pausing with his back to his grandpa as he remembered the feel of Isabel's mouth on his. "I don't know that I'd go so far as talking about love, though, Grandpa."

"No use denying your feelings, Son."

Daniel closed his eyes for a minute and then turned around. There wasn't any point in lying to his grandpa. "I know you're right, but I'm not sure how Isabel feels. I've wasted so much time already, and I can't stop the sinking feeling that my time is running out."

"Nonsense. You have a whole lifetime ahead."

"Not if she ends up back in LA." Daniel bent and helped Gus out of his shoes.

Kissing Isabel tonight had been reckless. Wonderfully reckless, but reckless all the same. It was only going to make everything that much more complicated. He never should have crossed that line, even if he was having a difficult time regretting it at the moment.

"You know, there are things such as planes and trains and automobiles." Gus leaned against his shoulder. "You could always use one to visit each other. Or maybe you could take this second chance to go with her."

Daniel was silent. Even after he had admitted to his grandpa what had held him back four years ago, he hadn't let himself think there was a possibility of another chance. At first he was trying to keep from getting hurt. When Isabel had first shown up, there hadn't been any point in entertaining a relationship. But that all changed the more time he spent with her. Still, how could it ever work?

"I don't know, Grandpa," he said finally. "My life is here with you in Mapleton, and I like it here."

"Yes, but you *love* Isabel."

Daniel couldn't deny it. If tonight proved anything to him, it was that. He loved Isabel. That love had morphed over the years, but it ran deep within him, almost as if it coursed through his veins alongside and intermingled with his bloodstream. His grandpa must have read his conflicted expression.

"Listen, Danny. Your life is where you choose to make it with the people you love. Don't use me as an excuse. If you love Isabel and the only way to make it work with her is for you to move, then I'd support you one hundred percent. That being said, I raised you to be smart. I don't want you throwing yourself at Isabel, no matter how lovely she may be, and giving up all you've worked for to build your life here if she isn't going to give you her whole heart in return." His grandfather turned after dropping that metaphorical bomb and started fumbling with the radio.

Daniel put his hand on top of Gus's and gave him a gentle squeeze. "Why don't we keep the radio off for now, Grandpa.

Most of your neighbors are probably asleep. You should head to bed, too. Can I help you with anything before I leave?"

"No, no. I'll be fine. You think about what I said, though. If you love Isabel, and if she loves you, too, then you should move mountains—or cities—for her."

·♥·♥·♥·♥·♥·

Driving to his house, Daniel's mind was flying through scenarios a mile a minute. His grandfather's message replayed in his head.

If you love Isabel, and if she loves you, too, then you should move mountains—or cities—for her.

He did love Isabel. He never stopped, as much as he tried to convince himself he had. The thought of leaving Mapleton made him sad, though. Could he do that? Pack up and say goodbye to this town? Turn down his dream job at *The Village Tattler*? He couldn't imagine not taking over for Gerald, not checking in on his grandfather, and not popping into On Deck Café for a serving of both the latest gossip and Julia's newest coffee creation.

Then again, he couldn't imagine life without Isabel, either.

And Gus had given his blessing, and Daniel could make new routines wherever he ended up. He'd been freelancing for long enough to know he could find work, and as much as he loved the local paper, he *would* give that all up for Isabel.

That is, if Isabel wanted him. And that was a big if. Daniel wanted to believe they'd kindled the spark he thought was extinguished forever, but he wasn't so sure Isabel felt the same. Maybe she was simply caught up in being home, and he was a familiar, friendly companion. The love he thought he was experiencing could have been nothing more than a fleeting summer romance for Isabel—a fun, comfortable fling while she was around town.

Daniel put his car into park and rested his head against the steering wheel. The two of them needed to talk. Because he may have been re-falling in love with Isabel Marshall, but love was a two-way street, and he'd been left in the dust once before.

Chapter 31

ISABEL

ISABEL SPENT THE REMAINDER of the weekend writing her heart out into book form. She shoved her warring emotions about Daniel aside and showed up bright and early on Monday morning to house number four, happy to have something productive to do that didn't involve sitting at a computer for hours on end.

They'd gotten some filming done here last week while she bounced between the third house and this one, but there was much more to do.

The creamy brick exterior of the fourth property was charming. She had already commissioned someone to build cedar flower boxes for the windows. She was going to get new house numbers affixed, and that was all the outside needed.

"Isabel, good, you're here. We need to talk." Horatio held the front door open for her and waited for her to join him inside.

"Uh oh. What is it now?" Isabel set her bag down on the refinished narrow plank wood floors. "This house is to die for," she said happily.

"It's the network. They're pulling the plug on our project here in Mapleton, and they want to meet with us to discuss the direction of the show. In person."

"What? When?" Happiness fled, and Isabel's stomach sank. She knew there was a chance it would come to this. She'd been in the business long enough to know how the network operated, but she was holding out hope she'd be able to finish up in Mapleton before she was called before the HoSt heads.

"The meeting is scheduled for this Friday."

"This Friday?" Isabel repeated as the room tilted. "But we won't have enough time to finish both this house and the last one."

"I know. I know. But I've done all I can do. My hands are tied, and if we don't make the meeting, I'm afraid HoSt will cancel us outright without giving us a chance to wow them with what we've been working on. We have to head to LA on Thursday."

"Whoa, whoa, whoa. What?" Grace walked through the front door with Samson on her heels, looking concerned.

Horatio explained the predicament to Grace and Samson, and Isabel was afraid to make eye contact with Samson. Her gut twisted at the thought of leaving him in a lurch. She'd promised to design and stage five houses, and now she was only going to be able to finish four—if she was lucky.

"Samson, I am so sorry," she said when Horatio finished his spiel.

"Me too," Samson said. "We really like having you around. I know I speak for the rest of Mapleton."

His comment hit Isabel hard, twisting her stomach the opposite direction and making the room flip on its end once more. While she'd been considering how she'd let him down from a business standpoint, Samson was focused on the personal side of her leaving.

Her eyes welled with tears as she imagined saying goodbye to her parents and Ford and getting one last cup of coffee from Julia's.

And leaving Daniel.

Again.

A single tear trickled down her cheek, but Isabel hurried to wipe it away.

All three of them were looking at her with empathetic eyes, but falling apart in front of Horatio, Grace, and Samson wouldn't help anyone.

"Okay. Here's what we're going to do." Isabel squared her shoulders. "I want to work overtime on this house so we can finish it up for you, Samson. Grace, call my brother and tell him

I'm demanding he film the reveal of this one with me. We need a
realtor's perspective."

Grace made a nervous face. "Is he going to hate me for this?"

"No. He and I made up, so you should be good," Isabel assured
her. "If not, tell him I'll find another realtor who is willing." Isabel
smirked. She knew she could play to her brother's competitive
nature and get him here. "Tomorrow, we're going to film at my
parents' house. We've got to get footage of my mom's garden.
I'll transplant flowers from there to here, and we can film on
Wednesday."

Horatio nodded his approval.

"Okay, then. Grace, tell Ford I'll be ready for him Wednesday
afternoon."

Isabel looked around the space again, a vision for this home
forming in her head, and she nodded. "If I only have four days
left here, we need to get to work."

The morning flew by in a blur. Grace coordinated with a local
furniture store to get the pieces they needed into the home
for staging. Isabel set to work crafting a feature wall with
peel-and-stick wallpaper. The outside of this house was darling,
but the inside lacked character. She infused a little life by adding
rustic, red Newport reclaimed brick wallpaper.

"I love this stuff," she said to no one in particular as the cameras
rolled. "It's easy to use and makes a strong statement with a price
point that can't be beat. If we were going to try to add a brick
wall here, we'd blow the budget out of the water. This has the
same effect at a fraction of the price. And if you change your
mind or grow sick of the pattern or texture you chose, you can
take the wallpaper down and try something new. Peel-and-stick
wallpaper won't damage your walls, so it's perfect for renters,
too." Isabel lined up a sheet and smoothed it out, stepping away

to assess her work and nodding before grabbing another sheet and repeating the process.

"Cut!" Horatio yelled. "Nice, Isabel. Really nice. We got everything we need on this project."

"I'm going to keep working," she told him. "I want to get the wallpaper up so we can move furniture around and stage in here. Then, I'll move on to the bathroom."

"Prepare your materials for the bathroom re-vamp, and we'll plan to film that after we're done in your mom's garden."

Isabel nodded. That would give them enough time to do finishing touches on Tuesday afternoon and stage the house so they could film with Ford on Wednesday.

Speaking of Ford.

"What's the good word on my brother?" Isabel asked as Grace ducked around the camera and walked over to her.

"He'll be here. He didn't sound thrilled, but he said he'd do it."

"Good!" Isabel smiled. She meant what she had said the first time she saw Ford after she arrived in Mapleton: she wanted to work with him. Now, she'd get her chance.

"Somebody's happy."

Isabel spun around to see Daniel dodging a cameraman and walking in her direction, two cups of coffee in his hands.

"Daniel!" The sight of him had her heart dancing, but the knowledge that she'd be leaving town—and him—so soon halted the pitter-patter. "What a nice surprise." She walked over, and he handed her a coffee.

"I thought you could use this. I tried to call but didn't get an answer. I figured you were working. Samson swung into the café, and he told me you were here. I hope it's okay."

"Of course. Grace, I'm going to take a little break."

"Take as long as you need." Grace winked before walking off toward Horatio.

"Let's sit on the porch for a bit." Isabel led the way outside and sat down on the second step. She took a long swig of coffee and closed her eyes, trying to find the words to tell Daniel everything she was feeling. "Gosh, this is good," she said of the coffee, leaving her eyes closed.

"I know."

She opened her eyes to find Daniel staring at her. The intensity of his gaze hit her like the sun burning through a magnifying glass, but he looked away after their eyes locked.

"Samson told me you're leaving," he said after a long pause.

Isabel sighed. "I'm afraid so. The network hasn't given us a choice."

"Are you anxious to get back?" Daniel stretched his legs out in front of him. His demeanor seemed casual, but Isabel knew a lot rode on her answer.

"Yes and no." She mirrored his pose. "It's strange, you know? I didn't want to come back home, but I found myself again in Mapleton."

Daniel's gaze was kind and hopeful. "I'm so glad to hear you say that, Izzy."

"But I have to go."

Daniel's jaw ticked, but Isabel pressed on. "I have to go and fight for my show and the new direction I want it to take," Isabel clarified.

"And what direction is that?" Daniel asked, lifting his hand and tucking a piece of her hair behind her ear.

Isabel's eyes shut at his touch. She didn't want to leave him. She knew that in the core of her heart, but she also knew she owed it to herself to fight for the future of her show. And she didn't want to make any promises she couldn't keep.

"I want to convince the network to let me focus on the little guys instead of the huge mega-homes," she said, finally opening up her eyes to meet his gaze.

He tilted his chin at her in question.

"HoSt pushed me to design for high rollers," Isabel said. "But Mapleton reminded me I like designing for regular people. That's where the magic happens. I've got to go try to win them over to my new idea."

Isabel chewed on her cheek. She couldn't get a read on what Daniel was thinking.

Finally, he gave a single nod. "I can't wait to see what you do, Izzy. I'm sure it will be extraordinary."

She turned and looked out over the yard before answering. "Based on your history, I'm sure you'll give me an honest review."

Daniel started, and she glanced in his direction, extending him a smile. "No, I mean it," she went on. "I've been thinking about the whole *Entertainment Magazine* thing, and you were right about me. I hadn't found my direction yet. I *was* stiff and mechanical. I'd like to think I've grown in the past two years, but something has to change, or I'll risk becoming exactly what you said I was. Again."

Daniel studied her. "You know, when I watched that episode, I couldn't breathe. You were so dazzling coming through my TV screen, and I couldn't help but think about how that beauty paled in comparison to the real deal. I thought I'd lost you then. You were out there, making your dreams come true, and I was sure you'd never look back. As time went on and we didn't hear from you, I figured I was right."

"Daniel, I—"

"No, please, Izzy. Just let me say this." Daniel's gaze was nothing short of imploring, and Isabel pressed her lips together, feeling like something weighty was going to come out of his mouth next.

"Having you back in town has been the second chance I need. I don't want to let you go again, so I'll do whatever it takes to keep you in my life, someway or somehow. Even if it means moving to California."

Isabel's mouth dropped open. She couldn't have heard him correctly. "You'd move to LA?"

"For you, yes. I want to be close to you, and I want to see where this relationship goes. Where *we* can go. I lost you once, and I don't want to lose you again."

Tears weaseled themselves into Isabel's eyes for the second time that day, and she tried to blink them back. It was too much.

"Daniel, I couldn't ask you to do that. To leave your grandfather and this town. Not now. Not after I finally see how much it all matters."

"That's the difference this time, Izzy. You're not asking me. You matter to me, and I'm telling you I would do it. For you. If you want me to."

Isabel was afraid if her heart swelled any further it would explode, and when she glimpsed the resolve in his eyes, something let loose inside of her.

Without giving it a second thought, she grasped around his neck, drawing him closer and capturing his mouth with hers.

Daniel sat still for all of two seconds before he kissed her back.

It wasn't the gentle reconnection of the night before. This kiss was filled with need.

And want.

Deep, soul-level want.

They sunk into each other, and when Daniel put his hand above her hip and squeezed, it sent a thunderbolt of electricity up her side. She felt the heat of his kiss whizzing to every last nerve ending in her body. She scooched over, leaning in to him, and he ran his other hand through her hair, tugging slightly as he deepened the kiss. Isabel needed to keep his lips on hers as much as she needed air to breathe. She couldn't get close enough. She was about to hop onto his lap when the sound of a throat clearing reached her ears.

Daniel jerked his head away from hers, and they turned to the street.

Ford stood there with his arms across his chest, eyeing the two of them with a mixture of amusement and disgust. "Can't you two get a room or something? She's my sister, you know, man?" Ford scowled at Daniel before turning his glare to Isabel.

"Ford." Isabel shoved her disheveled hair behind her ear, her words coming out a bit labored. "Didn't Grace tell you we didn't need you for filming until Wednesday?"

"She told me, but I wanted to talk to you. I have a life, you know. A real job. Not one that involves canoodling on porches during working hours. I can't be summoned and expected to show up because you need me here."

"And yet, here you are," Isabel shot back.

Ford's lips quirked. "Touché. I wanted to talk to you about what I would be expected to do on Wednesday."

"Aww, are you nervous?" Isabel teased as they stood, and Ford joined them on the porch.

"No." Ford scuffed his foot against the floor boards. "Maybe a little."

"You'll be fine," Daniel spoke up. "I did it."

Ford looked between the two of them. "Yeah, but Izzy and I don't have the same romantic tension to tap into as you two do, what with me being her brother and all."

Isabel smacked Ford's arm, heat soaring up her neck along with the strong desire to pounce on Daniel again and explore that romantic tension even further. She managed to exercise some self-control and, instead, poured all of her pent-up romantic frustration into an eye roll to end all eye rolls, which she aimed at Ford. "But you *are* my brother. That'll make for an interesting angle on its own."

"If you say so." Ford shrugged. "Can I see the house?"

"Sure," Isabel said. "But it's not done yet."

"I'll let you two get to work," Daniel said. "Good to see you, Ford. You'll be great on camera."

Ford shook Daniel's hand, and Isabel tried to collect her thoughts. The haze of romance she wanted to get lost in with Daniel evaporated as the reality of the decision she was faced with became painfully clear.

"Daniel, I—" She stopped herself, unsure where she was going with that sentence.

"It's okay, Iz. Think about it, and we'll talk later."

Isabel nodded, and Daniel descended the porch steps and walked to where his car was parked on the other side of the street. He turned as he opened the driver's-side door, and their eyes connected. When Isabel looked at Daniel, she saw not only her past but also her future—a future filled with joy and support and a handful of kids with grassy-green eyes, who loved baseball and books and antiquing.

She wanted that. She wanted *him*. But how could she agree to let him leave Mapleton? For her?

Daniel waved and smiled.

Isabel waved back, touching her still-tingling lips as she dropped her hand.

At the sound of Ford's cough, Isabel spun her head around.

Her brother stared down his nose at her. "You going to tell me what I just walked up on?"

"Nope." Isabel strode past him into the house. The truth was, she didn't know what to say about any of it, and she didn't know what she was going to do, but she did know that a lecture from her big brother was not what she needed right now. "Let's get to work."

Chapter 32

ISABEL

"SO YOU'RE LEAVING THIS week?" Her mom stared at her from across the kitchen table later that night.

"Yes." Isabel had wanted to break the news to her family before they heard it around town. But doing so wasn't easy.

"Does Daniel know?"

Isabel raised an eyebrow at Ford's question.

Ford mimicked her expression. "What I saw didn't look like a friendly, goodbye kiss. It looked like a *hello, it's nice to see you again, I want you in my life forever* kiss. And you won't talk about it," he added.

Her mother's mouth hung agape, and her father's bushy eyebrows were halfway to his hairline.

"Yes, Daniel knows." Isabel directed an overdone sigh in Ford's direction. "And I'm not talking about it because it's complicated."

"Didn't look complicated this afternoon." Ford pushed his chair away from the table. "But if there's something more going on, you need to lay all your cards on the table with him, Sis. Especially now that he's got the gig at the paper."

Isabel frowned. "What gig at the paper?"

Ford cocked his head. "You know he was offered the position of editor, right?"

Isabel flinched backward. "No. I had no idea. He didn't tell me."

"Huh." Ford shrugged. "Well, yeah. Gerald Mahoney is retiring, and Daniel's his pick to take over. Anyway, I've got to run. Late showing tonight over in Turner. When do you leave?"

"Thursday." Isabel's thoughts were hitched on Daniel, but she told herself to focus. "I'll see you Wednesday for filming, though. Right?"

Ford nodded once. "The things I do for my sister."

Isabel smiled at him as Ford dropped a light kiss on their mom's cheek.

She excused herself after Ford left. She needed some space to sort through her feelings. "I'm going to go upstairs. I-I've got some writing to catch up on."

"Okay, but don't think we're letting you off the hook about Daniel, dear."

Isabel's stomach wiggled in an uncomfortable way, but instead of answering her, she hugged Val's shoulders from behind. "I'll see you bright and early for filming, Mom. Bring your pretty smile!"

Upstairs, Isabel plopped down on her bed and stared at her feet.

Daniel had offered to move to LA. Isabel wanted to scream, "YES! COME WITH ME!" but doing so would have been selfish. Especially now that she knew he would be giving up a huge career opportunity.

Saying yes to him would be the thing the old Isabel would do. This trip home made her see the importance of family. Gus was all Daniel had in that department, and she couldn't live with herself if she was the reason the two were separated—even if Daniel said he wanted to come.

Isabel was emotionally spent. She lay back and closed her eyes, trying to relax the muscles in her face.

When her phone vibrated on the bed next to her, she palmed for it blindly, grateful for a diversion. Isabel held her phone up in front of her face and sucked in a breath. So much for focusing on something else. Daniel had texted her.

Are you at home?

Isabel typed back.

Just got done with dinner with my family. Why?

Daniel's response popped up within a second.

I'm outside your window.

Isabel scurried off her bed and peered out her window. Sure enough, Daniel stood on the sidewalk, looking up to her room. He gave her a sheepish wave, and her heart tore completely in two. One half soared, and the other half sunk.

Isabel held up a finger to let him know she'd be right down. She looked around her room, as if the answers to the major questions in her life would roll off the tongues of Nick Carter and the rest of the stationary Backstreet Boys crew immortalized in her old posters.

If only.

She gave her head a rueful shake before using her fingers to comb through her hair and making her way downstairs.

She hollered goodbye to her parents and left through the front door.

A smile spread over Isabel's face as she approached Daniel. She couldn't have stopped it if she tried. She wished she could throw herself into his arms and not think about the consequences. But that wouldn't be fair to him. He didn't deserve to be led on. At the thought, her smile wobbled. "What are you doing here?"

"Come on." Daniel reached for her hand, and an involuntary shiver raced from her fingers straight to her sternum, making her whole chest vibrate. "I want to show you something."

"Where are you taking me?" Isabel asked, curiosity temporarily outweighing her anxiety.

"Just wait."

They walked down her parents' street and cut over a couple blocks. Isabel pointed out her favorite features on different homes as they went. She could almost let herself imagine that this was like old times, with the two of them wandering the streets of Mapleton together.

But the pit in her stomach reminded her of the serious conversation she needed to have with Daniel. For now, she kept rambling. She worried if she didn't do something to keep her mind and heart occupied, she'd leap into Daniel's arms, consequences be darned.

"This white picket fence is to die for. Oh, and I always love these late-blooming hydrangea bushes, don't you?"

"I do." Daniel pulled her to a stop in front of house number five. "And here we are."

A crushing feeling of wistfulness came over her, and her shoulders sunk of their own accord. "This is a spectacular property. I wish I could work on it. I'm so proud of the stamp I've left on all of these homes, but we ran out of time for this one."

Daniel led her across the front yard and around the side of the house. When they turned the corner into the backyard, Isabel's mouth dropped open.

A giant weeping willow tree took up the entire corner of the yard, and the leaves were drawn aside to reveal a blanket and some pillows. Dozens of tea lights in white paper bags lined a pathway to the tree, making the whole backyard flicker with shadows gliding around like old-fashioned dancing partners in the romantic light.

"What is this?" Isabel turned to find Daniel studying her, and by the way he brushed his thumb and first finger together, she could tell he was anxious.

"Samson said you were sad to leave this one behind, and I figured you'd like to have a happy memory here to go along with the rest of the houses you've designed in Mapleton, so I thought, why not make a memory ourselves?"

Isabel was speechless. That Daniel went through the effort to put something like this together...she didn't deserve it.

"Do you like it?"

Isabel nodded and gulped down the tears threatening to fall. "Thank you."

She settled her gaze on his green eyes. What she saw in them was the promise of a future, if only she'd say yes. And she wanted nothing more than to give her "yes." But she couldn't. He was too good. She needed to tell him where she was at.

"Come on. I brought food." Daniel led her into the canopy of willow tree vines. He plucked a giant bowl of popcorn out from where he had stashed it under the tree. "I thought we could watch the stars and talk."

Isabel opened her mouth, trying to figure out where to begin. Daniel was watching her closely, and all she could do was shoot him a helpless look.

"What's wrong, Izzy?" Daniel asked quietly.

"Nothing's wrong." Her voice sounded funny in her own ears. Her usual tone was being crowded out with the thickness of the emotion swelling up in the back of her throat. She was frustrated with herself for making such a mess of Daniel's gesture. "This is amazing."

"Sit. Talk to me." Daniel eased down onto the blanket and waited.

Isabel hesitated for a beat and then gave in and obeyed. She snuggled against his side, and he put his arm around her shoulder. When she leaned her head against his chest, she couldn't help but dream of a lifetime filled with moments like this. The quiet of the night held them as Daniel held her, and the rhythmic beat of his heart lulled her agitated spirit.

"What's on your mind, Izzy?" The rumblings of his words in his chest tickled her ear. She needed to start explaining herself before she lost her nerve.

"Tell me about the paper."

Daniel linked his hands around her so her whole body was cradled in his arms. "What about it?"

"Are you the new editor for *The Village Tattler*?"

Daniel's breathing pattern changed. "Who told you that?"

"Ford mentioned it at dinner tonight. Why didn't you tell me? That's amazing news, Daniel."

Above her, she felt him shake his head. "It's not news yet. I haven't accepted, and no one is even supposed to know. I'm not sure how Ford found out."

Isabel couldn't help but chuckle at that, even though her heart felt like someone was turning it into lemon zest. "It's Mapleton. I'm sure word got out somehow."

Daniel exhaled. "I guess you're right."

They were quiet for a minute, and Isabel braced her heart for what she knew she had to do next.

"I want to be with you, Daniel. I do. But..." She searched for the right words, leaning back and looking up at him through her eyelashes.

Daniel stared down at her, his eyes pleading. "I'll come to LA. You say you want me to, Izzy, and I'll be there. I'm prepared to turn down the editor position and keep doing my freelance work. I can do that anywhere."

Isabel looked away, shaking her head quickly and trying to stave off the tears pressing against the backs of her eyes. His earnest declaration overwhelmed her. Daniel used his finger to turn her chin to him.

"Izzy?" He was begging her, searching her face for the answer he wanted to see.

The first tear fell because she knew she couldn't give it to him. "I can't, Daniel. You can't come to LA. It wouldn't be right of me to let you. I'm sorry for kissing you and for getting your hopes up. That wasn't right of me either. I'm so sorry."

Isabel's voice caught on a sob. She tried to remember why she was doing this when it didn't feel good or right at all.

"I wish it was different," she choked out, leaning her body away from him and pressing the heels of her hands into her eyes. "But everything is so up in the air with the network. I don't know what life is going to look like for me back out there. It would not be fair to tell you to pack up your whole world and come with me when I might be out of a job or working my tail off to try to save one. It would be selfish, and I don't want to be selfish. I couldn't live with myself if I knew you gave up your dream job for me. And I don't want to take you away from Gus, either. So, no. I don't want you to come. It's best if we just stay friends."

It was the truth, but Isabel didn't want it to be.

And she'd never realized how much the truth could, in fact, hurt until that very moment.

Chapter 33

ISABEL

WHEN ISABEL WALKED ONTO her parents' deck the following morning, bleary eyed and emotionally strung out, she found her mother chewing on her lip. Val's nerves were splayed across her face like graffiti on the side of a train car.

That won't do.

Her own emotional turmoil forgotten, Isabel walked over and slung her arm around her mom's shoulders.

"Ralphing roaches." Val grimaced, her forehead wrinkling as she turned to Isabel. "I don't know how you do this on a daily basis. I'm so nervous."

Isabel turned Val so they were facing each other. "Mom, look at me." Isabel waited for her mother to meet her gaze. "You are the most effusive, charming, entertaining person I know. The camera is going to love you. I love you, and I can't wait for all my fans to officially meet you."

"About that." Val gave her a shy look. "I caught up on your blog after Ford showed me how to read it, and I saw your article—or whatever you call it—about me. Did you really mean that?"

Isabel hauled her mom into a tight hug. "Of course I did. Don't you doubt it for a second. I meant every word."

Leaning back, Val's face had transformed and was now set with resolute confidence. "Alrighty then. Let's do this."

Soon, they were joking with each other and laughing their way through the garden as they had earlier in the month, Val in her giant sun hat and Isabel trailing dutifully along, listening as her mother shared all her tips and gardening tricks. Val was a wealth of knowledge, and Isabel had never been so thankful for her chatty nature. Her endless stream of conversation kept Isabel's mind from wandering to Daniel.

Together, she and her mom extracted a couple of hostas to transplant at the property Isabel was working on, and Isabel snipped a few stems for indoor use.

"This'll be a picture-perfect addition to the house across town. Thanks for letting us raid your garden, Mom."

"You know, I always believe flowers are for everyone, dear. A flower brings joy, and when it's shared, that joy is multiplied."

"And cut!" Horatio shouted out over the wind and rustling of the leaves. "Marvelous! Absolutely marvelous!" He strode over to hug Val. When he released her, Val reached for Isabel's hand with tears in her eyes.

"Thank you," her mom whispered.

Tears burned the back of Isabel's throat, too, and all she could do was nod.

The next day, Isabel stood with Ford in the living room of house number four. It took all that was left of her energy and most of the day, but Isabel finished the job. The late-afternoon lighting wouldn't be ideal for this final round of filming, but the tech crew brought in a couple spotlights to give the illusion of mid-day sun. No matter what, the house itself shined. They were filming what would be the final scene of the house, and the final scene she'd film in Mapleton.

Isabel was trying to keep her composure, but it was difficult to do when every time she thought of leaving town, it felt like someone was slicing off a piece of her heart. That, and when she scanned behind the camera, she saw her parents, Julia and Samson, and Daniel and Gus. Horatio had invited everyone who was a part of the process to come see their final hour of filming and join them for dinner after they wrapped. He wanted to celebrate a job well done.

What he didn't know was that Isabel was barely holding herself together, and sitting across from Daniel over a meal might be the end of her.

"You can do this," she mumbled to herself. "You've said goodbye to Daniel once before, and you survived. You can do it again. And this time will be different. You'll call and text and visit."

Maybe after she landed on her feet, they could work their way up to a long-distance relationship and see where things went from there.

As she thought it, her gumption failed her. They were at the point in their lives where, to have a real shot at the type of relationship she knew they were both looking for, they needed to be living in the same town—or at least the same state. Long distance would never satisfy.

Besides, Daniel would probably be scooped up by some other deserving woman by the time she got herself figured out, and she'd be left in the friend zone forever.

Isabel fought the urge to bury her head in her hands, instead turning her attention to Ford, who looked every bit the professional realtor he was in his crisp black suit and navy-blue tie.

"Ready to do this?" she asked him as Horatio took up his position behind the camera. Hilde rushed forward and powdered Isabel's face. Ford scrunched his nose in disgust.

"You don't need that stuff, Sis," he said, earning a glare from Hilde. From his unflinching expression, Isabel gathered that Ford couldn't have cared less what the makeup artist thought of him. "But yeah, I'm ready as I'll ever be."

"Rolling in 5, 4, 3, 2, 1 and action!" Horatio pointed to Isabel.

Isabel stood up straighter and smiled at Ford. "So, as you can see, Samson and his team opened this space up to create an airy floor plan." She gestured to the staircase.

Ford nodded. "That's a huge selling point for families."

"And we intentionally staged the house with the comforts of home in mind. No stiff furniture, just cozy, livable pieces, ideal for the on-the-go family who needs a comfortable place to return to at the end of each busy day. What do you think?"

Ford studied the room before turning and grinning at Isabel with a look of sheer delight on his face. For a moment, Isabel swore they were two kids, playing make-believe in their childhood garage.

"It'll sell in a heartbeat." Ford oozed cool confidence. "I can't wait to get a family in here and have them join the community of Mapleton."

"It's a one-of-a-kind place, that's for sure." Isabel's voice faltered.

Keep it together, she thought before turning and facing the camera. "And that's all we have time for here in my hometown. I hope you enjoyed your visit, and I hope we can come back very soon."

"Cut!" Horatio clapped his hands. "That's a wrap here in Mapleton."

Chapter 34

DANIEL

IF WEBSTER NEEDED A photo in its dictionary next to the word 'excruciating' in that moment, Daniel volunteered himself as tribute. Because for the last hour and a half, he'd felt completely gutted, looking on as Isabel did her thing.

It was a particularly cruel form of torture.

The only reason Daniel was there was because of Gus. Horatio had invited them before Daniel had known how things were going to end with Izzy. As it all turned out, he'd had half a mind to cancel, but he'd promised Gus the chance to see what went into making a real-live TV show, and his grandpa would have been disappointed to miss out.

Now, Gus sat in the passenger seat, recounting what they'd seen. He waved his hands excitedly, praised Isabel, and was all around thrilled to have been included in the production.

Daniel made grunts in response, but that was as much as he could engage in the conversation. All he was thinking about was Isabel and how she glowed under the lights. The joy and pride of a job well done was etched on her face, and that—mixed with the bit of remorse she displayed at finishing up her work in Mapleton—made her so human it was mesmerizing.

And excruciating.

"Daniel. Danny. Hello?"

Gus's voice stirred Daniel from his thoughts of Isabel.

He blinked. "What? Sorry."

Gus looked exasperated. "Son, I've been spouting nonsense for the past two minutes to see how you'd react, and what did I get? Crickets! What's got you all knotted up?"

"What do you think?" Daniel turned into the parking lot at Hal's.

"I'd guess it has something to do with that woman over there." Gus motioned, and Daniel tracked his finger to where Isabel and her family were walking into the diner.

Daniel hadn't told Gus what happened under the willow tree earlier in the week, not wanting to dampen the mood of the day or draw any extra attention, but he should have known it would be impossible to hide his feelings from his grandpa.

"You'd guess right."

"Have you told her how you feel?" Gus asked quietly.

"Yes." Daniel stared after Isabel's retreating figure. "I told her I would come to LA."

"And?"

"And she told me no. She wants to stay friends. I really thought she was feeling the same way I was," Daniel's voice cracked.

Gus stared at him, his eyes moist with shared sadness. "I'm sorry, Danny."

They sat in the car for a moment longer until Gus spoke again, his voice laced with a steely resolve. "I still think you and Isabel are destined to be together. Someway and somehow. Mark my words."

His grandfather may have been a hopeless romantic, but right now, Daniel couldn't buy in. Isabel turning him down was too fresh, and this was history repeating itself.

Dinner passed in a flurry of activity. Stories were told across the table with Val, Dave, and Ford reminiscing about Isabel's childhood, and Grace and Horatio chiming in with funny anecdotes from LA. Kylie showed up with her dad after they'd taken their seats, and it was really amazing to see the young teen bloom under Isabel's prompting—a bittersweet sort of amazing. Daniel hardly needed the reminder of how incredible Isabel was.

Someone asked Gus about the Brewers, and that topic of conversation lasted him the entire meal. Daniel was thankful all he had to do was sit silently and observe. Though he tried, he couldn't keep his eyes off of Isabel.

Izzy.

Her gaze kept flitting over to him, too. When their eyes locked, she would give him a sad, small smile before her attention was called away. She was the star of this dinner, just as she was the star of her show and her life. And Daniel was merely a spectator, no different from any of the thousands of faceless fans and friends who tuned in to her show each week.

"You have to tell us what's going to happen next, Isabel." Julia situated her chin in her palm and leaned on the table, waiting for Isabel to tell all.

Isabel set down her drink. "With the show, you mean?"

Julia nodded.

"Honestly, I'm not sure."

"We're going to fight for it," Horatio cut in. "We're going to blow them away with Isabel's idea to refocus our efforts on normal families and normal properties. No more outlandish homes."

Isabel gave her producer an appreciative smile. "But there is no guarantee."

Grace opened her mouth to say something, but Isabel cut her off.

"You know there isn't," Isabel said. "And it's okay. I've loved doing the show. Well, I've loved the idea of what it was and what it can be. We seemed to have gotten a little off track this season, and that's why I really want to pitch taking it in a different direction to try to make it something that others can love, too. But there is a good chance the network won't want to hear what I have to say. Or they'll listen and tell me, 'Thanks, but no thanks.' And if that happens, then that's that."

Was it wrong that a part of Daniel hoped for that? He couldn't help but think that if the network shot her down, maybe she'd come back to Mapleton.

But no. He would never wish for her dreams to be shattered. And he didn't think he could be satisfied knowing he was a consolation prize.

"What will you do then?" Samson asked, and Julia nodded. The whole table was hanging on Isabel's every word.

"I don't know. Start over, I guess. LA is full of opportunities. The TV show is one thing, and I'm grateful for it, don't get me wrong." Isabel nodded to Horatio before shifting her gaze to Julia. "But I want to be more like you."

"Like me?" Julia put her hand to her chest, her eyes wide. "What do you mean?"

"You serve people and take the time to get to know them. I've watched you over the course of the month. You've reminded me of the importance of personal touches. You all have." Isabel looked around the table. "I've tried to follow your lead and imagine the real people living in the homes we've designed here. I want to do more of that going forward. I'll find some way to do it, with or without the network. Hopefully, I can make Mapleton proud."

"I have no doubt you will," Samson said.

"Here, here!" At the other end of the table, Dave held up his glass to salute his daughter. The rest of the party followed suit.

Isabel had tears in her eyes as she clinked her glass with those around her. Her gaze settled on him, and it was all Daniel could do to not lunge across the table to her. His heart ached for its counterpart. She was so close and yet still out of reach.

As the dinner crowd dispersed a half hour later, Daniel helped Gus into the passenger seat of the car. He shut his door and turned to find Isabel walking in his direction. Behind her, Val and Dave were getting into their minivan.

"My parents are giving me a ride home, so I don't have much time, but I'd like to stay in touch—if that's okay." She dropped her gaze but not before he saw her glassy eyes. "Your friendship means the world to me, Daniel."

Friends. Somehow, that would never be enough for him. Somehow, it had to be. But he didn't think his heart could handle it.

"I don't think that's a good idea for me, Iz. Not right now, at least." Daniel tried to clear the emotion out of his throat.

Her face fell, but she nodded, looking at him with teardrops clinging to her eyelashes. "I should go."

Daniel heard the reluctance in her voice and wished she'd tell him she'd changed her mind and wanted him to come. He wished she would give up LA and stay in Mapleton. Either way, he wouldn't force her hand. He couldn't. And he couldn't live being half in and half out.

"My offer stands." He made one last effort to convince her.

Isabel's eyes softened. She held his gaze, and in that moment, Daniel tried to tattoo her in his mind—the curve of her cheek, the laugh lines by her toffee eyes, and the wave of her hair. He didn't know when he'd see her again.

"I know." She stood on her tiptoes and left a light kiss on his cheek. She turned before he could say anything else.

Daniel's whole body lurched, as if the marrow in his bones was trying to propel him in her direction. But instead of going after her, Daniel got into the front seat.

Gus stared at him expectantly. "Well?"

"She's leaving, and I don't know what I'm going to do."

Chapter 35

Isabel

Bright and early the next morning, Isabel lugged her suitcase downstairs and wheeled it out to the road. She had been up past midnight putting the final touches on the draft of *Feels Like Home*, and now she stifled a yawn.

Grace was waiting for her, all smiles and perfectly curled hair.

"You look way too good for five-thirty in the morning," Isabel grumbled before hoisting her bag into the trunk.

"Chin up, buttercup," Grace said around Val as she hugged the Marshalls goodbye.

Isabel embraced her mom and dad next.

Her mom squeezed her tight. "You just got here."

"I know. I won't stay away so long this time. I promise."

"Take care of yourself, pumpkin." Her dad wrapped his arms around her.

"I will, Dad." She gave her parents a firm nod, signaling she was okay, before climbing into the rental car. She tried and failed to keep from tearing up as Grace pulled away from her house.

"I thought you could use this." Grace dipped her chin to the center console. Two to-go cups of On Deck Café coffee sat in the cup holders, steam billowing from the openings of the lids. "I stopped by the café on my way here. I couldn't leave without one last drink from Julia. I'm going to miss this place."

Isabel's hands shook as she grasped the coffee, clinging to it as if she could hold onto the town it stood for, while they sped to the airport, leaving Mapleton behind.

"Grace," Isabel said after they drove in silence for a couple minutes, a mist in her mind suddenly forming itself into a full-blown thought bubble, complete with an idea.

"Yeah?"

"I need your help."

·♥ · ♥ · ♥ · ♥ · ♥·

After a cross-country plane ride, Isabel stood in the entrance of her condo in Los Angeles and peered around. Nothing about it had changed in the past month, but everything was different. With its bare walls and sleek furniture, her house screamed *sterile hospital chic*. It was the opposite of home. In comparison to her parents' house, which burst with life with all its colors and textures and well-worn comforts, her condo was like a wilted flower.

Isabel missed Mapleton. The flight from Wisconsin to California allowed for ample time to think as she talked through her plan with Grace. A plan that would completely change the course of Isabel's career and, hopefully, her life.

The last time she left the Midwest, she'd been so worried about making a name for herself she'd lost who she was. This time, she felt like she had rediscovered and rebuilt a part of herself with the help of those she left behind. But her job wasn't finished yet.

·♥ · ♥ · ♥ · ♥ · ♥·

The next morning, Isabel got up with the sun. With the time change, she should have been dragging, but she was wide awake. It was as if she could feel her synapses firing. Nerves would do that to a person.

She dressed in her most boss-lady attire—complete with a crisp white blouse and a black pencil skirt. She traced her lips and filled them in with a power-red lipstick. Sweeping her hair into a sleek French twist, she gave herself a onceover in the mirror before deciding she was ready. It was time to put on her figurative design-icon hat and make the network see they wanted to do business with her—even if it took them all in a new direction.

Isabel slung her oversized bag over her shoulder, making sure her laptop was safely stowed. Locking the door behind her, she opened the ride app on her phone to schedule a pick up. Isabel started for the elevators when her phone rang. She checked the caller ID and smiled.

"Julia! What a pleasant surprise!" Isabel answered.

"Hi, there! Is this an okay time?"

"It's perfect. I'm heading into work now."

"I was hoping I could catch you before your meeting." Julia raised her voice, and Isabel heard the noise of the café in the background. "I wanted to wish you luck. I'm sure you'll show the network what a valuable asset you are. They'd be crazy not to pick up your show for a third season! Oh, and Samson told me last night that he talked to Ford, and they're going to list the first four properties you worked on right away."

"Thanks, Julia. That means a lot." Isabel was touched Julia thought to call. "And how exciting! What's Samson's plan for the fifth house?"

"He's going to hold onto it for a bit, I think. Oh, shoot. I've got to go. My drive-thru traffic is picking up with the lunch rush. You're going to crush your meeting. I know it."

Isabel walked out in front of her complex to wait for her ride. "If I channel my inner Julia, I'll do just that."

"You be yourself. We're all rooting for you. Hey, everybody, say hi to Isabel." Julia's voice sounded faraway. Isabel could picture her holding out the phone toward the dining room at On Deck Café. The whole café shouted a greeting to her through Julia's phone. She stopped walking and closed her eyes to savor the virtual hug from Mapleton.

"You really are the best," Isabel said when Julia came back on the line. "My ride's here now, so I have to run. I'll let you guys know how it goes, but the meeting will probably take most of the morning."

"Can't wait to hear from you. Bye, girl," Julia said in her trademark Wisconsin way, her voice laced with the Midwestern twang of drawn-out vowels.

"Bye, Julia."

As she climbed into the waiting car, Isabel generated a text message, scrolling to find Samson's phone number. It was time to put the first part of her plan into motion.

> Hi, Samson, it's Isabel. I heard through the grapevine you're holding the fifth house off the market. Any chance you can keep it in your back pocket until we can talk? I have some ideas.

Isabel pressed send and reread her message. She'd kept things purposefully vague, but she was sure Samson would assume she wanted to come and decorate it at some point in the future. He wouldn't be totally wrong.

Isabel set her phone in her lap and chatted with her driver as they passed city sidewalks and skyscrapers. Before she made it to the network offices, Samson replied.

> Isabel, great to hear from you. If the Mapleton intel network is connected to LA now, I'm afraid no one is safe. I'd be happy to talk with you about the house. Name the time.

Isabel smiled, rubbing her hands together before tapping out a quick message.

> I'll be in touch! Thanks, Samson.

She stashed her phone in her purse as her car arrived in front of the HoSt office building. Isabel thanked the driver and took a grounding breath, her already snappy nerves kicking into high gear.

All her dreams for the future rode on this meeting and on her ability to convince a bunch of network executives that her plan for moving forward was in their best interests...and hers.

Grace was lingering outside the entrance, and at the sight of her, Isabel was instantly calmed.

"Morning, Iz. You look fabulous." Grace leaned in as Isabel approached and kissed both of her cheeks. "How're you feeling?"

Isabel stared up at the sleek, silver office building in front of her and squared her shoulders. "Ready."

Grace grinned. "Alright, then. Let's do this."

Isabel walked into the board room where an oval table took up most of the floor space. On one side sat six men dressed in black suits. They stood one by one and shook Isabel's and Grace's hands. Horatio gave her a hug, and she nodded at Jeb, one of the men who worked on their tech crew. He stood in the corner, ready to handle the streaming of their footage. After introductions were made, Isabel took her seat.

The network head spoke first.

"As you've been made aware, we have our concerns about the critical reception of *Inspired Interiors*. While you had a strong showing in your first season, the episodes that are currently airing are not only getting less viewership, the reviews coming in from critics are also less than stellar. Something needs to change. While we're always willing to work with members of our HoSt family, we brought you here to discuss plans going forward. If we can't agree upon a solution, we won't be airing a third season of *Inspired Interiors*."

Isabel sat in her chair, her back stiff. She knew this news was coming and had braced herself accordingly. She nodded once at the executive to let him know she understood and waited for Horatio to speak up.

As they'd discussed, Horatio started off with an explanation of what they'd been doing in Mapleton while Jeb cued up the footage. Isabel would say her piece when they were through. She only hoped Horatio wouldn't take it personally when she went off script.

Snapshots of the episodes they'd shot in Mapleton filled the projection screen in the conference room, and the image of her hometown filled Isabel with so much joy that no matter what happened with her show, she knew she'd be okay.

Her trip to Vintage Market rolled first, and Horatio was right. The footage was gold. He'd edited it so it flowed seamlessly with Isabel's tips and Daniel's jokes to portray the experience of a perfect morning out antiquing. Which it had been.

Isabel got lost in a daydream about Daniel and what he might have been doing right now. She wondered if he was at the café when Julia had called. Did he add his voice to the chorus of well-wishers? She hoped so, but she wouldn't blame him if he'd held himself back.

She tried to tell herself to focus, but the next thing Horatio played for the executives was footage of her describing the shelves she'd created for the second house. It did little to rid Daniel from her mind. Instead, she felt a blush creep up her neck at the memory of their time together in the basement.

From there, footage showed the aftermath of the storm and the village rallying together before moving on to the third and fourth houses. Isabel smiled as her mom appeared on the screen in her gardening hat, and Ford looked handsome as all get out, every bit the successful realtor he was.

An unfamiliar energy coursed through Isabel by the time the film ended. She recognized what it was: pride. For the first time in over a year, she was genuinely proud of her artistic accomplishments. Using the momentum generated from the footage, she stood and began her speech.

"Gentlemen, I hope the material Horatio and his team expertly compiled is as compelling to you as it is to me. You see, I didn't

want to go to Mapleton. It's my hometown, but I left it four years
ago when I came out here to make a name for myself. HoSt has
helped me in accomplishing that. Along the way, I buried my past.
I didn't think it was worthy of the future I wanted for myself.
But as you have said yourselves, things got stale. We were doing
the same old designs and styles of homes in LA. Our clients are
extremely wealthy, and there's nothing wrong with that, except
that it made our show not relatable at all. Something has been
missing, and I'm certain it is that something that is causing our
viewership to drop.

"When Horatio and Grace convinced me to go to Mapleton, I
rediscovered what that something is. Plain and simple, it's the
idea of home and heart and personality. Moving forward, I want
to take my own personal brand in that direction. I don't want to
stage massive homes for people who make millions of dollars.
That may be what makes me and the network the most money,
but it doesn't make for good TV. Instead, I want to work with
the little guy. I want to design on a budget." Isabel tugged her
shoulders back. "I want to move to Mapleton."

Horatio gasped. Isabel shot a look to Grace. Her friend gave her
a thumbs up.

When Isabel drove away from Mapleton with Grace, it dawned
on her. She wanted to transition to working on more modest,
everyday homes. It was what her original proposal to HoSt hinged
on—what she'd discussed with Horatio. It was assumed she would
do that in California. But what she really wanted to do was work
on properties in Mapleton. And why couldn't she?

She and Grace had spent the entire flight to LA sorting through
details, dreaming of what that sort of pivot would entail. The
more she dreamed it, the more Isabel wanted to make it a reality.

The men from HoSt were staring at her with curiosity clear in
their eyes.

"Horatio's footage speaks for itself," Isabel went on. "You see
what can be done in a small town. I want to shine a light on the
communities of small-town America, using Mapleton as my case

study. I want to continue designing houses for residents there. I can set up shop and work on flip properties, remodels, and assist those who need help making their current space work for them. There are also new homes being built south of town, so I'm sure I could dabble in designing those, as well. Really, the opportunities, as I see it, are endless. I am willing to let HoSt film my work there." Isabel took time to look each of the network heads in the eye and made it clear that the direction the show took in the future would be on her terms.

"I have built a following online that will thrive with or without this show. So, if you don't want to move forward with this idea, I will walk out of here and thank you for your time and what you've done for me. I am willing to do that. But if what you've seen today"—she motioned to the now darkened screen—"and what I've proposed to you sounds intriguing, then I'm ready to hash out details so we can put a plan together that's in the best interests of HoSt, myself, and my team."

Isabel sat down and clasped her hands gently on the table. Her heart was beating out of her chest, but she was pleased with what she'd said, and she wasn't about to blink first. She'd spoken her piece, and either way, she'd be on a flight to Mapleton later that night. That was all she wanted. That, and a certain man by the name of Daniel Smith.

If only he'd still have her.

Chapter 36

DANIEL

DANIEL SAT WITH HIS back to the door of On Deck Café. His fingers flew across the keyboard as he cranked out an article. He'd gotten to the café when Julia and Amanda opened the doors at five-thirty this morning, and he figured he'd shut the place down at nine o'clock tonight.

There was nothing like unrequited love to make a person productive.

At noon, the bell above the door jingled, and Marge Wilson strode inside, purpose punctuating her every step. She made a beeline for the counter and whispered something to Julia.

Julia turned in his direction with a frown on her face.

Here we go.

The news of his and Isabel's breakup—could he even call it that?—had made it to the café. Actually, it was remarkable it had taken a day and a half for the word to get out. He'd worked from home yesterday for this very reason, but nothing would keep the town at bay for long, so today he figured he'd face the music.

After handing Marge a to-go cup of coffee, Julia marched over to his table. "What happened?"

Daniel didn't take his eyes from his computer screen. "It sounds like you already know."

"Well, yeah. Marge was at Colony Elms, and she talked to Cheryl who talked to Gus who told her that Isabel sort of broke your heart." Julia cringed. "Again."

"That about covers it," Daniel said dryly.

"I'm so sorry. And here my big mouth made a show of calling her earlier. I'm sure that made you feel like crap."

"It's alright, Julia. I know you didn't mean anything by it."

"Well, I'm still sorry. I was really rooting for you guys."

"Yeah." Daniel glanced up and shrugged. "Me too."

Julia walked back behind the counter and put her head together with Amanda. Daniel readjusted his headphones. He needed to hammer out an article for *Brides of Wisconsin* about unique table centerpieces. But his gaze hovered on Julia and Amanda, and he finally decided to move on his original idea, as well. He rose from his seat and approached the counter.

"Well, what can we do about it?" Daniel heard Amanda say before Julia's eyes landed on him, and she nudged her friend in the side before turning to him.

"Daniel, what can we do for you?" Julia shot him an innocent smile.

Daniel rolled his eyes, sure that the two of them were up to their usual conniving. He didn't even want to think about what they'd have in store for him.

"Actually, it's your fiancés I need," he said. "I want to ask them a few questions about weddings."

"Are you serious?" Amanda snorted.

Daniel bobbed his head. "I want to do an entire exposé on a guy's perspective of the wedding planning process. Think your men would agree to let me do full-blown interviews?"

The bell rang over the door behind him, and Amanda and Julia looked beyond him.

"You can ask them yourself." Julia smiled as Samson and Seth approached the counter.

"Ask us what?"

"Daniel wants to feature you in the wedding magazine." Amanda grinned.

Seth groaned, and Samson's eyes bugged. "Heck no."

"Oh, come on!" Daniel explained his position.

"See, that wouldn't be so bad." Julia walked around the counter and rested an imploring hand on Samson's back. "I'm sure you guys can help Daniel out, can't you? He could really use it today," she said under her breath to Samson, but Daniel caught it.

"I suppose we can do that. Right, Seth?" Samson eyed Julia, and they had an entire conversation in that look—Daniel was sure of it. He had to work to tamp down his jealousy.

Seth groaned. "I guess. But you better provide beer, Daniel."

Amanda whooped. "I've got to be there for this."

"Oh, me too. For sure." Julia high-fived Amanda.

"I don't know about that, ladies. I'm afraid I won't get honest answers if you two are listening in."

Amanda stuck up her nose at him in mock offense. "Daniel, I always thought you were on our side! Besides, I'm sure Seth and Samson only have wonderful things to say about wedding planning. Isn't that right, babe?"

"Yes, dear." Seth winked at her.

Amanda swatted him, a playful glint in her eye.

"See, this is what I mean." Daniel pointed between the two of them, and they all laughed. For Daniel, it was bittersweet. His own heart longed for that sort of closeness with someone.

With Isabel.

Daniel gave himself a mental slap across the face. He needed to keep his focus on the task at hand. Not on pining after Isabel.

Amanda pouted, and Daniel conceded. "You and Julia can join us after the meat of the interview is out of the way."

That placated them, and with the interviews locked down, Daniel said goodbye and walked to his table to resume working.

Over the course of the afternoon, he kept his head down and ignored the looks the café patrons snuck in his direction. The baristas plied him with food and free refills. It was pity coffee, but he wasn't too proud to accept it.

When he finally looked at the clock on the bottom of his computer, it was after eight. Daniel stretched his arms over his head, taking in the café in front of him. His eyes were tired from staring at the blue light of the screen all day.

The bell over the door jingled, and Daniel turned to see Samson and Julia stroll back in. Julia had been done working for the day at two o'clock.

"You haven't moved from where I left you," she said when they walked over.

Daniel shrugged. "Busy day."

"You know what they say about busy days?" Julia's eyes twinkled. "They make for good nights."

Daniel shot her a puzzled look. He'd never heard anyone say that. What in the world was she talking about?

"Anyway! Come on, Jules. I promised you a late-night iced coffee treat." Samson shooed Julia away from his table and gave Daniel an apologetic look.

Daniel shook his head. Julia was something else.

He checked his email, responded to a couple of queries that came in for freelance work over the course of the day, cleared out his inbox, and gazed at his phone to try to conjure up a text from Isabel, which was stupid since he'd been the one to sever any chance of ongoing communication.

Daniel raked a hand through his hair and was about to shut things down for the night when the bell over the door to the café jingled again. This time, the whole dining room went silent, and Daniel spun around to see what was going on.

Isabel stood there, staring directly at him, looking tired and a little travel-mussed. She smiled tentatively as she raised her shoulders before letting her arms fall to her sides like Ally in *The Notebook*. "I'm home."

The café erupted in cheers, and people shoved their chairs out and rushed to hug her. Daniel held her gaze, afraid if he blinked, she'd disappear.

Even as she was pummeled with affection from half the village, she never broke eye contact with him.

His head reeled. She was here. In Mapleton. How? What did this mean? She'd said she was home. Was she in town for good? How had she gotten here? And so soon? Why didn't she tell him she was coming?

Daniel stood rooted to the floor as the crowd of well-wishers finally dispersed, and Isabel made a slow march toward him. She stopped directly in front of him and nibbled her bottom lip before staring down at her shoes. When she met his eyes again, she spoke quietly. "Happy to see me?"

Daniel's lips twitched. "That would be an understatement. Welcome home, Izzy."

He reached for her as she flung herself at him. They collided in a hug that was as hard and pure as a diamond. Daniel held Isabel tight against his chest, burying his face in her hair and inhaling her sweet honey scent as she snuggled as close as she could get.

The café erupted into another round of cheers. Amanda whooped from behind the counter, Samson whistled, and out of the corner of his eye, he saw Julia jumping up and down in glee.

When Daniel finally relinquished his grasp, Isabel looked up at him.

"It's good to be home." She shot him a coy smile.

It felt like the air particles around them were taking up more space than they had been a minute ago, pressing in against him with uncharacteristic warmth and static electricity.

"What's going on, Izzy?" Daniel searched her face, hoping she meant what he thought she did but unable to believe it until she spelled it out for him.

"I'm home. My past and my future are here, Daniel. I met with Samson, and I am going to buy the fifth property—the ranch house I didn't get a chance to work on. I'm moving my production team here, and HoSt wants to do a third season of my show, set in Mapleton. Can I have another chance with you? I've screwed this up so many times before, but I promise—"

Daniel didn't let her finish before he put his first finger under her chin, tipped her mouth up, and settled his lips against hers.

The kiss held all the emotion of lost time and the promise of future happiness. Isabel gripped his back, drawing him closer, and Daniel gladly obliged. He slowly speared his hands through her hair, letting his thumbs rest gently, reverently against her jawline. The noise of the café faded away as they drank each other in, speaking a language only the two of them knew.

When they finally surfaced for air, Daniel rested his forehead against Isabel's.

"I thought I told you to get a room."

Keeping a tight hold on Isabel, Daniel transferred his weight just enough to spot Ford standing inside the door, smirking like only an older brother could.

Isabel hid her head in the crook of his neck before she met his gaze again, a beautiful blush enhancing her already breathtaking features.

Daniel could hardly believe this was real. He tugged her into his booth on the same side as him. He didn't want to be separated from her at all, and even the other side of a café table was too far. "When did you decide all this?"

"I got about two miles from my parents' house on the way to the airport and asked myself, 'What am I doing?' Grace and I worked up a proposal for relocating to Mapleton, and the network bought it. By the time I was halfway over Colorado and we had a plan, I knew I'd come home either way, but now I know I have a job."

"And a new house. I can't believe it. Wait until my grandpa finds out."

Isabel's face took on a serious edge. "I want to spend as much time with Gus as possible now that I'm home. And with you—if you'll have me."

Daniel pulled her closer. "Izzy, I don't consider you a thing to be had. But I will always support you. I will always be there for you. And yes, I'd like to spend as much time as possible with you, too."

Isabel looked at him, eyes glistening with tears. "I'm sorry I didn't figure myself out sooner."

"We're together now. That's all that matters."

Daniel leaned down to kiss her. Because she was here. Because he could. And when she met his gaze, her eyes twinkling, he knew he'd move mountains to make sure they'd be together forever.

Chapter 37

ISABEL - 6 MONTHS LATER

ISABEL SLAMMED ON THE brakes and skidded into a parking stall outside Vintage Market. She was running behind schedule because she got caught up daydreaming about paint colors.

She was officially settled at home in Mapleton—a proud resident for the past six months.

The "Welcome" sign on the outskirts of the village would have to be changed to read "Population: 2,134." Isabel was going to put a bug in Samson's ear about it. As the new Village Administrator, he could make that happen for her.

Isabel had moved into the ranch she bought from Samson right away. It was a work in progress, but as part of season three of her show, she was making it her own. She thought it would be an extra-personal touch to give viewers a first-hand look inside her space. That was her focus, after all.

And that was also why she was at Vintage Market. They were filming a scene for an episode featuring her home office. Daniel was on tap to shop with her for an antique desk and some chairs.

She hopped down from her truck—which she was currently borrowing from her parents until she made up her mind about what kind of car she wanted to buy—and slammed the door. Tugging her parka closer to her neck, she scurried to the front entrance of the market. The parking lot was slick, and Isabel tried not to slip and fall on the ice.

Grace stood waiting for her, her breath visible in the frigid February air. Both she and Horatio gladly moved to Mapleton—at least for the months out of the year they spent filming. Bless her producer for getting over his initial shock at her proposal and jumping fully on board.

Grace opened the door for her. "You're late."

"I know. I know. Sorry!" Isabel hurried inside. She waved to the women staffing the market that day. They were used to her coming in and out with the crew by now. She'd been one of their most regular customers over the past half year, happily plugging their shop on her show and buying all her own seasonal and home décor here. Currently, everything was decked out in hearts and pink pastels in honor of Valentine's Day.

Isabel sloughed off her jacket and smoothed down her sweater. She approached the mirror hanging behind the front counter and dabbed at the corners of her eyes to make sure the mascara she'd applied at home had withstood the biting winds. Hilde hadn't moved to Mapleton with the crew, so Isabel reapplied her own peach lip gloss and was ready to go when Daniel strolled over to her.

"Hey, beautiful."

Isabel's throat went dry when she caught sight of Daniel staring directly at her with a look of admiration on his face. All the positive reviews in the world, all the praise from strangers and fans, would never make her feel half as good as one look from Daniel.

"Hey, stud." She turned and skipped her way right into Daniel's arms. She leaped, and he caught her. She wrapped her legs around his waist and planted a firm kiss on his mouth.

"Thanks for filming with me." She slid down his body but kept her arms folded around his neck.

"If that's the greeting I get, I'll film every day." Daniel pressed a kiss on her forehead.

He had become a frequent guest on her show. Horatio claimed he couldn't have cast a more in-sync duo, and Isabel agreed.

She was so grateful he was a good sport about filming. It wasn't like he didn't have other things going on. He was excelling as editor of *The Village Tattler*, and he was in high demand as a freelance writer. His wedding piece on real-life grooms' perspectives went viral, garnering the attention of several national publications. And yet, he always showed up for her.

Daniel was everything she needed in a partner. Someone who challenged her and kept her grounded. Someone who called her out when she got too big for her britches, but also pumped her up when she needed to be reminded of her worth. He'd helped her set up her charity foundation which aimed to provide scholarships and internship placement to young creatives who hoped to pursue a career in the arts. She had Kylie to thank for her inspiration there, and Daniel, too. His goodness made her want to be better.

Since she had returned to Mapleton, the two had only fallen deeper in love with each other. She'd included a chapter in her book—set to publish later in the year—about their love story. Based on the teasers she was starting to share online to drum up interest in preorders, she was pretty sure it was going to be her fans' favorite part. They wouldn't be alone—it was her favorite, too. Isabel couldn't wait to see what the future held for them. Though, right now, she wasn't too concerned about what came next. She was perfectly content to rest in Daniel's embrace.

"Okay, love birds, cage it up until the cameras are rolling." Horatio ambled over to them. "Let's get this show on the road, shall we?"

Isabel dropped her arms from around Daniel's neck and felt for his hand, interlocking their fingers.

"Let's do it." He raised her hand to his mouth and kissed her knuckles.

"And rolling." Horatio nodded to them.

Isabel started walking down the first aisle of the market. "Today, we're on the hunt for a personal piece," she said. "I want to find the perfect desk for my home office."

"What style are you looking for? Ornate or classic?" Daniel asked.

Isabel beamed at him. "Listen to you! Date a designer long enough and you'll start to think like one."

Daniel grinned at her, waiting for her to answer his question.

"I'm thinking something classic, but I'm guessing I'll know it when I see it. This piece has to be both attractive and functional. I'll use it a lot. After all, I pen a blog post each night, so this is where I'll do that. And I'm planning to use greens for the wall color and accents in this room. A warm wood tone would work well."

They turned the corner, and Isabel gasped. "There!"

She dropped Daniel's hand and strode to the back of the booth. Underneath a stack of old books and a lamp that looked like it had seen better days was an elegant oak writer's desk.

"Daniel, look at this!" Isabel squealed. "It's in pristine condition, and it's exactly what I was envisioning."

The legs tapered as they neared the ground, and the front was simple with one drawer. The vintage pull was the cherry on top, or rather, on the front, of the piece.

"I love it. Aren't you going to smell it to make sure it passes the sniff test?" Daniel kidded.

"You read my mind." Isabel winked. She took a step forward and opened the drawer. "That's funny. What's this?" Sitting directly in the center of the empty drawer was a small black box.

"What?" Daniel came closer to check it out for himself.

Isabel gently lifted the lid, and realization dawned on her. "Oh my goodness." She covered her mouth and turned to Daniel.

He grabbed the ring box from her and dropped down onto one knee.

"Isabel Marshall, you are the most beautiful person I know. I love everything about you, from the way you care deeply for your family and your friends and this town, to the way you waffle over paint colors and sniff old pieces of furniture. I want to spend the rest of my life loving you. Will you marry me?"

Daniel took the ring from the box. She couldn't process how stunning it was. Standing there, staring into Daniel's eyes, so full of hope and adoration, she only saw him.

"Yes!" She exhaled, though she was pretty sure she didn't have any air in her lungs to get rid of. "Yes, I'll marry you!"

Daniel stood and wrapped her in his arms before letting her go to slide a flawless oval diamond ring on her fourth finger. He sealed his promise with a lingering kiss.

When Isabel leaned back, she could barely see through her happy tears. "How'd you know I'd choose that desk?" she asked in wonder.

Daniel's eyes danced. "You date a designer long enough, you start to think like one."

Isabel felt her own eyes widen with awe, and she laughed. This moment was beyond any one of her wildest dreams.

"This desk reminded me of you...and of home," Daniel went on. "So I knew it had to be it."

"Well, you're right. I love the desk, and I love you the most. I can't wait to build our home. Together."

Later that night, Isabel sat behind her newly purchased desk and stared down at the sparkly diamond on her finger. The walls of her office looked like camouflage. She'd tested out more than a dozen different shades of green in search of the exact tone she wanted—the one, as it were, that would remind her of Daniel's eyes—but that decision would have to wait.

Outside her office, her family and friends mingled at the engagement party Daniel had secretly put together for her. Isabel sighed with contentment and gratitude. She couldn't help but marvel at what a gift this second chance in Mapleton was—for so many reasons.

Beyond her relationship with Daniel, she'd worked hard over the past few months to show her family how much she valued them. She never missed a Sunday dinner, usually coming early to catch some of the afternoon Packers game with her dad. She and her mom had made a habit of trying out new recipes together. Their best effort so far was a homemade chicken pot pie.

Isabel and Ford were building their relationship back to where it had once been, as well. She helped him stage the houses he was trying to sell, and they had weekly lunch dates at Julia's café. Isabel was encouraging him to pursue getting his state real estate broker license. She was so proud of the business he built and even prouder of the man he was.

She couldn't wait to join Ford, her parents, and especially Daniel in celebration, but first, she had a blog post to write.

She touched her ring once more to make sure she wasn't dreaming before getting started.

I've been signing this blog Love, Inspired *for the past five years. Over the course of that time, I've found inspiration all around me—in buildings with cool architectural features, in the color of the sunset, in the kindness of a neighbor, in my family and my friends. So many things have taught me lessons about not only design, but life and all that goes into making living worthwhile.*

Today has been the best, most inspiring day of my life so far. While working on a project for my own home, the love of my life surprised me with a promise to love me forever. Needless to say, I said yes, and now Daniel and I are engaged! I can't wait to grow together with him in life and love.

You see, he's inspired me to be me. To hold on tight to what I love. To cherish it, to nurture it, and to never take it for granted. He reminds me to be humble, but to also reach for the stars. I'm so thankful for his love and his belief in me. It's a beautiful thing to feel supported and encouraged in what I do. I pray you surround yourself with people who inspire you to be your best self and to follow your dreams, too.

Because while design is intensely personal, it's also intensely communal. We create spaces for people to live. And while we may live alone—I did that in LA for nearly five years—hopefully, eventually, we find people who will share our space with us, who we open our home to, and who make life worth living to the fullest. Whether that's a romantic partner, a family, or a group of friends that's like a family, people are the reason for the design of homes and spaces.

This people-first design mindset will shine as the episodes of season three begin to air next week. We've poured our heart and soul (and home!) into the making of the third season of our show, and I've loved every minute of it. I hope you do, too. Be sure to watch the episodes later in the season. My expert producer and team captured our engagement on film, and we can't wait for you to see it! I'm off to celebrate love. So, until next time, dear readers, happy designing.

Love, Isabel

Epilogue

ENTERTAINMENT MAGAZINE

Review: *Inspired Interiors* – Season 3 premiere.

The first episode of the third season of Inspired Interiors *aired on HoSt network earlier this week. Regular viewers would have been quick to notice the detour from past seasons. Indeed, season three is slated to take place in Ms. Marshall's hometown, Mapleton, WI.*

The show began with a welcome to the village and featured local businesses and residents. We then got a peek into Isabel's own house before she began work on a neighboring property, helping homeowners Ashton and Kristy Klink remodel their guest bedroom and office into a functional playroom. The episode was full of helpful, relatable tips and tricks, and Ms. Marshall shined in both her knowledge of the tasks at hand and her bubbly, down-to-earth delivery. With the change of locale, she literally is the girl next door.

It's obvious Isabel has learned much over the course of her already illustrious career, and if this debut episode of season three tells us anything, it's that she's committed to bringing the focus of home design shows back to actual homes and the people who inhabit them. It's a breath of fresh air, and we can't wait to see what she does next.

Review Summary: Helpful. Heartwarming. And Homey. Five stars.

Disclaimer: This editorial was written by Isabel's fiancé, Daniel Smith, who in the past has remained nameless. But suffice it to say, from now on, he'll be a vocal supporter of his future wife's work. Entertainment Magazine stands behind Mr. Smith's statements, for as biased as they may be, they are also the truth.

·♥ · ♥ · ♥·♥·♥·

Acknowledgments

All glory to God, now and forever.

Hey! You read the acknowledgements section in the back of books? Cool! Me too! So, I'm going to start off by thanking you, sweet reader. Thanks for being here and for giving *Good To Be Home* a chance. I hope the story made you smile and filled you with that fuzzy, fizzy feeling inside.

I owe a massive thank you to my amazing cover artist, Ana Grigoriu-Voicu at Books-Design. I had a vision for the cover of this book, and you delivered and then some. I'm so thankful for your willingness to continue to bring Mapleton to life with your designs. Your work is exquisite—everyone says so!

To my beta readers, Amanda K, Amanda S, Andrea, Jennie, Liz, Maggie, and Meredith. You read this book well before it was ready for publication, and your honest thoughts and feedback helped me to mold it into something I'm truly proud of. Without you, Isabel might have remained unbearable and mean, and no one wanted that! I'm so grateful to you.

To my editor, Jenn Lockwood. Thank you for your time, attention, and enthusiasm for this project. You made it all shine.

To my local library and my favorite librarians, especially Tracy, Julie, Ann, and Holly. Thank you for putting my books in circulation (a literal dream come true) and for being so supportive of me as an author, but most especially for everything you do for our community. I admire you and your work!

To my book club ladies, I'm forever inspired by you and by our discussions. Thank you for being the friends you are.

To my family—Mom, Dad, Luke, Ben, Bailey, my in-laws, grandpa, aunts, uncles, and cousins—you guys are the very best. Thanks for talking through title ideas and plot issues and reading everything I write, whether romance is your usual genre of choice or not. Thanks for texting me play-by-play responses to my stories and making me laugh and for being so excited about my books. Knowing I have you in my corner means the world.

To my incredible kids. I love you. You've taught me more about forgiveness than perhaps anyone else. Thanks for bearing with me when I fall short and for putting up with me playing the playlist for this book over and over and over again.

To Nick. You're my favorite. Thank you for giving me a second chance when I needed it most. I love you madly.

About The Author

Leah Dobrinska earned her degree in English Literature from UW-Madison and has since worked as a freelance writer, editor, and content marketer. As a kid, she hoped to grow up to be either Nancy Drew or Elizabeth Bennet. Now, she fulfills that dream by writing mysteries and love stories. She's a sucker for a good sentence, a happy ending, and the smell of books—both old and new.

Leah lives out her very own happily ever after in a small Wisconsin town with her husband and their gaggle of kids. When she's not handing out snacks, visiting local parks, and doing projects around the house, Leah enjoys reading and running. Find out more about Leah and connect with her through her website, leahdobrinska.com.

Book Club Discussion Guide

1. What were your initial impressions of Isabel and Daniel? Did you understand Isabel's hesitation about returning to Mapleton? Why or why not? How did Daniel's explanation of their history make you feel?

2. Who was your favorite character? Why? Which character underwent the most growth and change throughout the story?

3. How does Daniel's relationship with his grandfather and Isabel's relationship with her parents and her brother impact the storyline?

4. Do you have experience living in a small town? In your opinion, what are the pros and cons?

5. How do the *Entertainment Magazine* reviews in the prologue and epilogue frame the story?

6. The theme of forgiveness plays a key role in the novel. Daniel tells Isabel, "That's the great thing about forgiveness, isn't it? Once it's offered, you don't have to dwell on your past mistakes. It's like the slate is wiped clean...even when we feel unworthy or like we don't deserve it." Talk about a moment when you experienced forgiveness. How did you feel? Have you ever been inspired by someone else's ability to forgive?

7. What other major themes were explored throughout the story?

8. Is there anything in the story you wish had gone differently?

9. Share your favorite quote or scene from the story. Why did it stand out to you?

CPSIA information can be obtained
at www.ICGtesting.com
Printed in the USA
LVHW102055080822
725440LV00004B/38

9 781737 448327